D0354171

HELEN HALL LIBRARY
CITY OF LEAGUE CITY
100 WEST WALKER
LEAGUE CITY, TX 77573-3899

DISCARD

MAR   2002

The Way to Somewhere

a novel

Angie Day

HELEN HALL LIBRARY
CITY OF LEAGUE CITY
100 WEST WALKER
LEAGUE CITY, TX 77573-3899

Simon & Schuster
New York London Toronto Sydney Singapore

SIMON & SCHUSTER
Rockefeller Center
1230 Avenue of the Americas
New York, NY 10020

This book is a work of fiction. Names, characters,
places, and incidents either are products of the
author's imagination or are used fictitiously. Any
resemblance to actual events or locales or persons,
living or dead, is entirely coincidental.

Copyright © 2002 by Angie Day
All rights reserved,
including the right of reproduction
in whole or in part in any form.

SIMON & SCHUSTER and colophon are registered trademarks of Simon & Schuster, Inc.
Grateful acknowledgment is given for excerpts on pp. 15, 91, 163, and 213
taken from Restoring Antique Furniture by Richard A. Lyons. Reprinted
by permission of Dover Publications. All rights reserved.
For information regarding special discounts for bulk purchases,
please contact Simon & Schuster Special Sales:
1-800-456-6798 or business@simonandschuster.com
Designed by Karolina Harris
Manufactured in the United States of America
10 9 8 7 6 5 4 3 2 1
Library of Congress Cataloging-in-Publication Data is available.
ISBN 0-7432-2332-2

Acknowledgments

I would like to acknowledge the chain of good will that made this happen—from Greg Battle to Tiffany Ericksen to the one, the only, Jennifer Sherwood, without whom I'd have never progressed beyond Chapter 2. I also want to thank Alisa Wyatt and Katie Hobson for their perceptive reads and sound advice; Tracy Fisher and Alicia Gordon for their unwavering support; my editor, Marysue Rucci, who helped me make this book more my own than it was in the first place; Ari for taking the time to talk transoms with me; the Day clan, the California Girls (Sarah Rogers, Anne Enna, and Carolyn Hoecker), and Clay McDaniel for having faith in my choices in life; Rob Barocci for believing in me even in the days of Sofa Girl, and for being my source of exclamation points ever since; Greg Blatt and Eric Zohn for fighting my legal battles; George Plamondon and Kevin Chinoy for helping me develop a character who I got so sick of I created Taylor to beat her up, and who along with Mike Hodge, Greg Waldorf, and my brother Aaron have the dubious distinction of being among the first to back me up; Howard Mansfield, for writing *The Same Ax, Twice*, an insightful and moving work of nonfiction that became a well of inspiration for me; and finally, Mr. Russell and all the teachers I've had over the years who made me think that this was possible.

For my two Roberts and Geraldine

The Way to Somewhere

To build a Shaker-style rocking chair, you need:

2 back posts
2 front legs
1 back seat stretcher
2 side seat stretchers
1 front seat stretcher
1 back rung
4 side rungs
2 front rungs
1 lower back stretcher
1 upper back stretcher
1 backrest
2 rockers
2 dowels
Cloth tape

It is this process of building from a pattern or a plan that leads people to romanticize the precise, guided hands of a carpenter. Someone who lives in a world where everything has a purpose and a place to go.

• • •

I am surprised every day that I am living out of order. Because there are also rules that apply to people, expectations of relationships. How we live. How we love. How we die. And in what order. Something like:

First years structured by two loving parents, peppered with birthday parties.
And then your first love comes in high school.
But you leave him in college, chasing your first sex.
And then you graduate and begin a career that you love.
And leave your first sex to search for your first true love.
And then you get married.
And your father comes to the wedding.
And your mother comes to the wedding.
And they give you away together.
And your first year of marriage is rough, but you make it.
And then you have a kid. Most likely two kids.
And losing your parents is horrible, but you make it.
And watching your kids grow up and leave home is difficult, but you make it.
And watching your spouse die before you is devastating, but you make it.
And then you're old, but you've got your two kids who take care of you.
And your grandkids who call you Bamma instead of Grandma.

I am amazed that so many expect this order, when so few have experienced it.

I made my first rocking chair when I was twenty-two. I chose my stock (birch). I cut and shaped the pieces myself. I turned the legs, rungs, and stretchers. I bent the wood for the backrest and back stretchers. I drilled the mortises in the legs and posts. I sanded and assembled the frame. I applied the finish. And I wove its back and seat until, finally, I'd constructed something I'd want to sit in. It wasn't a perfect piece of work, but it served its purpose. Of rest. Contentment.
Except I was never content.

Instead, I spent all my time dreaming in it. Imagining future after future. Futures where the rocking chair resembled something more like a La-Z-Boy. Made out of top-grain black leather. A right arm with a convenient beverage holder. A left arm with roomy storage for remotes. It would be modern, at home in the showroom window. Free from the responsibility of back-story. With a reclining feature, so I could kick my feet up. And nap.

But each time, when I was done imagining my future, I would wake to find myself sinking further into my woven seat.

Because I am, I would learn, exactly what I built.

I am that first rocking chair. I am that bureau with the chipped paint and worn brass handles. I am that door that I hauled cross-country because I thought that's what moving meant. That door with all the bumps and bruises.

Is me.

Restoring, as the name implies, is the act of bringing something to its original condition. Restoring does not permit improving or changing, which means that the restorer must overcome the temptation to change the original, even if the change might add convenience. It would be unthinkable, for example, to replace a worn turnbuckle with a magnetic latch or to replace a warped or cracked board at the back of a cupboard with a piece of plywood. Such changes would greatly reduce the value of the piece.

"Rules and Tools for Restoration of Antique Furniture,"
Restoring Antique Furniture: A Complete Guide,
by Richard A. Lyons

red-white-and-blue bombs

When Mr. Candesa agreed to hire me, he thought I was a twelve-year-old boy. I came recommended by the soccer coach in the church league, which was all boys except for me, so I suppose his mistake was understandable.

Mr. Candesa was a history teacher at the Catholic high school. He was real skinny with a weak voice, but his eyes were set so deep and dark that somehow he still managed to be intimidating. You just knew not to piss him off. His wife was a balloon of a lady who sunned in a tent dress on a pool float built for two, but no one ever teased him about her. Or made a joke about Vietnam. Or about ice cream.

"Taylor," he said matter-of-factly, as he checked me over the first day I showed up for the job. I was wearing a baseball cap, and my short hair just peeked at the edges.

"Yes, sir."

He took a sly look first at my chest, then at my crotch, hoping a small bulge in either place might betray my identity. It didn't. He looked up at my face, still confused; I'd been called Mount Taylor long enough to know that girls weren't meant to be as tall as I was. Finally, embarrassed, he focused on the Skoal logo on my forehead. "You a boy, son?"

"No, sir." When I was six and had the chicken pox, I told my mom my dick itched, but she'd since informed me and my brother J.J. of our differences.

"You were supposed to be a boy," he said.

"That's what my dad says, too."

"Oh." I could tell he thought that explained a few things. Like why I was a soccer player. Why I was the reason Mark Brocada got his front teeth knocked out. Why I wanted to work on an ice-cream truck for the summer. "Get in," he said, gesturing to the candy-colored truck waiting in front of his house, so clean it hurt my eyes to look at it.

That summer Mr. Candesa and I sold red-white-and-blue bombs more than anything else. Mickey Mouse ears we sold the least. And after just three days I was hearing "Camptown Races" even when the truck was sitting in front of the Candesas' house, closed for the night.

Every day I'd meet him at noon in front of his house, which had a lawn and so many flowers planted that I wished I didn't have to live in an apartment. He was always five minutes late, carrying a vanilla-colored bag he'd filled with history books. Once we hit the road, it was my job to explain the ice cream, take the money, and sweat a lot, while Mr. Candesa read his books in the front seat. He was "struggling through his dissertation," he told me.

Our first stop was always Maplewood, this big pool they had in his neighborhood. It was so nice that to be let in, you had to show them a little tag that proved you were from around there. Little squirts would run out to the parking lot as soon as they heard our truck's song, change spilling through their small hands. Next came a few mothers declaring that they were going to treat themselves just this once. And then came Priscilla Banks and her giggly friends, smelling like tan shoulders and coconut oil, pointing to the pictures of ice cream while eager twerps, mostly from my summer soccer team, bought the girls whatever they desired. Then the fancy girls would leave and the boys would talk to me.

"Why are you selling ice cream?" our goalie Jacob wanted to know.

"I still make soccer practice," I said.

"I'm not talking about that. Don't you get sick of hearing that song all day?"

"Camptown Races," I said.

"My dad says it's not legal to work until you're sixteen."

"Maybe your dad's a numskull like you," I said, then turned to a little kid who showed up every day with no money and treated him like a real customer, asking him if he'd like some ice cream, just so I wouldn't have to talk to Jacob anymore.

At the end of the first week, Mr. Candesa asked me if my dad ever took me swimming. I explained that my dad was a plumber who worked too much to take me to the pool, but that was a lie. I think Mr. Candesa felt sorry for me, because the next week he got me a pool tag. After that, a couple times a week when we were at the pool, Mr. Candesa would lift his head from his papers and books, usually on our second stop there later in the afternoon. "Twenty minutes," he'd say, and I'd take off my T-shirt and shorts and run out to the pool in my orange one-piece that I wore to work every day just in case. I'd drop my towel on one of the pool chairs, then me and the guys would do cannonballs off the diving board while Mr. Candesa tanned in a lounge chair and flirted with the lifeguards until it was time to go back to our route, which was exactly the same, every day. And I liked that at first, driving in a pattern, knowing every turn.

Really I worked because my family was broke, and I still wanted things. Expensive things. Like a new baseball glove. My mom bought me a stained blue glove at a garage sale, which explained my punching Mark Brocada, because he always teased me about it. I also wanted a new pair of jeans, since mine were way too short. And I wanted to get away from the divorce. My parents told me once that they would never divorce, since we were Catholic, but they talked and screamed about divorce all the time.

When I told Mr. Candesa once about my parents fighting, he told me that he never fought with his wife. That he knew since the first day he saw her that she was The One. It was all in her smile, how it drew you in, sucked you in. "You got a nice smile, you know that?" he said, really looking at me for the first time. "In fact—you know what?—you might actually be pretty." He looked some more. "Yeah," he said, "you are." For that entire day he just kept looking at me and chuckling to himself, until finally all his laughing had worn out the compliment.

"You're a loner, aren't you?" Mr. Candesa said gruffly one day. He was driving the truck while I stared at his thick bare feet pushing the pedals.

"I got a brother."

"I mean friends," he said.

"I have friends."

We pulled up to a light and stopped. He turned and looked me straight in the eye. "Those boys aren't your friends."

"We play soccer together." They were the closest things to friends I had.

The light turned green and I was relieved when his attention returned to the road. "You got to learn sooner than later that boys aren't your friends. Ever. Especially at your age. Especially since you're pretty."

I just sat quietly. A little girl wearing nothing but flip-flops was running after our truck, but he didn't see her and I didn't say anything. He shifted in his seat and cricked his neck uncomfortably. "You know what urges are?"

I nodded weakly. I could define an urge. Like the urge I had to smack him upside the head so he'd stop talking about weird stuff.

"OK," he continued. "An urge is what those boys have towards you and you don't know it."

"They don't like me that way," I said dumbly, thinking about the curvy girls in tiny bikinis who smelled like vacation.

"You go ahead and think what you want to," he said, in a way that meant he didn't mean that at all. "But even if they don't like you that way, even if you're *like* a boy, *you're a girl*. And a twelve-year-old boy plus *any* girl equals urge, you see?"

I didn't.

By the last week of the summer I'd made close to three hundred dollars. I didn't tell my brother J.J. because lately he'd developed a ten-

dency to steal things. And I didn't tell my parents because my money
wasn't going to become part of the family fund. I was sure of that. I hid
it in a maxi pad box in my top drawer, underneath my underwear. I decided at the beginning of the summer that I wasn't going to spend any
of it until August 8, my thirteenth birthday.

The morning of August 8, before work, I went to Target and I
bought a Spalding glove, a pair of Lee jeans, eight bags of Fritos, a
pocketknife, a sleeping bag, and a bikini. I hadn't planned on the
bikini, but it stared at me from the row of mishung suits. It was red-
and-white striped with a blue band around the edges. Another girl had
returned it to the rack. "You're too heavy for that," her mother kept
telling her, as the girl whined that she just *had* to have it. Before I
could think, I took it right off the rack and walked to the dressing room
to try it on. It didn't look right. The saleslady knocked, asking if I
needed anything, probably thinking I was lifting the suit. So I opened
the door while I still had it on, with my underwear tucked in as best I
could. "My," she said, "don't you look nice in that one. What I
wouldn't do for a muscular little body like yours. And those long legs."
She shut the door again, shaking her head to herself.

I looked in the mirror one last time. Really quick, since I hated mir-
rors. And all I could think was *How do I stand in this thing?* I tried to
put my hands straight at my sides, then on my hips. Then I tried to put
one hip out a little to the side, and make a serious face. And then I
caught my own eyes in the mirror and just felt dumb.

Still, I decided to buy it, the saleslady's words echoing in my head.

Work on my birthday started out the same, since Mr. Candesa
didn't know it was my birthday. He came out carrying the vanilla bag
filled with books, his wife draped in a cantaloupe dress smiling and
waving good-bye as we pulled out. We went to Maplewood and sold
out of red-white-and-blue bombs, and everyone started complaining
because nobody liked the chocolate-banana ones. It was especially hot
that day, and humid, one of those days where everybody is irritated at
everybody else for everything. Which was why I was so surprised when,
after Priscilla walked away with her yogurt stick, Mr. Candesa said,
"Twenty minutes."

I pulled off my shirt and shorts while Mr. Candesa stared at me. "Whoa," he said, and looked away. "New suit, huh?"

"It's my birthday," I told him.

"Well, then," he said. "Forty-five minutes."

I nodded, happily, and headed out to the pool, my Yosemite Sam towel wrapped around my hips. I looked over to where Mr. Candesa was perching himself on a lawn chair. I decided I was going to sun myself. I walked by the deep end, found my own lounger, and spread open my towel.

I felt thirsty and treated myself to a lemonade at the refreshment stand. On my way back I heard Jacob say, "Look at Mount Taylor." I pretended not to hear. There was a group of about eight guys, mostly ones I knew, and they were staring at me. First they were talking to themselves, then all their jabber focused on Jacob. He got out of the pool and walked over to me.

"Wanna play catch?" he asked, while all the other guys looked on.

"Buy me a pretzel, and I'll think about it," I said, doing my best imitation of the flirty girls I saw every day at the truck. I'd never done anything like this before. But I figured it was my turn.

He looked all over me and then took off walking, while I heard "sucker" yelled from the pool. When he returned with a pretzel, I took just one bite before I was bored. From my lounger, I watched them doing cannonballs off the diving board for a few minutes, measuring who had the highest splash. But I got tired of watching. So I walked over to the diving board to get in line, trying my best to ignore the stares. "Whose splash is highest so far?" I yelled to them as they hung near the ladder at the side of the deep end. They pointed at Jacob who got out of the pool to gesture how high his splash had been. It was pretty high, but I'd done higher. Slowly I walked about two-thirds down the length of the diving board. I breathed in and took two long and careful steps followed by a double bounce at the end of the board. I knew that the lifeguard would blow her whistle if she saw the double bounce, but I didn't care. I was flying off the board. I was so high that I could feel my stomach sink a little in the air as I formed myself into a ball. I landed with a huge splash. I remember smiling underwater, feeling the liquid glide over my teeth. And then coming up and shaking my head as I resurfaced. And then looking over at the guys to make sure I'd beat Jacob's splash. And then realizing that they were all laughing at me. My stomach sank again, this time in panic, as I looked down. My top was gone.

I dove back underwater and saw my stringy top drifting down toward the drain. I was almost out of air by then but knew I had enough left to grab it and go. Then a blur passed in front of me. Jacob grabbed the top, carrying it in slow motion to the surface. For that moment I was completely still. I just relaxed and drifted down, feeling myself move back and forth, pulled into the slow rock of the water. And then I ran out of air. I shot up to the surface, gulping it in, trying my best to keep my shoulders below the water.

The lifeguard was too engrossed in her conversation with Mr. Candesa to notice that Jacob was waving my top at me from the side of the pool, expecting me to lunge forward and try to grab it from him.

"Give it back," I shouted.

"Come and get it," he said as the guys looked on and laughed. He gave the top a little wave, taunting me.

I swam closer, still treading water, low enough so I could keep my chest hidden, close enough so I could see him throw my top into the rusty blue trash can.

And then I don't remember deciding what I was going to do next. I just did it.

I climbed out of the pool as fast as I could and I ran. I ran past all the boys pointing and laughing at my pale, nubbed chest. I ran past the mothers who were frowning at me, confused and concerned, yet still doing nothing—just walking in a quick circle, trying to find someone else they could tell to help me. But it was too late. By then I'd run through the gate. And into the ice-cream truck. I threw on my T-shirt, which I'd left in the back, and that's when I noticed the keys, dangling out of the ignition.

I thought for a minute. I thought about waiting for Mr. Candesa, finishing our route. Maybe crying later, once I got home, but not before.

And then I just stopped thinking and turned the key. I pushed on the gas as hard as I could, like I'd seen Mr. Candesa do. It made an awful, scraping sound, but it started anyway. "Camptown Races" blared. I shifted the gears and pushed the gas, but somehow I was still surprised when the truck started to move, that my pushing on the pedals was actually making this big thing go wherever I wanted it to go.

By the time I made it to the driveway, I was laughing to myself. The kind of laugh that you see in the movies done by the bad guys. Only I wasn't a bad guy. I knew that. I was someone who was going to drive somewhere far away. Maybe I'd drive to Montana. I'd heard that there are the fewest people there of any state—that there's only land for miles. The streets were so empty that day, I knew I could do it and never be traced. Never be found. I had eighty-seven bucks in my bag, and I was going to drive and drive and drive away.

When I got to the first red light, a perm-haired lady in a Cadillac pulled up next to me and stared. The kind of stare that lets you know someone's sizing you up and you're failing. I stared right back at her, then rolled my eyes.

Five minutes later I'd made it to Highway 6, this big flat country road with nobody ever on it. "Camptown Races" was still screaming, and every now and then some little kid would run out of his house, hoping I'd stop. But I didn't. I was too busy thinking about how it'd feel to throw a brick right through Jacob's window. And that's when I felt it. A jolt as the truck hit something.

And then the screaming started.

I don't think I'd ever heard a sound so bad. It was just yelping and yelping and yelping, louder than barking, louder than "Camptown Races" even. I pulled the truck over as best I could and saw the mess I'd made. The sickly little mutt dog was on her side, barely moving, except her mouth. She yelped for about a minute more and then she stopped. I had her head in my lap by then, and I swear I saw everything, the whole world, pass right through her.

And then I couldn't move. Everything just felt so still once the yelping stopped. The silence seemed more like a sound. A beautiful sound. Like thick, quiet air, taking over everything. Even me. And around me there was not a car, not a person in sight.

I know it sounds dumb, but I didn't know what to do. I wanted to get help, but she was dead already. I wanted to drive away, but I couldn't just yet.

I decided I'd bury Betsy. I'd named her by then. She was pretty heavy, so I had to pull her to the edge of the ditch. Then I pushed her as hard as I could, and she slid down into the water.

And that's when the man showed up.

"You look awful young to be out here by yourself." He was one of those men who always dressed like he was on his way to church. He was wearing a button-down and slacks and was clutching the keys to the brownish Pontiac that he'd parked behind the truck. He had this smile frozen on his face, like people get when they're trying to coax an animal into a cage, making sure they don't move too fast and upset the beast. He looked me over with a quick glance. I was covered with blood. I just nodded and lied.

"My dad. He just hit a dog."

"Your dad, huh? Well, then, can you tell me where your dad is?"

I told him about what happened. About how my dad and I were talking about my birthday party and all of a sudden this stray dog came out of nowhere. "She was so fast, she just looked like this big streak." And about how my dad tried so hard not to hit her that he nearly swerved the truck right into the ditch. And about how I got so scared I cried. And about how my dad went to get help and left me with the truck, since it wouldn't start. "I think all her guts and stuff messed up the engine."

The man looked at me sideways, then walked slowly around to the side of the truck. He wiped the sweat off his brow, and I noticed that he had huge circles of sweat under his arms too. "Why don't I try to start it, then," he said. I could tell by the way he said this that he knew I was lying. He just wanted proof before calling someone. I was wondering who he'd call first. The cops? My mom? My dad?

He leaned into the truck and gently turned the key. And it started on the first try. He stuck his head out the truck's window and told me it appeared to be working just fine. "I think you'd better come over here," he said.

But I was already gone.

I'd run down the dirt slope towards the edge of the water in the ditch, thinking I'd just lie low so he couldn't see me. But then I saw the old sewer hole that had been carved in the side of the ditch, above where the water was, and I went for it.

By the time I'd crawled inside the hole, my whole body felt like something different. I could feel the rush of the blood going through me. Everywhere. The sewer's ridged metal was smelly and made my hands rusty touching it, but I didn't care. I just sat there for what seemed like forever, still as I could be.

About two hours later, I heard Mr. Candesa come to reclaim his truck. I heard the cops asking him if he wanted to file a complaint. A couple hours after that I even thought I heard my mom, but when I peeked I saw that it was only Mrs. Candesa.

When the sun had gone down—all the way down—I grabbed a dead tree branch, pulled out my new pocketknife, and started scraping off the edges of the wood. I made a cross for the dog, tying two pieces of the branch together by breaking off some of my shoelace. And I carved her name in it. While I did this, I thought about my birthday. About days in general. About how you can wake up one day and be one thing, and by the time the day is done, you're something else altogether. Or maybe I'd been this way the whole time, the kind of kid who could get away, but that was the first time I knew it. I put the cross right where I'd hit Betsy, and I began walking along the side of the road, listening to my feet crunch the grass with every step, wondering how long it'd take me to get to Montana.

driving

We'd just found a big, fat rat in the toilet. He'd climbed all the way up the pipes, only to get stuck halfway out of the crap hole in the bottom of the bowl. The rat's body was just long enough so that when he stretched as hard as he could, he could barely get his nose out of the water. My brother J.J. found him first, and told me not to look, which is exactly why I did. And once I started, I couldn't stop. We watched the rat stretch and breathe and stretch and breathe again and again until finally the fatso got too tired and sank to the bottom of the toilet we were supposed to clean.

J.J. clumsily knelt beside the toilet bowl, trying to get a closer look at the dead rat. It looked strange to see somebody as tall as J.J. crouched over that tiny toilet, staring inside like he was studying a science project or something, his hair so long I was afraid it was going to touch the water. I knelt beside him.

"We should go get Dad," I said. Dad was outside by our covered parking spots playing with his cars. For as long as I could remember, my dad was obsessed with little car and truck models. He'd spend days putting the stupid plastic things together, just so he could run them around in circles in the parking lot for a while, then put them back in his closet in boxes that he wouldn't let us touch.

"Dad's an idiot," J.J. said, his eyes still fixed on the rat.

"Dad's a plumber," I pointed out.

"Well, then you go get him if you want him here so bad," he said.

I didn't move. "Maybe we don't need Dad," I said, somberly.

I guess J.J. knew I was still upset from this morning. Because just then he looked at me like a dad should. "You can't take that fight too serious," he said. We'd woken up to our parents fighting. From what I could gather, someone called my dad at 6:00 A.M. with a plumbing problem. He told them he couldn't work on Sundays because of his religion, then went back to bed. And Mom was mad because she knew he was lying just so he wouldn't have to get up early. And because we needed the money. And because she *did* go to church, and none of us did, as usual. So about a half hour before we found the rat, Mom had stomped off to pray for all of us. And while she couldn't punish Dad (at least not exactly), she did punish us. The rule was that if we chose not to go to church, we had to clean the whole apartment—which is how we ended up cleaning every Sunday.

I hate Sundays, I was thinking as I stared at the rat in the toilet, wondering how long it would take before he'd bloat like a frog. Maybe even pop.

J.J. continued to explain their fighting to me as he dug around in the closet, looking for something. "They're just married. And no matter how you look at it, marriage stinks."

"Why?"

"Because everybody stinks a little. And most people stink a lot, that's why."

"Then why did they get married?" I said. It was something I never could figure out. My parents weren't the kind that ever talked about "the good old days." I knew they met while working together in a factory in Kentucky. I assumed that one night they'd gotten drunk and had sex, and that my dad married her because she got knocked up. And that they moved to Texas because her family was going to come after him.

"You think too much," J.J. told me, and he reached into the toilet with plastic grocery bags over his hands. With a quick jerk he pulled the rat through the hole. "I think I broke the fucker's back."

The rat looked tiny in J.J.'s enormous hands. He grinned at it, then held its dead body out in front of my face. "Touch it," he said.

"No way," I told him, then touched it anyway. It was cold and damp and dead, basically. And I remember realizing, right then, that we were poor. I had lice once, and finding this rat sort of felt like that. Like if people at school knew about this, they'd know that one time I saw my mom stealing pickled eggs at the grocery store. Or that once when I was six, we got kicked out of our apartment for having no money. We were poor. Just like that. Some times were better than others, but we would always be the kind of family that would have rats in our toilets.

J.J. just stared at me. I think he thought my eyes were watering because he'd made me touch the rat. "Want to go for a ride?" he asked, as he pitched the rat into the garbage.

"We're supposed to clean, remember?" I told him.

"Fuck cleaning," he said.

As we walked down the stairs to our parking spots, I could see that Dad was still there. The remote control car that he had been playing with was now under his chair, as he focused on building a new one, on this little foldout table that he'd dragged outside.

I never could get over how funny he looked working on his models. He was about six foot five, even bigger than J.J. and way bigger than my mom, who was already shorter than me. And he was thick. His neck. His fingers. Everything about him was oversized. I was thinking this as I walked past him, hoping he didn't notice that we were getting into J.J.'s car. But, of course, he did notice, since he was sitting right next to it.

"Taylor," he said. "Come here a minute."

At first I was scared, thinking that I was about to get in trouble for leaving. Until I saw that he was working on his Ferrari's tiny interior. He handed me one of the little pieces. "It goes right there," he said, pointing to the spot that was too small for his hands. He glued up the piece in my hand, and I put it exactly where he wanted it.

"Just think," he said, as I finished my duty. "When this thing's done, I'll have touched every piece." And then he asked me to get him a beer.

"Actually," J.J. boldly chimed in, "we were about to go to the store. We're out of Comet," he lied. I looked at J.J. with my eyes bugged out,

as if to tell him not to push it. But Dad had already checked out for
the day.

"OK," Dad said, not looking up from his plastic sports car. "Sure."

I knew that later that night J.J. would get it from my mom. She would
yell at him for not taking better care of me. For smoking and skipping
out when we were supposed to clean and for being a bad example in
general. And my dad would sit in his chair, watching TV, acting like
nothing was going on around him. As focused on the TV as he was with
his models earlier in the day. Focused enough to tune my mom out.

But that hadn't happened yet. Because right now, Mom was still at
church. And Dad was doing models. And J.J. was taking me for a drive.

J.J. worked at Burger King for a year so he could buy his heap of a
car. It was a blue Monte Carlo with the slightest hint of sparkle, just
enough to make it look like a giant, beat-up bowling ball. J.J.'s bowling
ball. We got in.

Inside it smelled faintly of cigarettes. With a quick sweep of his arm,
J.J. pushed all the garbage off the seats. McDonald's wrappers, chew-
ing gum wadded up in school papers, a plastic cup with a brown ring
of dried-up dip-spit inside. I hadn't ever been on a date, but I figured
this was what it's like. Somebody making room for you.

"Where are we going?" I asked him. I was hoping he'd say we were
going to the record store, or to get a donut. But he didn't answer my
question. Just kept driving.

Part of me wanted to talk to J.J., but he was one of those people who
lived most of his life in the quiet, and I didn't want to interrupt whatever he was thinking. Instead, I stuck my head out the window like a
dog and watched the strip malls pass by. Just one year ago, there used
to be these fields behind Sunny Acres, our apartment complex, where
I could actually pick berries. They grew wild out there. But now the
fields were gone, and in their place were just more and more apartments, more and more stores. I decided to start counting Targets, but
before I got to even two, J.J. pulled into a gas station.

"Wait here," he told me.

Minutes later he came out carrying a pair of sunglasses and a bag of
Fritos. He opened the Fritos and threw the sunglasses at me.

"Did you steal these?" I asked.

"Maybe I did. Maybe I didn't," he said, but from the look on his face I could tell I'd hurt his feelings a bit. "I just figured you'd need them."

I glanced at myself in the rearview mirror to see how I looked in my sunglasses. The same. The car sputtered to a start and we were off again.

I held the steering wheel as J.J. lit up a joint. I half-expected him to pass it to me, but he didn't. Same as always. He believed that pot wasn't good for me, which I thought was funny. Him being so protective. Keeping me away from things that he obviously thought were fine for him.

"Where are we going?" I asked again.

"Why does it matter?" was his annoyed response.

I shrugged, then returned my focus out the window again, making myself dizzy watching the white-dotted lines zip past. And next thing I knew we were on the freeway. *Where are we going?* It really could have been anywhere. In the fifth grade I had to do a report on Houston. I wrote about the Astrodome, Astroworld, the Galleria, NASA, the museums. I also wrote about good Mexican food. And about how we had the Oilers and the Astros and a hockey team. But that was just for a dumb report. Because really, to me, Houston was just a tangle of freeway that led to a thousand places that all looked the same.

At least that's what I thought.

Until that day with J.J.

When we turned into this neighborhood that for a minute seemed more like an amusement park than a place to live. It was a long street lined with huge, thick-trunked trees. All along the street were houses so enormous I couldn't even imagine what they would be like inside, how many servants, how a day would be passed. At the end of the street there was the biggest mansion of all, endless and white. Its entrance was marked by huge white columns bursting from the ground, announcing to all who entered that they were in the presence of majesty.

And we were.

"Oh my god. How many people do you think live in that house?" I asked, pointing to the mansion at the end, which I noticed also had a guard station at its driveway.

"That's a country club, stupid. Welcome to River Oaks," was J.J.'s response.

I'd heard of this neighborhood, a place so ritzy that you really had to be somebody (a rich somebody) to live there. But I'd never seen it. And couldn't have imagined it. House after house as big as Sunny Acres. Even the people keeping the grounds seemed happy. There were tall old trees and birds and paths to walk on and people smiling, and we were right there, passing by it all.

Every time we'd turn the corner, we'd see a bigger house with a larger lawn, or maybe the lawn was smaller but the front of the house was more ornate, looking more like a decorative box than a dwelling.

The music was still screaming out of the car, and I honestly couldn't think. I just sat, mouth agape, looking at the tall old houses with windows that sighed and front doors that beckoned. And then at J.J., who I knew then was sharing his secret spot with me.

He pulled the car over in front of this huge gated house. "Do you want to drive?"

"You know I'm not old enough," I said, thinking of all the trouble I got into when I stole the ice-cream truck. But immediately I regretted saying no to J.J. I *did* want to drive.

"You know I don't care," he said, mocking my tone.

I stepped out of the car and was walking around to the driver's side when I saw it. It was by the garbage cans at the corner of the front gate. A photo album. Half of it was in the shiny metal can, and half of it was hanging out. As if someone had marked a page in a book by draping it over the can's edge.

"Hold on a sec," I said to J.J., and I walked over to investigate, making sure nobody was looking. I grabbed the album out of the can and walked back to the car, slipping into the driver's seat as if I'd been driving for years.

"What the hell is that?" J.J. wanted to know.

I opened it up on my lap, the car still running. The photo album was pretty but had a cheap clasp that had broken, so most of the pages were slipping out. I put them back in as best I could while I looked at the pictures inside.

They were all of the same family. And it looked like they were on a cruise. Most of the pictures were of their kid, who was about eleven. It was the kid getting a lei put around her neck. The kid sitting on a deck lounger in her bathing suit. The whole family in front of a sunset, standing beside the captain.

"Why do you think they threw this away?" I wanted to know.

"How the fuck would I know that?" he said.

I put the album between the two front bucket seats.

"You're keeping it?" J.J. asked. "What the fuck for?"

"I'll throw it out later," I told him, lying. I knew that later that night I would flip through it a hundred times, wondering how it would feel to be that kid. On a cruise of all things. With two parents who seemed to get along.

"Just focus on the road, Tay," J.J. said, helping me with the steering wheel as I jerked the car around the block a few times. Always going too fast or too slow. Always braking too soon or too late. Finally, just when I'd gotten the hang of it, he said it was time to head back and took over driving again.

"We haven't gone down that one," I said, pointing to another street.

J.J. obediently turned the car onto one of the grandest streets we'd seen yet. House after house from different eras. Some bigger than others. All with fresh paint and living yards and mailboxes with names on them.

In one yard, two Mexican men were diligently trimming the bushes until they were shaped like poodle legs. The men waved as we drove by, which seemed to be the custom in this neighborhood, a custom that I was completely unfamiliar with. In my neighborhood you'd be more likely to get the finger.

"A different world out here, isn't it," J.J. said, without any hint of bitterness.

We drove past a house that had a fountain in the front yard. A woman in a bikini with the straps pulled down around her shoulders sunned on a wooden lounge chair, oblivious to the world. "It is," I said. "It really is."

finding maria

Her name was Maria. She was Mexican. She lived in a town called Querétaro until she was eight, when she came to Houston to live with her mom. She moved into Sunny Acres the summer before I started high school. She was my first real friend. The first time I saw her, she was holding a baby on each hip like mothers do. I remember feeling sorry for her, thinking that she had two kids already and didn't even look as old as me (fourteen).

I was really surprised when she showed up in my algebra class that fall. I spent two weeks staring at her long black hair in the seat in front of me before I got the courage to ask her, "How old are your kids?"

"My kids?" she said, raising her eyebrows, looking at me like I was nuts.

I told her I'd seen her at Sunny Acres, by the pool, with babies. She couldn't stop laughing. Normally I'd be mad if someone just laughed at me like that, but Maria was the kind of person who always made you feel like she was your friend.

Maria had two brothers and two sisters. She called them all by their names with "ito" or "ita" tagged onto the end. Carlosito. Florita. She was the oldest, and she took care of them way too much, according to my mother. "The Mexicans aren't like the Chinese," my mom said. "The Chinese just want sons sons sons. No son. No future. But the Mexicans always want the firstborn to be a girl, so that they've got a nanny for the next twenty or so kids." I told my mom that Maria's mother gave her extra money to baby-sit, but she said all that did was prove her point.

Maria's apartment looked exactly like mine. From the outside, and the inside.

On the outside, the whole three-story complex was painted dark brown. And all of the balconies were lined up perfectly out front, as if they were stacked on top of each other. And they all had two windows in the same spot, with matching burglar bars. And on the ground floor there were covered parking spots for each family. We each got two. And they were all the same size.

On the inside, there was a brown carpet that ran through the whole place. Except the kitchen, where there was brown-and-beige checked linoleum. Each apartment was a perfect square, with three bedrooms, two bathrooms, and a living room with a kitchen in it.

We each had a medium TV, a junky sofa, an old lounge chair (for our dads), and a little dinette table that was meant to be folded up but stayed open all the time. And the rest of the furniture was different but still similar, in that it fell apart easily and didn't match at all. It was like a garage sale that you lived in all the time.

We called them our dollhouses, because they seemed like they were made in the same factory. We only wished that we'd gotten our apartments fresh out of the box, instead of the hand-me-downs that they were, with dirty walls and stained carpeting.

I tried fixing up our place once by rearranging the furniture in the living room. I got in so much trouble that I never did it again.

But Maria was allowed to decorate her place. In fact, her mother encouraged it. She mostly decorated their apartment with collages that she made out of magazines. She could do anything with some picture cutouts, glue, tape, and paper. The first thing she ever gave me when we were friends was a collage of all these pictures of dogs. She knew I'd never had a dog, and that I wanted one, badly, but wasn't allowed. She had two stray dogs that hung around her apartment, that she called Garfield and HK, for Hello Kitty. She thought things like that were funny, naming your dogs after cats.

She used to dress in all sorts of colors that didn't go together. She'd try to get me to wear maybe a bright pink sweater or maybe her really yellow sandals, but I didn't like anything but jeans and T-shirts mostly.

On Friday nights we would walk to the movies together for a double feature. We'd pay for the first one. The second one was whatever we could sneak into. Later, when we got to my apartment, we would talk about what we liked and what we didn't like about each, and then we always had to decide which movie was better, using the taco system. Three tacos was the best, and so far only *Sixteen Candles* got that.

After a while, people at school started calling us Taria, both our names mushed up together like we were one person. Maria used to roll her eyes at people when they said that. Me too. But we both liked it. We even told each other so one night when she slept over.

Maria told me that I was funny. She used to give me a sentence and see if I could say the same thing but better. Like if she said, "Priscilla Banks is a bitch," I would say, "I'd rather file my nails with a cheese grater than talk to Priscilla Banks." And she would laugh and laugh.

I showed Maria the photo album I'd found in River Oaks. I'd marked out my favorite pictures from the cruise. At first I was embarrassed that I'd kept it, but Maria told me that she knew why I would keep such a thing. But she also said that I was missing the point entirely. "They threw it away," she said. "What's so perfect about that?" I understood her point, but it only made me want to keep the album more. It seemed too sad for me to throw it away for the second time.

Instead, we buried it in an empty field as part of our next time capsule.

We made these time capsules about once a month. Inside of a shoe box we would put little scraps of stationery where we'd written our predictions. Then we'd tape up the box and bury it. Sometimes I would predict where Maria would be in five years, or ten, or fifteen. Sometimes she would predict where I would be. Like this time she predicted that in ten years I would be married to a doctor and living in River Oaks. And then I predicted that Maria would be a famous interior designer in a big city somewhere, maybe Los Angeles. We were pretty sure that some of our predictions would come true.

Dear Maria,
I wanted to talk to you in person, but I can't. I'm too mad. I can't
believe you left me there. I'm not mad about you letting Todd sit
with us at the movies. I mean, he was there too. But, you left me
there. I was totally worried. I even got the movie house manager
guy to look for you. We went into the bathrooms, out in the parking lot. I thought you'd been abducted or something.
    I overheard someone in school today saying that you and Todd
are some couple now or something. And I guess that's OK. But if
you two being friends means that you're going to leave me everywhere, make me walk home by myself while people like Sheryl and
Priscilla yell out the window at me, then I guess I'm not really that
happy for you. I just think you're being really selfish right now,
and I don't want to talk to you again until you apologize.
Your best friend,
Taylor

My mom knocked on the door while I was writing this. I told her
three times to go away, but she wouldn't listen. So I explained what
happened. And she tried to make me feel better by telling me that I
shouldn't be surprised. Because Mexican girls develop earlier, and
start having desires at an earlier age, and that my time would come
soon. And then she told me about the time that she had a fight with

her friend Annette over a boy named Dion. And I just sat there, still, wishing that I could be someplace where people didn't have stories that they passed on as if they were your life.

I nodded as she told her Dion story, pretending to listen, knowing that if I made my mom feel bad, she would stay even longer in my room, telling me about her own life. She loved to turn things around like that, turn my problem time into her problem time. But tonight, I was so attentive that she left after half an hour, feeling better about herself.

Immediately I went to Maria's apartment and put my letter through her mail slot. That way, I was thinking, we could have a fight about it by tomorrow. And Maria could tell me she was sorry. And it would be done. Back to the way it used to be.

my life would be like this:

By the end of freshman year at Jefferson High, when I was fifteen, I was up to two cigarettes a day. The first one I'd smoke at home, usually outside when Mom and Dad were yelling at each other. Most times, their fights started about him not working enough and her not working at all. And then ended something like this:

> Mom: *I should leave you, you lazy no good piece of crap.*
> Dad: *Fine. I'd love to see how you'd support yourself.*
> Mom: *I don't need you.*
> Dad: *I said fine. Just tell me when you want me to leave.*

And then he'd turn on the TV, right then, just to piss her off. And she'd go to church. And probably cry. She loved to cry. It used to make me mad, but now it happened so often that I just felt sorry for her. It seemed like she was the only one who didn't realize that at one point in her life, she'd had a better personality. But after years of trying her hardest and still never having enough money, she chose to lay herself in the Lord's hands instead, her favorite excuse for giving up. "I'm going to let Jesus drive from now on," she told me once, and I imagined Jesus cussing at the crappy gears of her Chevy Citation while she napped in the back. After church, her mind more at ease again, she would drink until her words started to slur. And Dad would stay outside of the apartment as much as he could, either working or playing with his model cars.

The second cigarette I'd smoke during lunch at the side of the phys-ed building. There was an old generator there, and I'd climb on top and stare at this picture someone had drawn in black Sharpie. The drawing was of a man walking down a long road and looking back over his shoulder, making sure that it was only him on that open road, that there was nobody else there with him to mess it up. It was signed Gaff.

It was also around then that Mom took to worrying about me again. After Maria and I stopped hanging out because of Todd, Mom told me that I "gave off signals" that I didn't want to belong. She knew that most kids tended not to talk to me, because every time she came late to pick me up after school, I was waiting alone. I'm pretty sure she was late on purpose, hoping that I'd make friends in all that meantime. But what Mom didn't get was that I didn't care if I had friends. I didn't want to talk about homework and nail polish and who stuck their hands down George Redd's pants. And from what I could tell, this was the only kind of conversation you could get at Jefferson. No thanks.

I was also by myself after school, since J.J. was away at Texas A&M. He'd decided to go to college, and—when my dad refused to pay for it—he surprised all of us by saying that he'd take a job and pay for it himself. So now he was at A&M, working two jobs and getting by, just like he always managed to do. And I was here, miserable, with my mom hawking my every move, out of boredom as much as concern.

And I was bored, too. I'd quit the high school's soccer team after just two weeks, because girls' teams suck, basically. And I'd taken to read-ing Faulkner, even though I could never figure out what was really go-ing on, just that someone was not quite dead yet and somebody else was playing with sticks or whatever. And I was bored.

Which is why I started volunteering at the Houston Cancer Clinic. When I told Mom I wanted to do it, I thought she was going to start singing some hallelujahs or maybe even hug me. I told her I wanted to help people. That I realized I'd been wasting my time by just watching TV and now I wanted to make a difference. I'd thought about it be-forehand, how I'd talk her into this, and I decided to think like a TV commercial and I know it worked because the next Monday after school she drove me the forty-five-minute trip out there, even after

Dad told her he did not approve. "We're too broke to be working for free," he said, again and again. But she was determined. I was going to turn out to be a good girl.

What I didn't tell anybody was that really it was all about death. On TV and in the movies, people were dying all the time. And I don't mean dying like you walk into your ninety-four-year-old grandmother's bedroom and realize that she "slipped away" in the night. I mean dying like drowning in the sea when your fancy cruise ship goes down. Or dying all tucked away, like if Boo Radley found out he had AIDS and couldn't tell anybody, and died with nobody knowing about it just like he lived. I'd never had anything like that.

And our school had never had that one tragedy that some strange part of people longs for, although they'd never admit it. Some tale of death, like maybe about some Betty Lou who got lit on Meister Brau and destroyed her cute little Volkswagen Rabbit in a big crash. And then every time people drove over the skid marks in the future, they'd retell the story of the wreck and the funeral, where maybe a pallbearer was so taken by sadness that he dropped his part of the body, and the casket opened in front of the whole crowd, who to this day swear they saw her wink.

But no such thing.

I got the volunteering idea during driver's ed on a day so rainy that all you could see out the front windshield was a big gray blur with flashes of passing light. Mr. Wu was telling Priscilla to "puu ova" because she was freaking out—something she seemed to do more often now that she was a cheerleader. I was in the back with Billy Talkington, who was cute and popular but picked his nose right in front of me because he knew that he'd never want to date me and that Priscilla was too busy driving to see. We were swerving all over the place. "I can't pull over! Billy, help me." At that point I was wishing something would happen, even with me in the car. It didn't have to be a death. I'd have settled for a good injury just then, like Priscilla having to cheer without a leg, and everybody would come to the games so they could say how proud they were of Priscilla on her one leg, still smiling and bringing light to all those football players.

And that's when it hit me. There I was, waiting for an accident to just happen, not realizing that *waiting* is what comes to those who wait. So I decided not to wait anymore. I wasn't going to kill anybody. I wasn't crazy. But there were places that attracted tragedies, where you could watch death happen, right there, up close, and people thought you were a better person for it.

My boss at the cancer clinic was Mr. Peabody. When he talked he waved his hands like a gymnast and rolled his eyes, and he always seemed to be confiding in somebody about something. "You will find your experience here, Taylor, to be what I call a *life* challenge. This ain't no scooping ice cream at the mall, I'll tell you that."

On my first day at the clinic I learned what death smells like. First it smells like pee, a little trickle of pee that you can't trace to its source exactly, that sort of hangs in space. And then add to the pee a little bit of sour milk. And a lot of vitamins. And just a touch of bad food and bad-food breath. Death.

Aside from my smell education, that first day was three hours of boring. I toted carts in and out of the rooms, delivering things like mail, or newspapers, or guests. And I figured out what I really wanted for myself.

I really wanted Annie's job. Annie started the same day as me, and I couldn't stand her from that first minute. She was one of those girls who didn't talk; she chirped. It was "gaawsh" and "golly" that punctuated her meaningless conversation. And on top of that she dressed only in the colors of cotton candy, so of course she got the job of talking to the patients. She'd go from room to room and chirp at all the dying people.

I was pretty sure I didn't get her job in the first place on account of I was already tagged as something else, something other than cheery or pleasant. Mr. Peabody nicknamed me Sour Puss that first day, and I was wearing my ratty shorts. Mom had debated buying me something nice, but ultimately she decided to spend the money otherwise. "Lord, listen to me worrying about your appearance," she said. "You're a *volunteer*, for God's sake. If there's any place where people see your inside, and not your outside, Taylor, this should be it." Instead she bought herself a foot massage to knead away all the tension of my father, she said. Then made me promise I wouldn't tell him. So, for my first three-hour day, Annie saw death and I saw only pieces of it. She saw what was going through their minds, and all I saw were hands, grabbing mail from me, or asking Annie to take a letter or something from me and read it. I wanted to talk to them—*What's it like to die?*—but only Annie really got to, and she wasn't even enjoying it.

I followed Annie into the bathroom and knew she'd booted when she came out of the stall and rinsed her mouth, smiling all the time, even though her hands were shaking so much she couldn't reapply her lipstick. I told her she'd get used to the living dead, and she smiled fakely. When we emerged from the bathroom, Mr. Peabody, who seemed to know what was going on, thanked me for helping out with Annie. By then it was time to go home. Mom was only ten minutes late picking me up.

On the drive home, Mom took me to McDonald's. She leaned over her tray of fries, undetected catsup clinging to her wrinkled elbows, and congratulated me. "It takes a very mature and developed person to give yourself away like you did today." I just nodded and scarfed my nuggets.

I thought about the time I stole the ice-cream truck. I thought I was mature then, since I'd managed to get away from everybody and walk home by myself. But that night, when I saw my mom after I'd been missing for hours, well, I bawled like a baby. And even though I know I wouldn't bawl like that now, I'm also smart enough to know that something will always break you into a child. Like what happened to Mom on that same night. When I walked in the door feeling proud of myself, Mom was in a drunk lump on the kitchen floor, rocking back and forth, squishing my dried-up birthday cake between her fingers. Younger than me she was just then.

Still, I sat quietly, munching my fries, letting her enjoy her moment, wishing that maybe I'd get promoted on account of Annie's yellow belly. Then my mom said it.

"Don't you think you should start thinking of someone to take to the Sadie Hawkins dance?"

"I didn't go last year," I said.

"Which is why maybe this year, I was thinking, you could get an earlier start."

"I don't want to go."

"There are tall boys, Taylor."

Once my mother overheard someone calling me Mount Taylor, and she was convinced that the experience had made me weird, that my whole life has been an attempt to be short somehow.

"I'm not going."

"A girl as pretty as you should have a boyfriend. You should."

I wanted to tell her that the last thing I needed was a boyfriend, or anybody else for that matter. I would have thought she'd have learned that by now, with the help of my father. Still, I said nothing.

"Trust me, Taylor, you don't want to be a loner like you are all the time. You can't live a life like that."

"So I should find someone to argue with instead? Like Dad?"

She looked at me, incredulous. I thought she was going to hit me or yell at me, but instead she just shook her head. "You're so young, sometimes. So young."

My wishing worked. The next Wednesday Mr. Peabody told me Annie had decided not to come back. Her parents thought the clinic was too traumatic for her and decided instead that she would take riding lessons. Mr. Peabody said he thought I should stick with my volunteering and "shine through" to all the patients. "I should have known that you'd be better at this. The misfits are always the toughest," he said, almost like he was talking to himself.

Later that day I met Mr. Reynolds. I remembered him more than the other patients because he wouldn't tell me his last name at first. "I'm Mr. Idiot," he said, so soft I almost missed it. "I want you to call me Idiot."

Mr. Idiot was staring out the window. At what, I wasn't sure. It was an empty parking lot, the one in the back of the cancer clinic, where no one parked. You'd think they'd have tried to give dying people something prettier to look at, but it was just blacktop and yellow stripes and an unusually high number of handicapped parking spaces. Mr. Idiot's arms were polka-dotted on the insides. They looked like little twiglets that had broken off the main tree of his body and fallen out through the sides of his robe. What was left of his white hair was poofing up in the middle in a way that was more sad than funny. With a huge effort, he raised his finger like E.T. to the window, then let it drop.

"Kid," he said, looking at me, his voice sounding like the outline of a picture instead of the picture itself. "You a boy or a girl?"

I was thinking to myself that he was in even worse shape than I thought. Still, I answered. "A girl."

He paused, contemplating whether he should say what he was thinking. He decided to offer it up. "I remember this room, but did it always have that window there?"

What? "As far as I know," I said, then paused. How do you keep up a conversation like that? "Do you like it?"

"Can't see that much, really. Can only see those dogs there."

No dogs in sight. "Yeah. Those are some dogs." I looked into his eyes long enough to see that he was really enjoying his dog vision. "I especially like the purple one," I added.

"Oh, yes," he said, then paused, feeling silly, which looks weird on an old man. "Why am I here and none of my family is here?"

"You have cancer."

"That's right," he said, remembering. "I have lung cancer." A pause. "You smoke?"

"No," I lied.

This is what I learned about Mr. Idiot over the next few weeks:

Mr. Idiot grew up in Tuscaloosa, Alabama. Lost his virginity there. But at sixteen he realized he didn't like anybody there anymore. "I don't like many people," he told me. "You may think me unkind, but I'm being honest. You see, me, I'm a thinker. When I was your age I thought about war. When I got older I thought about love. When I got older than that I thought up my writings and my business. But I was sixteen when I learned that most people in this world don't think— they fight, they fuck, and they consume." I smiled a little to myself, glad that he'd say *fuck* right in front of me. It was what I liked about him. That he just treated me like a person, not a kid.

So at sixteen Mr. Idiot ran away, because nothing was ever going to happen in Tuscaloosa. Nothing for him, anyway. Because he knew too much. He'd seen pictures of what other places were like. Good places. Places where you had to be smart to fit in. Places where you could really learn something, really do something, instead of just sitting still and growing a big butt in front of the television.

He joined the Navy to get out of Tuscaloosa, was how he put it. Not long after, he took up smoking, took up loving women, all sorts. And he lived out his traveling itch. Since then he'd spent his whole life wandering places, and writing some journallike things, up until the time he got tired of loving so many women and decided he could settle down. He started his business, which had something to do with advising people who want to start businesses in foreign countries.

Then he married this lady Anita, which surprised the hell out of me considering how much he talked about those other women and the "independent spirit," as he called it. But he explained that his wife was the only person more independent than he was. She started her own public relations firm from nothing and now had lots of money and people who worked for her. "She was the first person other than myself I could love because she was the first person I respected more than myself. Not a needy bone in her body."

"Why am I here and none of my family is here?" He asked this daily. I wanted to tell him it was because he'd married the type of woman who would throw out photo albums. But I didn't.

"Anita is coming over later," I told him, hoping it was true.

"Did the boys call?" he wanted to know.

"The boys" were the two sons he had with different women. Earl was in Japan and Josiah lived in Milwaukee. They were never close, he admitted, but he wrote them twice a year and had been sending them money since as early as they could spend it. But even with the money and the cards, I never met Josiah or Earl. "No," I said. "But I'm sure they will."

In Greece they drink alcohol that tastes like black licorice, and sometimes they eat a meal and then smash all their plates on the floor and on people's heads. In Spain people don't eat dinner until ten at night and then they go out until the sun comes up and then they sleep until they have dinner again. In Venice people get around on boats instead of cars, because the whole city is divided by canals. And in Mexico there are pyramids that you can climb, that were made by the Indians ages ago but are still standing strong. And Mr. Idiot had seen it all first-hand.

One day I'd finished up with the boring patients and their naggy relatives within an hour, which meant I'd have two hours with Mr. Idiot. With a shaky hand that day he passed me a piece of paper. At first I thought that maybe he'd put me in his will. I was about to get rich enough to eat out every night and stay in fancy hotels whenever I wanted, in whatever city I happened to be in that day.

But it wasn't a will. It was a list. "Of what you're going to do," he explained.

Where You'll Go: *Egypt and Russia and Austria* (and about thirty other places I couldn't locate on a map)
What You'll Do: *ride a donkey, fall in love, leave your love, fight for your own cause, build your own bookshelf, ride a motorcycle, scream in a church, keep a journal and once a year read the journal from ten years before . . .*

It was just a dumb piece of paper, but for the next three days I read it more than anything I'd ever read before. I kept it taped on the inside of my binder so I could look at it whenever I was bored and imagine all those things I'd never seen before.

• • •

The next time we had driver's ed, things were weird. Priscilla kept chattering to Billy, and he just sat still, not looking at me or her. So finally Priscilla shut up and I was so relieved by the lack of noise that I became oblivious.

Until I heard Priscilla's voice. "I've already been to Austria," she said from the backseat. I jerked to a stop three feet ahead of the stop sign. In the rearview mirror I saw her fake a yawn. "Boooring."

"What made you think about Austria?" I asked, already feeling the answer in the pit of my stomach.

I heard that evil coo of a voice. "Places I'll go: Egypt, Russia, Austria . . ."

"Put it away."

"Finland, Venezuela . . ."

"I said give it back."

"Oh, and this is good," she said, my binder spread open on her legs. "What I'll do: ride a donkey?" She laughed with too much effort, flipping her hair with such a head toss that for a minute I thought I had hit another car.

"No fighting," said Mr. Wu. "You fight, you don't pass class."

Finally Billy spoke up. "Put it away, Priscilla."

"What are you going to do to me, Billy?" she said, fluttering her overmade-up eyes. "Huh?"

"You're a bitch," he said. Just like that.

Priscilla threw the binder on the floor, leaning forward just enough to brush Billy with her overgrown chest. She whispered in my ear. "Keep your stupid list, you weirdo."

I threw the list away that night. First I memorized it, and then I threw it away. I told Mr. Idiot that I'd retaped it inside my new journal I'd just bought, which was two lies in one but made him feel better anyway. Not that he remembered.

The next day I was smoking a cigarette, looking at Gaff's work, when suddenly I realized that there was somebody standing next to the generator.

"Got another one of those?" I heard Billy say from behind me.

"No," I said. I had half a pack left, but there was no way he could tell.
"Mind if I stand here for a minute?" he asked.

"Free country," I said, and did my best nose exhale, feeling like a dragon in control of my lair, this little top of a generator that was my kingdom.

He leaned against the generator, which hit him at about his shoulder. "Cool perch," he said, and I nodded.

"You going to that dance?" he asked.

"You mean the one where the *girls* ask the boys?"

"Yeah, that one."

"What do you think?" I said, inhaling coolly, pulling in my cheeks, pretending I was J.J., who smoked cooler than anybody I knew.

He shrugged and waited, I guess for me to ask. I thought about it for a quick second. I thought about girls in expensive dresses sitting on one end of the gym while the boys sat on the other, talking about where they could drink afterwards and whose tits were looking good. No way did I want to go.

He waited just a bit more, and I could hear his breath, nervous almost. Finally he gave the generator a knock with his thick knuckle. "Later," he said.

"Later," I said back, not realizing that that would be impossible.

"Leonard Reynolds?" Dad said. "You're wiping the butt of Leonard Reynolds?"

"Now, Bill," Mom reprimanded, as she fixed herself a Scotch and soda.

"I don't wipe his butt, Dad," I said. "We just hang out. I cheer him up."

"Taylor," he said, "you're a lot of things, but I'd hardly describe you as a sunny kid." Then he sank into his big chair, pulled the recliner handle, and turned on the TV.

"Bill." Mom again. "Why do you have to hurt her feelings?"

"He likes me," I continued. "What's the big deal anyway? You used to play trucks with him or something?"

"People like Leonard Reynolds only drive the real thing."

"Well," Mom said, "even rich folks need good plumbers."

"He'd never call a plumber like me. His kind call *technicians*."

"Maybe if you got out of that chair once in a while you'd look good enough to be a technician, too," my mom said, never letting anything just drop.

"Maybe," he said, and then lowered his head, pouting. They always did this. He'd run her ragged with insults, then she'd bite back, then he'd pout while she got a little drunk. And at the end of the night, after I went to bed and they thought I wouldn't notice, he'd sleep in his recliner and she'd get the bedroom. And all night long he'd watch these movies that he kept locked in one of his toolboxes, where all these men just yelled and yelled until I could hear the yelling in my dreams.

But as wrong as my dad is about most things, he was right about Mr. Idiot.

Turns out Mr. Idiot was once hailed on the *Today* show as the voice of the sixties. He wrote about his travels for years and completed a collection of books that Mom says now feels a hundred years old, instead of just twenty. "But he made a mint, I'll tell you that. For a while he was living large. Can you imagine living like that? Having money to spare?"

If I were Mr. Idiot my life would be like this:

I wouldn't come back when I stole the ice-cream truck at thirteen. I would hitch a ride or hide in the back of a delivery truck. Once I got to Montana, I would lie about my age to get a job waiting tables at a pancake house. My first hundred bucks I would use to buy a banjo, which I would learn to play through diligence and hard work. After three years spent saving money and losing my virginity to a ski instructor, I would leave and it would be easy. I'd miss my dog Getgo more than any of the other waitresses who knew my age yet kept my secret, or ski instructors whose calls I never returned, or hippie friends who dug my poetry, which I read on Thursday nights at the local bar.

I would use my three years' worth of money to buy the cheapest ticket to anyplace in Europe, equipped only with a backpack and a foreign language. I would return ten years later, three languages in tow, no ties to speak of, no place to go but everywhere. I'd maybe get a job, in TV or something, and I would be good. I would become famous in time, the kind of famous where not everybody knows who you are, but every now and then someone would tap me on the shoulder. *Aren't you Taylor Jessup?* they'd ask, and graciously I'd explain that I didn't give autographs but appreciated their familiarity with my work, whatever that would be. I would live this way, happily, adventurously, for many years. I wouldn't carry a compass because no one, nothing, not a machine and not myself, could know what mountain I would climb next and in what direction.

"Why am I here and none of my family is here?"

I'd gotten good at this. "Your family is touring with Michael Jackson, just like you were until you got sick." This was one of his favorites. He'd ask, "How was I when I was a Jackson?" and I would describe to him the suit he used to wear, with the purple and orange sequins, that zipped up the side, and how the doo-wop was his specialty and then he'd try it for me. "Doo-wop," he'd say in his wrinkled voice.

"Fuck Michael Jackson," he said today. "Who the fuck are you?" His eyes were hard. His twiglets shook when he tried to shift in his bed. "Jesus Christ," he shouted. "Move me! Aren't you going to move me?" I hadn't been allowed to, but he was making so much noise that I felt like I had to do something. "Ring my goddamn buzzer. Jesus!" I touched his hand. I'd never done this before, but I thought it might calm him down. He winced, trying and failing to move his arm out from underneath my hand. "Jesus!" he shouted. "Get the fuck out of here," he said. "Get me a nurse. Jesus!"

Later Mr. Peabody saw me crying, quietly. He said, "Taylor, hon, I should have told you. I feel like this is my fault. The cancer spread," he said. "Mr. Reynolds may not be here when you get back next week."

"Oh," I said. I thought about Mr. Fleming and Mr. Gilbert, other patients who'd died in the past two months, and I tried to figure out why Mr. Idiot was so different.

"I've lost five friends this year," Mr. Peabody said, handing me a Dr Pepper. "Can you believe that? And it wasn't all about cancer, either. Do you know what AIDS is?"

"It's killing all the gays," I said, repeating what I'd heard on TV.

"And then some, and then some," he said, like a sigh.

"Why do you have so many gay friends?"

"Birds of a feather, baby," he said, and wheezed his way into a laugh. "I've been flying all my life."

"Oh, sorry."

"This ain't a sorry occasion, Tay." He took his time, judging his words. "Tay, did you ever think maybe you were attracted to girls?"

I thought about this. I did. And then I told him, "No." I first learned what gays were when I started being called one on account of how I looked and how athletic I was and how much I hated boys. All that teasing didn't make me realize I was gay, that's for sure. All it told me was exactly what I knew all along. That no one understood me.

"You really liked Mr. Reynolds, didn't you?"

"Mr. Idiot," I said. "His name is Mr. Idiot."

That summer I ended up getting more than I had wanted. I got my death experience, and I got my high school legend. And I knew I wouldn't want either again. But still I finally understood something that I never would have gotten from the television: that there are some aspects to our deaths and our legends that we choose ourselves.

Because if I were Mr. Idiot, my death would be like this:

My last coherent conversation would be with a young girl named Taylor. She would hold my hand even though it was slimy, and she would tell me lies she thought I wanted to hear, like, "Your sons just called and are trying to get to you as soon as possible." She would reintroduce me to my spouse, whom I hadn't seen in two weeks because of a once-in-a-lifetime reunion with college friends in Paris. This Taylor would tell me that she wished she'd known me before I was sick. Before I saw purple dogs out my window and thought I was the lost Jackson.

I would tell this young Taylor about my life, what I could recall. And I would describe my life's lessons to her, thinking they were original. I would drop the names of a famous few and tell her to set her standards above the ordinary so that she, too, could live the privileged life that I had. I would tell her not to believe in any emotion that can be expressed in a Hallmark card, not to buy into the American ideal, not to marry too young or have too many kids, and not to smoke, the one idiocy I myself had bought into. "Don't believe in God," I'd say, "but don't turn yourself into one either."

My funeral would be quick, efficient, and well performed. When all would be said and done, the last heave-ho of the dirt covering my casket, the world would miss me no more than I missed it. Only Taylor would cry at my funeral, partly out of guilt for being such a morbid jerk of a kid, but mostly because no one else at the funeral was. And that was the saddest thing she could imagine.

When Billy Talkington got shot in the back on a duck hunting trip with his stepbrother Coy, just about every high school and family in the city of Houston went into shock over the accident. It was like our own JFK. People hung ribbons on their trees. A fund was created in his name. All the things I'd hated before. But somehow, they were real. Even I cried at the funeral, remembering that day by the generator, and fearing that my old wish for a Priscilla accident had been diverted somehow, as if some satellite to God had gotten its signals mixed up. That this was all my fault, for wanting to get close to something that I didn't need to see.

There were several eulogies, from Greg Waldorf, who talked about the day Billy hit a grand slam to win the state pennant, to Betsy Harris, who read a poem he'd written to her about the stars once when he was camping. Billy had done nothing extraordinary in his life, I knew that. He was runner-up for MVP one year in baseball, his grades were awful, he smoked a load of pot, and he didn't get along with his mother. But people were crying. Even Mr. Wu. Everybody. And I'm pretty sure that everybody else imagined their own funeral just then too, assessed their lives for that split moment, hoping that if they ever got shot in the back, somebody would stop by and look at their cold, hard face in the casket and cry, saying, "I shouldn't have looked. I don't want to remember her that way."

the newbie

Surviving those two—Mr. Idiot and Billy Talkington—was like having a TV in my head all the time, playing each death over and over again and again. I'd think about that moment at the generator, when Billy wanted me to ask him to the dance. What if I had? Would we have been making out the weekend that he went hunting and had the accident? I would imagine Mr. Idiot, stressed out because he was seeing purple dogs. With no one there but me to tell him what was going on. And it'd make me want to cry.

There was only one way I could think to stop the death-TV that was playing nonstop in my head, even in my dreams. And that was Maria. It'd been almost six months since we'd stopped being friends. Since I'd had any friends, really. And enough was enough.

I followed Maria home from school every day for a week. It wasn't until the seventh day that she finally turned around.

"Taylor," she shouted. "You are such a weirdo!" I have never been so relieved to be called a name. She was laughing when she said it. She stopped in front of 7-Eleven and waited for me. "Todd and me aren't going anymore," she told me, just like that. I already knew, because I'd seen her eating lunch by herself lately, too. But I didn't tell her that.

"I'm sorry," I said, which was a lie, but one I figured she'd want to hear.

"I caught him feeling up Alaina Fontana," she said.

"Oh." I thought about telling her that I thought he was a bit of a jerk-off, but I didn't. I'd save that for later.

"So, you don't have to follow me around anymore," she said.

"Sorry."

"OK," she said. "Try this: Maria says she's sorry for being a bad friend."

It only took me a second to go back to our old game. "Maria says she's so sorry that she would walk on her knees through the school parking lot, in her underwear, singing 'Beat It' to prove it to me."

"You are so fucked up."

I raised my eyebrows at her. She didn't used to cuss.

But Maria now did a lot of things she didn't used to do. I'd heard people at school talking about how Todd and Maria did it on the football field one night. It turns out it was true. That afternoon, she made me swear not to tell anyone, and then laid out all the gory details. At first it was fun, but by the time we headed back home, I couldn't have endured one more detail about Todd's dick. Because all this talk about Todd and the football field was reminding me that I was already more behind in life than I was last year. That's what I was thinking when I opened the apartment door and saw my mom, drunk on the couch, not noticing that her robe was falling off. That's when she told me.

"He's gone," she said. Then again, "Your father left us."

"What?" I went into the closet in their bedroom, and all of his models were gone. She wasn't lying.

I came back to my mom, joined her on the sofa, where she was still sitting, numb. I wanted to know how we were going to pay for everything, whether we were going to have to switch apartments again. Whether he had left any sort of note, or something, for me. But I didn't ask her any of these things. I couldn't speak, really. Or even cry.

She continued. "Did I ever tell you that your father had a big important dream?" I had no idea what she was talking about. "He left me—and you—to become a newbie. Isn't that just the best?" she said, so drunk her eyes looked like they were about to roll back inside of her head.

"What are you talking about?"

"He's going to be a truck driver, honey. Gonna live on the road."

"Is he ever coming back?"

"He says he's going to come through when he can. Isn't that nice of him?"

"But, what were you fighting about that was so bad that . . ." I was about to cry by now, thinking about what might have made him snap. They'd always hated each other. Why did he have to leave now?

"He doesn't want our way of life, sweetie," she said. "He's got bigger things to do than us."

That night I called J.J. at college. He told me to remember that none of this had anything to do with me. That Mom and Dad lived in a fucked-up world where they made all of their own fucked-up decisions. And that part of being a kid is that you have to go along with their fucked-up world, at least for a time. "But don't forget," he said, "that it's *their* fucked-up world. And not yours. And that *they're* the ones who created it, OK? And as long as you remember that, this whole thing will pass through you like a vapor, man." But even as he was pretending to be a grown-up, I could tell that he was really upset. Almost like he didn't believe it. He kept telling himself (and me) that Dad was probably just letting off some steam. That if Mom said our apartment was going to be his home base, then it was probably true, and she was just overreacting. That Dad hadn't really left us. He'd just wanted to change his job and didn't want to have to run that decision by anybody else, especially not Mom. I knew J.J. wanted to believe all this. Still, I could tell by the way he was talking that he must have smoked two cigarettes during our conversation, which made me think he wasn't doing such a great job of convincing himself that he was right.

I hung up the phone feeling better, knowing I had J.J. on my side, but still pretty sure that I'd never see my dad again.

I sat in my dad's old chair all night, staring at the TV. I thought about going over to Maria's, but this was my thing. At least for right now. So I spent the night flipping through channel after channel, trying to figure out what it had been like to be my dad. Click. Click. Click. Until, finally, I fell asleep to the noise of the TV.

burning down the shed

If I'd never burned down the shed at Maplewood, then I wouldn't feel compelled to explain how I made a pup tent; but I did, so I will.

It was the beginning of my senior year in high school. I was seventeen, like the magazine. That age where, so I was told, things should start making sense. This was the year to think about college. To get sentimental about saying good-bye to high school friends. To start acting like a grown-up, whatever that means.

My life felt nothing like the magazine's. Kids would talk in the hallway about their college applications and scholarships and how many clubs they were in, and something about it seemed really gross to me. I made good grades, mostly because even trig books were more interesting than spending time with anyone at Jefferson. But what did those mean? That I studied? That I was good at memorizing things? It all just seemed silly to me. Senior panic. Dumb parties. Fact was, I wouldn't miss a thing about high school once it was done. And to me, college just seemed like more of the same.

"I want to go to Montana," I told my mother one night. She was on her second drink, sitting in front of the TV in Dad's recliner that she used to hate so much. That she still hated, even as she sat in it. Ever since he'd skipped out on us, she'd taken over his lazy ways that she used to complain about all the time. I was pretty sure she'd have started playing with his electric trucks if they hadn't been the only things he'd taken with him.

"Montana?" she said. "Is this a joke? A good way to run your mother into the ground? As if your father taking off wasn't bad enough. Now you want to leave, too. That's real ripe. Glad you've thought this through."

"I'm almost eighteen" was my brilliant response.

"And what about your job?" she said.

I was busing tables at Buster's, a twenty-four-hour eatery filled with pancakes and eggs and drunk late-nighters who didn't tip. "I'll get a new job once I get there," I said.

"Just like that, huh?" she said, in her most sarcastic voice. "And how will you pay for your move?"

I shrugged. "I'll figure something out."

And then her sarcasm faded as sadness sank into her face. Guilt. That look that all mothers seem to know how to give. "You've done so well at school, Taylor. Why give all that up?"

"I just said I was thinking about it," I told her. "It's not like I've got a plane ticket or anything."

That night I thought about my father. And my thoughts were far from good. Ever since he took off, he was in the way. When he'd been around, he could be ignored. But now that he was gone, it was like he was coming down on all of us. Especially my mom, who was clinging to me like I was her last hope.

The next morning Mom got up early and cooked me breakfast, something she only did when she wanted something. As she plopped a pile of pancakes on my plate, I gave her that look that told her I knew what she was doing.

"Taylor, I have an idea."

"I figured so much," I said.

"I want you to visit your brother. At college." My mother had never graduated from college, and she said the word as if it contained some sort of mystique that she assumed was as interesting and forbidden to me as premarital sex.

And in a way, it was. I'd asked to visit J.J. before, and she always said no. Ever since she found his secret place where he stashed not-so-artistic

porny mags and fresh pot buds in a Skoal can, she'd deemed him a bad
influence.

"So," she said, "why don't you call him?"

"I'll call him later," I said.

"Oh, come on, honey. Call him now."

"Mom, it's seven in the morning."

"Well, I'm sure he's got class, right? He's got to get up sometime."

I told her I didn't want to two more times before I finally gave in.
When I called, J.J. picked up the phone, half asleep. This is what we
said:

J.J.: *Hello?*

Me: *It's Taylor.*

J.J.: *It's seven in the morning, you fuckhead.*

Me: *Mom made me call.*

J.J.: *What's wrong?*

Me: *Mom wants me to visit.*

J.J.: *Why?*

Me: *Because I'm a senior. And that's what seniors do.*

J.J.: *Can we talk about this later? When I'm awake?*

Me: *Sure. I have to go to school anyway.*

All day at school I figured J.J. would come up with an excuse so he
wouldn't have to put me up. But he didn't. That night, while I was at
work, he called and told my mom which weekend I should visit. I was
sort of surprised. I missed J.J., but neither of us was the kind to keep in
touch in any regular sort of way, and part of me assumed that I was just
a dopey younger sister who he didn't really give a crap about. But his
calling back confirmed what I always had hoped was true.

That J.J. was the nicest person I knew.

And it wasn't just because he used to take me on drives, or because
I could always call him if I was upset. I think what I liked about him
most had nothing to do with me. I loved that you could never write
him off. Just when I was sure he was a stoner who'd never amount to
anything, he surprised all of us. First, by wanting to go to college. And

second, by getting in. And third, and most astonishing, by paying for it
himself. Maybe he was doing it for the wrong reasons, to prove he
could. But I didn't care. Everybody had been wrong about him, and I
found that thrilling.

I always pictured that the first person I fell in love with would be like
me, only a guy and opposite in some respects. Like maybe instead of
being too tall, he'd be too short. Or maybe instead of being pretty
smart, he'd be dyslexic or something. But Luther wasn't like that at all.
He was nothing like me.

Everybody wanted to be around Luther.

He was my brother's roommate. The first time I saw him was the
weekend I was visiting. J.J. had picked me up at the bus station Friday
night. I couldn't believe it, but J.J. had cut his hair. It was still longish,
but it was clean, neat, maybe even stylish.

"What's with the hair?" I asked immediately.

"Everybody assumed I was a stoner," he said.

"You are a stoner," I told him.

"Exactly," he said, as if he'd made a point.

He took me to a party in some guy's backyard, and when we walked
outside, I saw Luther sitting on a picnic table, with a few people
around him. He had a cigarette in one hand and bubbles in the other.
He took a quick drag on the cigarette then gently blew a cloud of bubbles, each one filled with a swirl of smoke. Luther turned and saw J.J.
and me. He shrugged his shoulders in this sheepish, adorable way and
waved as we approached.

"You must be Tay."

"Taylor."

"Taylor, sorry," he said. "I'm Luther. Do you want this?" he asked,
gesturing to the cigarette in his hand. I shook my head no, as J.J. took
it from him to smoke.

"I'm J.J.'s sister," I said. *Why did I say that?*

He smiled the most amazing smile. His teeth were big and white,
and seemed to match his preppy clothes, except there was a little

crooked one that stuck out in front, which only made him look more perfect, more defined. His hair was blond and dropped into his face. He brushed it away with his thick, muscly hand. "I know who you are," he said, and walked away with the most magnificent stride I'd ever seen. He was six foot four at least, which was just right, since I was getting past six feet myself.

When he came back he had a beer in his hand, which he gave to me. "I think that pitcher was enough beer for me for the time being," he explained. And then J.J. went to talk to some girl, and I was alone with Luther.

Luther was from a small town called Winthrop, Texas. He had one sister, and he spoke to his mother every other day on the phone. He was studying biology because he wanted to be a doctor someday. And he used to volunteer at a camp for kids with muscular dystrophy. It was then that he realized how he wanted to do something positive with his life through medicine, just like his father, who Luther claimed was the most generous man he'd ever known.

I told him about how for a year I volunteered at the Houston Cancer Clinic. And that that's why I finally stopped smoking. "About once a week," I told him, "I'd have this nightmare where my lungs were wheezing and I was so skinny that my pants wouldn't stay up. During the whole dream I'd walk around and around the clinic, pulling up my pants."

"Is that why you quit volunteering?" he wanted to know.

"I quit because of money," I said. "I had to get a real job."

"You've got a heavy head for your age," he said later.

"No heavier than it ought to be" was my response.

We stayed talking that way until J.J. came back to ask if Luther wanted another beer. He said he didn't but suggested that maybe I did. I looked at the beer in my hand, which was still over halfway full, just as J.J. shook his head no, as if I'd asked for one myself. "One beer and that's it," he said, pointing to the one in my hand. "And you shouldn't even be drinking that one."

"Geez," Luther said as J.J. walked away. "I never thought he had an ounce of discipline in him."

But I wasn't surprised. Or mad. Because I was used to J.J. being protective of me. And because J.J. knew that I never had really drunk before, except for a couple sips here and there. I'd told him once that to me drinking was what all the people I didn't like at school did at parties I didn't want to go to. So I stayed away from it as a point of principle. And I couldn't blame J.J. for not wanting a first-time drunk on his hands.

So I stayed sober, while they both got so drunk I ended up driving home. As we were getting out of the car, Luther grabbed my hand and squeezed it. "You're the only nice girl I know, Taylor," he slurred.

I didn't see Luther all of Saturday. J.J. and I just walked around. That's when I told him everything I knew about Dad. That I'd only talked to him on the phone once and that it had been completely surreal. That while we talked, Dad just kept saying how great everything was. And he was throwing around the lingo like it was magic to him. His handle (CB name) was Hot Rocket, whatever that means. His rig (truck) was a Big Mack (Mack truck). He'd been to Guitar Town (Nashville), Spud Town (Boise), Choo-Choo Town (Chattanooga). He'd chatted up coffee beans (waitresses) at the chew 'n' choke (restaurant), and squeaked by when the Smokys were thick (lots of cops). One night he even met a nice two-stool beaver (fat woman) who used to be a philosopher. I told J.J. that I'd wanted to ask Dad what the term for family was but didn't have the nerve.

"You should have," he said. "I'd like to hear the bullshit answer he'd come up with."

Then I told him about the postcards that my dad had been sending to me and my mom, sometimes in an envelope with a little check attached. The postcards always had pictures on the front, to show us the last place he'd been. And on the back, he'd write a thing or two about the place, as if he were traveling for all of us. J.J. took it all in, then told me never to forget that my dad was a motherfucker. I pointed out that Dad was still sending money. And that sometimes the notes were nice. But he told me that anyone who walked out on a family could never get above the level of motherfucker in his book. Then he tried to soften what he was saying. He told me how proud he was of how I was handling everything. Which would have been the highlight of the weekend, if only I hadn't met Luther.

The last time I saw Luther was on Sunday. He and J.J. and I went to get enchiladas together. I don't remember what we talked about, really. Just that I loved the way he ate, switching his fork and knife as he cut, wiping his hands every now and then on a napkin he'd laid casually across his lap. He had more manners than anyone in my family but wasn't so mannerly as to seem stuffy.

When they dropped me off after enchiladas, the last thing Luther said was "Come back and see us sometime, Taylor. Maybe by then big brother here will let you have a few drinks." And then he winked. Not a cheesy wink. The kind of wink that let me know that we were both on the same side.

I waved, hopped on the bus, and looked back just in time to see him bend over to get into the car.

I guess you could say I overthought the whole visit. Because in a daydream haze I decided that, given one more weekend, I could get Luther. And it wasn't just some game I was playing. I really wanted him. I was tired of being my own little protest group, not trying this and not trying that because it reminded me of all the people I didn't like. I deserved all this stuff, too. I deserved to know what a guy felt like.

Or I at least deserved the chance to try to get him. I wasn't sure what I'd do with him once I got him, but after the next weekend I would spend with him, if you asked him what girl he'd most like to spend a week alone with in Greece, he wouldn't say Charlotte or Anne or Carolyn. He'd say me. "Taylor Jessup." And his face would grin at the thought of me and my long neck (which he said made me elegant) and my long legs (which he said were sexy).

Now, when you start to like someone who's older, it's natural to want to show yourself in your best light. Your oldest light. Like, you'd never dream of wearing a high school T-shirt on a college campus. So, with that in mind, I picked up a few things for my next trip out to see them. I bought just the tiniest bit of makeup, so I could look older. And I bought a new R.E.M. T-shirt. And, feeling dumb and naïve for staying away from beer for so long, I decided I'd better learn how to drink.

That's when disaster happened:

It was my favorite kind of day outside. Just cold enough to wear a sweater and be comfortable. I decided that this was going to be the day I learned how to drink. I know it sounds dumb, but at the time it seemed like a practical idea. I wanted to boost my tolerance so I wouldn't look like a kid.

I got some wino to buy me beer and cigarettes. Even though I'd given up smoking since the days of Mr. Idiot, they were the only tool I could think of that might help me sober up before I went home to my mother.

I loaded up my backpack and walked over to Maplewood. It's really empty this time of year and close enough to Sunny Acres that I could walk. Outside of the fenced-in area where the pools are, there's a little playground and a shed. I sat down by the shed and opened up my first beer. Once I got halfway through, it tasted pretty good. By then I was enjoying both the beer and the time alone. I was thinking about where I might be five years from now. I'd be twenty-two. Would I be graduating from college? Or would I be in Montana breaking horses or something? Would I be with Luther? Probably not. Would I still be a virgin? Definitely not. Would I still be in touch with my dad? Or would he have disappeared out of all of our lives by then?

I was having a pretty good time until about halfway through my second beer. That's when I started hearing things. And I don't mean "hearing things" like I made them up. I mean like there were really things to hear. By the third beer (and the second pee in the bushes), I knew that the voice was coming from inside the gates. In the pool. It was a voice coming from the deep end. It sounded like a little girl, drowning. She'd come up for air, make a little squeal, then go down again. I got up and walked along the chain-link fence, half-expecting to see her, but there was nobody there.

It started getting dark, and that's when I began to feel queasy. At first

I tried to talk myself out of feeling sick. Tell myself that I was making it up. But I wasn't.

I went back by the shed, sat down, and leaned against it. I was hoping for sleep. But every time I closed my eyes, my head would start spinning again. I remember feeling so dumb just then. *Why in the hell did I do this to myself?* But then I also remember being glad that Luther wasn't there to witness this—which I guess is why I'd done it in the first place.

Ten minutes later and I was even dizzier. I thought maybe smoking would help sober me up, so I lit up my first cigarette, apologizing out loud to Mr. Idiot as I did it.

Then I got cold, so I lit the second one.

Then I got sleepy again, so I lit the third.

And then I fell asleep.

I remember waking up, opening my eyes a little, and thinking, *That is the most beautiful light I have ever seen.* For a minute, I thought it might even be God. The whole sky seemed like a halo. And then I felt the heat and heard the sound of something being eaten alive. It was the shed, flames dancing up its side. I got up and started to look for something to put it out with. Anything. And then I had to hurl. I took a few steps back and made a gnarly mess of puke. When I looked up at the fire again, I could tell that there was nothing I could do. I checked around the edges, and the whole little shed was surrounded by cement. I was pretty sure it wouldn't spread.

But still I wanted to do something.

I figured that there must be a phone or an extinguisher or something inside the chain-link fence, where the pool was. I tried climbing the gate, which was about eight feet tall, but I was too drunk. I fell back down before I could make it to the top.

And that's when I heard the sirens.

I remember, even in my haze, assessing the situation. It was empty beer cans and me, and it was pathetic, really. And too hard to explain. So I ran.

I only made it to the bushes before I had to yak again. By then, there were cops and firemen, so I stayed there, hiding myself as best I could. Which apparently wasn't very well. A cop found me less than a minute

later. In a stern and self-important voice, he asked me to tell him what
happened. I remember looking up at the fat cop, thinking how good it
would feel to puke. I told him, "I don't know," and then I barfed again.

"How do you suppose this shed started on fire?"

I said "I don't know" again, and then my eyes started leaking. I was
crying so hard that I was making blubber noises.

"It's a little late to be sorry now," I remember him saying. And the
next thing I knew I was in the car headed downtown.

At school, to everybody except Maria, I became "that girl." That girl
whose dad took off to follow his dream of being a truck driver. That
girl who eats alone every day and never wears makeup. That girl who
works at Buster's on the night shift, even on school nights. That girl
who burned down the shed, and might even have to go to jail. "What
a psycho," I heard some bowhead girl say.

I looked up *psycho* in the dictionary. Not that I didn't know what it
meant, but I wanted to see what it officially meant. "Someone who is
mentally ill or unstable," Webster's said. I decided that I was not a psycho but just someone going crazy because the rest of the world was
psychotic. How else do you explain all these kids I went to school
with? Kids who got cars on their sixteenth birthdays, and got good
grades despite the fact that they never really did anything. Who
watched dumb shows on TV and dressed like the people in them. Kids
who never had to look at anything standing from someplace else.
Who'd never looked back on anything in their lives because there was
always someone there telling them, "You're perfect just the way you
are, honey bun. Just follow the rules, go to college, do what everybody
else does, and you'll be happy." Now, *that's* psychotic.

Some people can make fancy things out of words, but I can't. At least
not when I have to speak them in front of other people. By the time I got
a trial, not even my mom believed the fire was an accident. After a
while, even I got to thinking I'd done it on purpose. Like maybe the

whole way I remembered it was a lie. I knew I was good at lying to every-body else, so why wouldn't I be good at lying to myself? Which is why I was so surprised when this lady judge decided it was an accident. I was free to go. "And I suspect by the trail of vomit you left, Miss Jessup, that these courts won't catch you drinking anytime soon?" I was given a ticket and probation and was glad that the whole thing was over.

Or at least mostly over.

People at school were still talking about me. But I'd grown used to it. People would say stuff, and Maria would find out who said what and then dare them to say it to her face, threatening to beat them up if they did. Maria loved this kind of shit. She'd always detested most of the people at our school. Because after her Todd days, they'd declared her a slut. And back then, she'd never really done anything about it. Just pretended it didn't bother her, even though it did. But now that it was me who was getting so much of their talk, she was fighting to the death, saying all those things that are sometimes harder to say if you're defending yourself but come easy when it is in someone else's name. I was glad to have her at my side, even if their words weren't as impor-tant to me as they were to her.

I should have known that my mom was up to something, the way she kept cleaning the apartment, scraping at things that would never get clean. And she hadn't cried all day. She told me to keep my Friday night open, because she had a surprise for me. I guess she was still hopeful for me. And for once, I was grateful for that.

At nine o'clock Friday night, the front door opened and a big bag of laundry walked in, followed by J.J. and then Luther. J.J., in an attempt to draw attention away from his haircut, hadn't shaved in days. Luther was even taller and cuter than I remembered. He gave me a shy, crooked smile and then a high five. "Tay!" he said. "How's the nicest girl I know?" J.J. just rolled his eyes as I blushed, partly because Luther was in the room, and partly because I was wearing old warm-ups that were way too big. Mom had told me earlier to change but hadn't told me why. So I'd ignored her and now regretted it.

• • •

"Have you heard from Dad lately?" J.J. asked later over our sausage-and-macaroni dinner. Mom nearly choked. Dad was off limits, not to be talked about.

"J.J.," she said sternly. "We have company."

"I don't mind," Luther said, so kindly that at that moment I wanted to tell him everything.

"Well, Luther," my mom said, with acid in her voice, "I do mind. And this is my home."

"Yes, ma'am," Luther said, and took a special interest in his sausage.

"He's my dad," J.J. persisted. "I just want to know if he's planning to visit. Ever."

"We haven't heard a word from him in months," she said curtly.

Now I knew this wasn't true and said so. "He called three days ago," I said. "From Portland."

"Shut up, Taylor," Mom said. "Both of you just shut up."

By then Luther was clearly wishing he was someplace else. "Excuse me," he said, and he rose from his chair to have a dip on our little balcony.

Once the glass door had slid shut behind Luther, my mom whipped around to J.J. "I was just trying to have a nice dinner. Do you know how long it's been since I've had a nice dinner? Your sister here, she's so busy setting things on fire that she doesn't have the time to talk. And you. Oh, I don't know. Your father's gone. G - O - N - E. Not 'away.' Not 'coming back for a visit.' He's gone. There. Are you happy now?"

"I just wanted to know if you'd heard from him. That's all," my brother said.

"Your father," she said, in her most sarcastic tone, "has more important things to do than pay attention to this family. He is a man of the road. A real traveling man. Living out that big dream of his." By now her voice was so shrill it was becoming unbearable.

"You're being ridiculous," J.J. told her.

"Life is ridiculous," she said. "Haven't you figured that out yet?"

• • •

Mom locked herself in her room for the rest of the night, while me, Luther, and J.J. played Scrabble in the living room. Luther had just spelled AHOLE, which I thought was pretty funny. My next turn I spelled out SHITZ, using the Z to get me to a triple-word square. I glanced over at Luther, who was staring right at me. Just then J.J. got all serious. "Tay," he said. "Can we talk for a minute?"

"What's with you?" I said, as soon as J.J. and I got into my room.

"I should be asking you the same thing," he said.

"It's not like I kissed him or anything," I said.

"Kissed who?" J.J. had no idea what I was talking about.

"Never mind."

"Kissed who?"

"It's nothing."

"You know why I came here this weekend, Tay?"

"Because you were worried about Mom."

"Because I was worried about you."

"I'm fine," I said, trying my best to be convincing.

"Oh yeah. Well, last I heard, people who are fine don't go around setting things on fire."

"It was an accident."

"Oh. OK. Sorry," he said, sounding more like my mother by the minute, with a mean tone. "Sorry. I forgot. You didn't start a fire. You just got so drunk, by yourself, that you puked four times."

"Three."

"Taylor!"

"Why do you have to bring this up? Just now I was having a good time. But it's like nobody will let me just forget about what happened."

"Taylor. It's because . . . because you have to at least acknowledge that it was a fucked-up thing to do. I mean, you were by yourself, outside, wasted and burning things."

"It was an accident."

"What were you thinking?"

I thought about Luther. About how good his butt looked in his

Levi's. About how he said I was the only nice girl he knew. About how this was just a dumb idea that got way out of hand. "Nothing."

"Look. I know this year has sucked. I mean really sucked. But when I saw you last time, when you visited, you were having fun. You were talking to people. I was, like, you know, happy you were there being my sister and stuff. And now you're some wack job I don't understand again."

"I am not a wack job. Everyone else is a wack job. I looked up *psycho* in the dict—"

"Just stop it, OK? Don't try to philosophize your way out of this one."

"Fine." Out of nowhere I started to cry. I hate that. Like all of a sudden your lip starts going crazy and that's it. You're done.

And, of course (what I hate even more about crying), he finally started being nice again. He sat down next to me on my bed and started scraping at a Charlie's Angels sticker on my bed's hand-me-down headboard. Finally, he gave up on the sticker and looked directly at me. "Tay, Mom needs you right now. She really does. And it's not that hard to help her. Look, all she wants is to think you're OK so she doesn't have to think about you anymore."

"That doesn't sound so great."

"Maybe it's not great, but it's easy."

I tried to lean in for a hug or something, but he didn't know how to give a hug any more than I knew how to take one. "Tay, there's somebody really cool in there. I know it."

I've been living with my family all my life, and there are still a few things they don't know about me. Like at night, when I can't sleep, I sit on the kitchen counter and eat cinnamon right out of the little jar. That's what I was doing when Luther came into the kitchen that night, wearing nothing but his boxers and a T-shirt.

"Gross," he said.

You'd think I would have been all panicked just then, knowing that he'd snuck up on me, sort of, but I wasn't. That's what I liked about

Luther. He just seemed natural. At everything. I shrugged. "You should try it before you're so sure it's bad."

While I was sticking my finger in my mouth, he hopped up on the counter beside me and stuck his finger in the jar, right where it was sitting in my lap. He licked his finger, then scrunched his nose a little bit. "The best thing I can say about this little snack is that I am not, at this very moment, vomiting." He hopped off the counter in one grace-ful motion. "I'm gonna make you something."

Next thing I knew he was digging through the pantry until he came across a little container of green sugar crystals, the kind you put on Christmas cookies. "Now we're talking," he said.

He hopped up on the counter again, this time so close I could feel the hair on his left leg tickle my right knee. He grabbed the cinnamon from me and started pouring the green stuff right into the jar. He capped the top, shook it a bit to stir, then dipped his finger right in.

"Nasty!" I was laughing.

"I tried yours."

"OK," I conceded, taking my turn.

We sat there, like that, side by side, sort of laughing and sort of not laughing, for what seemed like forever. Nervously I started swinging my legs. At first real soft. And then a little harder until my heels were thudding against the cabinet. I was giggling, finding the whole thing pretty funny, when I caught him just staring at me. The kind of stare that makes you aware of every part of your body.

"You're a hard one to figure," he said, not laughing at all. "Tell me what's going on in there."

"In where?" I said, not sure how to take his new serious tone.

"In the mind of Taylor Jessup."

I thought about telling him that it was his butt. His legs. The way he was leaning forward on the counter as he talked to me. "Nothing, really."

"Lie."

"What?" I asked, not understanding.

"That's a total lie," he said, not in a threatening way. More like he was saying he could see right through me.

I just shrugged.

"J.J. told me you're pretty smart."

"I guess so."

"So you're smart, and you're pretty." Did he really just say that? "And still you're setting things on fire."

"It was an accident."

"Your family, you know, they're worried about you."

"And what about you?" I said, my eyes not leaving his.

He met my stare for what seemed like minutes, then looked away, grinning. "I don't worry about you at all."

"Then why are you lecturing me?"

He paused a moment, calculating his words. "It's not an easy place here, is it," he said, more like a statement than a question. "I mean, with your dad, and . . ."

I shook my head no as he stared at the floor.

"You'll be out of here soon enough. Don't forget that," he said.

I rolled my eyes, then leaned forward awkwardly, my hair falling in my face. I had to lean forward because I'd felt this nervous laugh working its way out, and I didn't want to hurt his feelings. But I guess from the sound I made snarfing my laugh, and from the way I was hiding my face, he thought I was crying. Before I knew it he'd pulled me to his chest, rubbing the top of my head like a puppy. "Shhhhh," he kept saying, and I just stared out, my eyes open so wide that it felt funny to blink. "Shhhhh." I felt him scoot a little closer, and now he was rubbing my back. *Was this really happening?* I decided it was.

In one clumsy move I put my hand on his leg and I just kissed him. I thought it was one of those take-you-by-the-neck sexy kind of kisses, like Molly Ringwald gives Andrew McCarthy in *Pretty in Pink*. There was a quick second where we were kissing. I was sure that I felt his tongue in my mouth. But next thing I knew, he was pushing me off the counter.

"Taylor. I think you're getting the wrong idea here." Already he was looking over his shoulder to see if anyone had seen us. "I know you're having a tough time right now, but this . . . this isn't going to help anything. I guess you just misread everything, and that's OK, because I know you're young and you'll learn soon enough, but." He was walking backwards towards the hallway as he stammered, all the time his eyes focused on me, serious, nervous.

And I was giggling.

I guess my eyes told him what I was giggling about. He glanced down at his boxers, where the pup tent he'd raised about a minute before was slowly receding. He looked back at me, panicked.

We stayed eye-locked for what seemed like forever. I wasn't sure whether he was going to move in and sweep me into his arms or yell out for J.J. to call off his sister. Finally, slowly, he walked to where I was sitting. He put his hands on my knees, leaned in, and kissed me on the cheek, right near my ear. I was concentrating on the heat and the wetness of his lips evaporating from my skin when he whispered, deep and low. "You seem like a girl who can keep a secret," he said. I nodded. I didn't need to tell anybody. Knowing it myself was thrilling enough.

I remember one time, when I was pretty young, I spent about one hour being noticed. I'd just gotten a new bikini, and had sprouted a new body a few weeks before, and all these guys who before then thought I was anything but a girl started to pay attention. I think I might have even been sexy that afternoon. At least a little. But by the end of that day, when the guys' idea of sexy turned out to be more ambitious than my own, I vowed never to wear tight pants. Never to wear tight shirts. Never to show my legs if I could avoid it. I decided I was more of an "it." When I got to high school, and all the girls wanted to talk about was jackass boys and who did what with whom, I decided to stay an "it." It seemed easier, I guess.

But after I saw Luther's tent, something inside of me just took off. I kept thinking that there was a chance I might actually like all this stuff. Which is how I ended up having lunch with Charlie Simmons.

While he sucked down his chocolate pudding pack, I asked him if he would take off his glasses for me. You'd think I'd asked him to strip off his undies the way his whole face seemed to shrink in embarrassment. He pulled his frames off, slowly, and then froze, silent, awaiting assessment.

He looked exactly the same without his glasses, just with more visible pores. "You're not bad looking," I lied.

Two days later and we were making out on the generator. His tent wasn't as big as Luther's, but it was still there. I didn't touch it then, but I knew I was going to pretty soon. While we were in the heat of making out, I pretended he was Luther, and I remember just then, just when I'd mentally transformed even his meager body into Luther's stony one, this Luther leaned in to me and said, "I think I love you."

the whole bed

Graduation day. Four hundred kids sweating in hot robes, partly from heat, partly from anxiety. Four hundred names called. Four hundred big moments.

I was the one who tripped up the steps to the stage and rolled my eyes just in time for the photographer. I then obediently joined everyone else in the crowd, where we listened to the wise words of our valedictorian, Joyce Dixon. Maria and I once deemed Joyce most-likely-to-be-mute, yet still she forced a crowd to listen to her read (and I mean read) a painful ten-minute speech on the importance of having friends as we face the future.

During her speech I thought about college. I'd been thinking about it a lot lately, but I remember, during that speech, thinking that I'd figured out what college really is.

I decided that college is a place where certain people go and other people don't. People who can afford to go, do. People who can't afford to go, don't. People who have no real stress at home, no real stress in school, no real stress in life really, go. People who have brothers and sisters to take care of, who weren't always the most focused when they were younger, who "grew up" before they had to, don't. People who believe, like believe in "getting ahead," believe in being first, believe there is such a thing as being first, go. People who stopped believing a long time ago, don't.

If Maria, the smartest person I knew, couldn't go, then why should

I? And if other yo-yos at school were planning on going, people like
Lisa Lemme who thought that long hair that frizzes when it's humid is
a tragedy, then I didn't want to go. *She can "get ahead" all she wants to,*
I decided. *I'll stay behind where people are less than perfect but still
worth my time.*

And then I thought about Montana.

Which reminded me of my dad.

Dad didn't come to my graduation because he was on the road, but
he sent a postcard from Oakland, Nebraska. On the front was a picture
of a wooden horse. On the back he told me that Oakland was the
Swedish Capital of Nebraska and that the horse on the front was called
a dala horse, something that Swedes used to make out of leftover
scraps of wood to give to their kids. Then he added, "You graduated.
Love Dad." Mom was there in her best dress, an A-line number that
had started as yellow in the early seventies and now had more of a
creamish hue. She had been looking forward to this day all year. "My
second baby to graduate high school." She kept referring to it as my
special day.

Which is how we ended up at McDonald's, quietly eating our Big
Macs. Quietly until I told her: "I put a lot of thought into this, Mom. I
did. And I don't think I'm going to college."

"But what about Texas A&M?" she said, her face falling. "And that
scholarship?"

I tried to tell her. I did. I tried to be nice about it. I told her about
how unfair it was that Maria and people like Maria didn't get to go.
About how everybody I knew who hated learning, and who hated
thinking especially, was planning on going. "It's like some hoity-toity
club of people who want a degree just so they can take over their
dad's business or get an educated husband. It's just, if you ask me, it
has nothing to do with learning, and everything to do with class. And
that's bullshit."

She was so upset by this that she didn't even yell at me for cussing.
She stared me down, angry. "What's your father going to say?"

This phrase used to be a threat, but we both knew that Dad was so
absent these days he wouldn't even have an opinion on my future.

Which only made it worse. My mother had no sooner threatened to tell my father than her face tightened. "I just . . . it's important, Taylor. I could have done so much if I'd gone."

That night I called J.J. and told him I wasn't going to go to college.

"Whatever you want," he said, as I realized that maybe that wasn't why I'd called after all.

"Do you like it?" I wanted to know.

"Not right now, I don't," he said.

"Why not?"

"Did you call to talk about you or me?"

"I don't know. I just . . . Do you think I'm making a mistake by not going?"

"I can't answer that for you."

There was a long pause. I imagined him in his apartment. Was Luther there? Had he told J.J. what happened that night? My thoughts were interrupted by J.J.'s voice again. "Taylor?"

"I'm still here," I told him.

"I may not come back to school next semester."

"Why not?"

"It's a long story," he said.

"Just tell me."

I could hear him sigh. "I'm broke. And I'm working at night, and in the day. It's just, it's not worth it for me, you know? I don't even do that well."

"Oh" was my response.

"Don't tell Mom."

"Does she have any idea?"

"I'm just going to tell her I failed out."

"But that's stupid."

"It's just easier that way, OK?"

"OK," I said.

• • •

Two weeks after I graduated, my dad swung into town for the first time since he'd left, to sleep on the sofa, empty our fridge, ask my mom if she'd gained a little weight, and talk about how sorry he was that he didn't visit sooner. My mom wasn't buying it. She was giving him the silent treatment. I wasn't as strong. I was curious to see what he was like now, after all this time on the road.

When my mom had left to do some errands, I sat down with him in the living room, wondering what he would say to me. At first, it was nothing.

Then, finally, "You going to college?" he asked as he clicked through the TV channels, sticking on college basketball.

I shrugged.

"Shrug," he said. "You shrug your way through everything, don't you?"

"I don't know," I said loudly, clearly. "Is that better?"

"It's expensive," he said. "So don't go just to go. Because that'll be a waste of my money."

"My money," I said.

"Excuse me?" I could tell he was pissed, but I didn't care. I was pissed, too.

"I said, 'My money.' If I go to college, I'll be paying for it myself. Just like J.J. Don't try to act like Santa Claus, all right? Because lately you're more of a Houdini."

Then he yelled at me like I'd never heard him yell before. He wanted me to give him one good reason why he shouldn't be pushing trucks. All of us sitting around like baby birds waiting for him to drop food in our mouths. My mother not working even though she knew we couldn't afford it. Encouraging my brother to go to college, when what he really needed was work. And me, getting into trouble when I had everything he'd never had.

"You mean like a loving family?" I said.

"Taylor Jessup, I have never hit you. But I will tell you, the urge has never been so strong as it is now."

"Well, I'm not going to college."

"And I told you already. I don't care. It's your life, Taylor. That's the best advice I can give you." He took a moment to scratch his shoulder and drop his head. "It's taken me forty-seven years to figure that out. I just got my life. And now I'm giving you yours. Trust me. 'I don't care' is probably the nicest thing I've ever said to you."

I think Dad thought his visit would be good for my mom. As if he were blessing her with his occasionally concerned presence. Of course, this wasn't the case. She was a silent bitch for the days he was there, trying to ignore him with such difficulty that she appeared to shake from the effort at times. And the day he left, right after he walked out the door, she locked herself in her room, only to reemerge a few hours later and cook us a pot roast, which had been his favorite dish. She and I ate it together in absolute silence, like we'd been doing since our talk at McDonald's. The only difference was that this time my mom picked at her food, worrying that my dad was right, that she *was* putting on weight.

Finally, a few days after our pot roast feast, she broke her personal vow of silence with these words of forgiveness: "How are you going to support yourself without a degree, Taylor?"

I listed off all the things an eighteen-year-old could do for a living: Be a waitress. Hotel check-in girl. Ski instructor. Roller coaster operator. Secretary. Bartender. Waitress. I was running out quick.

"You forgot a few," she said. "What about working in a factory? That would be nice. Or maybe prostitution. Hey, have you ever thought about prostitution?"

I reminded her that she never went to college.

She feigned surprise. "You know, you're right. You could have everything. Everything I have. Two ungrateful kids. An apartment. A husband who's never home. An unemployment check. All this could be yours."

"I'm not you," I told her.

"Fine, Taylor. Fine. Go change the world. Go become a millionaire without college. Go on and make your miracle."

"Fine," I said. I had saved up four hundred bucks. I could work. I'd be fine, right? Better than fine.

• • •

It's amazing to me that no matter how different people are in a family, no matter how different they look, or act, how different their problems are, there's always something that the whole family has in common. And I'm not talking about a fucked-up family history. That's too easy. I'm talking about a trait, something that we all do alike even though we'd like to think we're different.

I am from a family of pretenders. I had become pretty good at pretending that I knew everything about college and how dumb it was. J.J. was pretending that he'd failed out, since that was less embarrassing than admitting that he was too broke to be a normal college kid. Dad had pretended for years that he was part of our family. And Mom was pretending that this whole Dad thing was just a phase.

Until now. Somehow my not going to college changed her. It was as if I was the last thing she was really hoping for, the last dream she was pretending still had a chance of actually coming true. Her daughter would have a better life than she did, she pretended. But now it wasn't true. My presence at the kitchen table searching through the want ads every morning taught her that.

And so she stopped pretending.

She stopped pretending that Dad was a good husband and decided to open up to her friends.

Except she had no friends.

But instead of pretending she had friends, she went to find them.

First she called the three women she used to play poker with on Tuesday nights. She'd stopped playing with them almost four years ago, but they were all she had left. It got so depressing I had to leave the room, as one by one my mom called the friends she'd had when things with Dad were bearable and she felt like going out at night. And one by one, there was an awkward, superficial conversation followed by a sigh as she hung up and moved on to the next one. She even started calling people from the church but gave up when someone said, "Could you spell *Jessup* for me?"

She was still barely speaking to me, but with no listeners on the other end of the phone, she had no other choice. I was up late watching *Cheers* when she sat down next to me on the sofa, adjusted her curlers, shifted on the cushion until she'd achieved the posture of a lady.

"I think it's another woman," she said.

"What are you talking about?"

She tried to look at me but couldn't, instead focusing on a thread hanging from her pink cotton robe. "I think your dad is with another woman. Maybe even more than one. And I'm not going to lay down dead anymore. I'm going to find out for sure, and then I'm going to . . ." She trailed off, trying to figure what the bigger punishment would be for him. Her leaving or her staying. "I'm gonna track him down."

One month after graduation, Maria and I were already bored. We decided that Houston sucked. We started calling it Armpit City since it was even more humid than it was hot. Any city dumb enough to be built on a swamp deserved to be left, we decided. If my mom was leaving for a few days, then so was I. So were we.

Maria had a new boyfriend named Diego. And he had a car. And a motorcycle. And a friend. Carlos. I'd had no luck with a new job yet, not even at Denny's, so we took off to see what New Orleans had for us. The guys would drive us there for the weekend, and after that, if we liked it, we'd stay. For good. I'd really been wanting to go to Montana, but it was too far, and Maria hated the cold besides, so I figured that we at least had to go *somewhere*.

Everybody but me got drunk on the way there, which is how I ended up driving for most of the six hours. We pulled into a Holiday Inn at six o'clock on a Thursday night. The minute we got to our room, Carlos and Diego lit up a joint. I'd never smoked one before, and I'm pretty sure I did it wrong, because I didn't feel anything. I just got real quiet and annoyed because all anyone else could do was giggle, at everything. And I didn't feel like giggling at all, what with my family falling apart like it was.

I should have left then, but instead I agreed to drive us to the
French Quarter. Two hurricanes later, I couldn't have cared less about
my mom. Or my dad. Or his other woman. We were dancing in the
street while a fat man played the piano, the rolls of his body bouncing
in time with the music. We watched little kids tap-dancing in the
streets and saw people drawing portraits. And the music was everywhere. I figured that this was what hallucinating felt like. Like existing
on some plane of music and color and laughter and being a little bit
dizzy but still standing upright, enjoying it.

Maria and Diego split off to get a tattoo in the shape of Texas, and
they weren't gone five minutes before Carlos kissed me. We were
dancing in this tiny hole of a place with people's IDs stapled against
the wall. There were three long-legged, tall-haired, majestic black
women swaying back and forth as the music pulsed its beginning. One
of them stepped to the front and began her breathy intro: "I want you
to think back, way back, to your very first time." It was a song about losing your virginity, and her husky voice seemed the perfect guide.

Carlos pulled me closer. He was twenty. He had thick stubble, and
I felt it caress my cheek. Maybe this would be the night, I was thinking. *I don't even know this guy, but wouldn't that be the perfect way to
lose it? In New Orleans.* "Giving him something he can feel," the lady
was singing, and I started to wonder how he would look down there. If
his beard was different than the guys' I'd seen, wouldn't the rest of him
be different, too?

Next thing I knew he was kissing me harder. "Taylor," he whispered
in my ear. "*Qué linda tu nombre.*"

I didn't know what it meant, but it sounded good to me.

That same weekend, my mother packed an overnight bag, threw it into
her Chevy Citation, and headed to Sport Town (Shreveport,
Louisiana). She'd lied to my dad's company, saying I'd fallen very ill,
and found out where he was headed next.

At the first truck stop in the area, she approached a bored, fat
trucker slurping coffee at the counter and asked him for a favor. He

jumped at her suggestion, eager. When he found out all she wanted was to use his CB, he agreed to it anyway.

"Fat Joe to Hot Rocket," he called out, and then asked for my dad's twenty (location).

Carlos and I made out on the dance floor until my face was burning from his emerging beard. He grabbed my ass with both hands, pressing himself against me. "We need to leave, Taylor," he said.

I opened my eyes again and immediately felt dizzy. "OK," I said. OK.

There were so many people in the streets that I clung to Carlos's arm. I felt complete strangers pressing against me. Breathing on me. Sucking in my air, and my space. I had to get out of there, fast. "We have to find Maria."

"Maria's her own problem," he said.

"But how will they get back?" And I'd no sooner said it than I realized I had no idea how I was getting back either. "I can't drive," I said, thinking I was too drunk.

"Neither of us can drive," he said. "They took the car a while ago Come on."

Next thing I knew we were in a taxi and my head was in his lap. He was rubbing the top of it like a dog, trying to coax it towards the growing bulge in his pants, but I fell asleep. As we pulled into the hotel, Carlos woke me with a soft kiss on my cheek, and I felt awake all over again.

Giggling, we peeked through the curtains before we went into the hotel room, not sure if we were interrupting something. We saw the empty beds and ran in, jumping on one of them. Staring in my eyes the whole time, he stuck his hand up my shirt. I'd just about decided that he could be the one when there was a scream. A loud scream. Maria's loud scream. Coming from the bathroom.

And Carlos just kept kissing me.

I pushed him off. "What are you doing?" he shouted at me.

He'd no sooner said it than I was pushing open the bathroom door. And then I couldn't move. I just. Froze.

I never understood why people had such a hard time with the word *fuck* until then. I'd always imagined sex like something in the movies, so *fuck* didn't seem dirty or anything. But Diego was fucking her. There was no other way of putting it. The shower was running, and she was leaning against the tiled wall of the shower, spread-legged, her back to him. Diego was behind her, his eyes closed as if he could be ramming into anything. Her eyes got as big as golf balls when she saw me. Diego didn't even notice.

I shut the door and stared at Carlos.

"You're one crazy bitch," he said.

"I thought something was wrong."

"No, baby. Something was *right*. That's why you heard her carrying on like that."

I lay down next to him, not sure what to do next. He moved on top of me and began unbuttoning my pants. "Sounds like maybe we have a virgin in there," he said to me softly, more like a question.

Just then I knew how young I was. How dumb I was. How little I knew about anything. But just for that moment, I didn't want to learn. "I'm not a virgin," I lied. "But that doesn't mean I'm going to add you to my list."

"*Puta*," he said, under his breath, not quite in a mean way. He rolled off of me, and I rolled onto my side, trying desperately to fall asleep. I used to dream about this. What it would feel like. To sleep next to someone else. Next to Luther, maybe. How I'd feel his chest rise and fall each time he breathed. How we'd be close.

"I'm going out again," Carlos said. And next thing I knew I had the whole bed to myself.

"New Orleans sucks too," I told Maria as soon as the guys had dropped us off at Sunny Acres. But she was still gloating that she had a new boyfriend who was twenty-four and drove a motorcycle. Whoopee.

"Taylor, you're just mad that it didn't work out with Carlos. I love New Orleans."

"Are you going to see him again?" I wanted to know.

"Diego? I told you. We're like, a couple."

"OK."

"You really don't like New Orleans?"

"I don't want to move there."

"But, Taylor, we *could*. Don't you get that?"

"Yes, I get that. But, I mean, we've been there already," I said.

"What about Cincinnati? Diego has a friend who runs a bike shop. We could work there."

"Cincinnati is a place you run away *from*, Maria. What about Montana?"

"It's cold in Montana!"

"It's cold in Cincinnati, too."

We weren't fighting, really. But something was clear. "Do you love him?" I wanted to know.

"Yeah. Taylor. We're, uh, we're leaving for Cincinnati in three weeks, I think. Carlos is coming, too. You sure you don't want to go?"

Mom cased the truck stop for three hours. Just parked her little car and watched the people go in and out. "I couldn't figure out what your father liked about these places. I mean, the people go in and out, in and out all day long. Going noplace. I couldn't wait for him to show up."

And finally he did. It was dark by then. She was in the middle of chastising herself for thinking she could actually find him—out of all the truck stops, all the places. But, finally, she saw him come out of his rig.

Was there some lady, naked in the back? She figured there was. She figured there was either a naked one inside the truck or one in the restaurant just waiting to take her clothes off for him. But there wasn't.

She told me that she watched as Dad paced all the trucks. There was one with the light on. He peeked in. Exchanged a word with the driver. And then hopped inside.

"I was thinking," she told me. "I was thinking that I was the dumbest lady around. I couldn't help crying. He wasn't leaving me for somebody else. He was just leaving me to leave, you see? I was jealous of someone taking my possessions, but I'd never had him anyway. That's what I was thinking."

And, in typical Mom fashion, she started feeling guilty for suspecting him. He came out of the other guy's truck about fifteen minutes later, and Mom followed him inside the restaurant. To apologize, of all things. As far as I could tell, through all her crying, the conversation went something like this:

Mom: So, I followed you.
Dad (nervous): I noticed.
Mom (crying): I can be a crazy woman.
Dad nods (eyes shifting).
Mom: So. I just. I don't know what to say. I feel so foolish. I saw you go into the truck with that man and . . .

She is crying uncontrollably with guilt. With shame. She'd lost faith. She was such a bad wife. She was such a bad person. She was such a—

Dad (soft, seeming guilty as all get-out): You did?

Mom was just crying now, sobbing. For everything. For having a husband she didn't trust. For having a marriage that just plain stunk. For having a life that was nothing like what she'd imagined.

And Dad, well, he started crying too.

Dad (like a baby): I'm so sorry.

So now, they're both crying. Only now it's Dad more than Mom. He's just bawling and people are staring.

Mom: What are you sorry for?

She's hopeful now. He's apologizing. For being a bad husband. For being away. Maybe she does love him still.

Dad (after a long, awkward pause): I didn't want to be a queer.

They call them good buddies. Big burly guys who like to suck dick. And all the rest. My dad is one of them.

Three weeks after road-trip weekend, and Mom wasn't doing well. I was doing even worse. I'd gotten promoted to waitress at Buster's and was trying to be good at it. Trying to remember the abbreviations, run my food as soon as it came up, and keep peace with the customers, who were ordering me around like I was their slave child.

Friday was about the worst day ever. I'd just stopped having to train with Clarice, the head waitress, and I had my own station. And who should sit down but Priscilla and her parents. She acted like she didn't know me and ordered a chicken sandwich, then changed her order at the last minute to a salad. No croutons. Dressing on the side.

Just about that time her parents recognized me. "Why, you were in Priscilla's class at Jefferson, weren't you?" While they asked me where I was going to college, Maria walked in with Diego, trying to get me to go for a ride on Diego's bike before they left for Cincinnati. And I was just standing there while her mom told me all about Priscilla attending the University of Texas. "Are you thinking of pledging a sorority?"

"I just told you. I'm not going to college."

"I thought you were kidding."

"Well, I'm not," I said and then went outside to talk to Maria while the Priscillas gossiped about my ill-breeding.

Maria was high, like she always was lately. She asked me if I wanted to smoke a joint, and I told her no. I was working. Just then Mr. Davies, the manager, walked outside and caught Maria all high and me right there with her.

"Taylor, the wait staff is not to go outside."

"I'm sorry."

"What is that you're smoking?"

"I'm not smoking," I said, just as Maria let out an "uh, oh."

"Let me see you in my office."

By the time I'd gotten fired, Maria had already left. I was hoping she'd still be there, waiting for me. Waiting for me to tell her the truth about my dad, my family. But she was gone. For good.

On the walk home, I was actually hoping my mom was there.

Until she was there, in front of me, drunk. "Taylor," she said. "I need you. I really need you to do something." She gave me five bucks and told me to go to the store. "I need to know," she said. "I need to see it for myself." I called J.J. He wasn't around.

So I went.

I went into the 7-Eleven, just like she wanted me to. I scanned the titles, then asked to see *Men of Iron*. The old guy asked for my ID, and I realized that turning eighteen did count for something. Porno. He

passed the magazine over the counter in disgust, and I paid for it while
a mother and son team bought matching Slurpees and gave me dirty
looks. "It's for my mom," I said loudly. I didn't care just then. I didn't
care about anybody. Because if anybody cared about me, I wouldn't be
alone on a Friday buying a gay porny mag.

I was crying before I got home. Those pictures. Some man oozing
into another man's mouth while he stood in front of an eighteen-
wheeler. Another guy jerking off his little piss ant dick. Two guys fucking. I tried to imagine my dad, and realized that was why my mother
was going insane. I handed her the magazine, and she said one thing
after opening the pages and bursting into tears. "And you think college
sounds bad?"

I must have spent all of August on the sofa, watching TV and not
watching TV all at the same time. I'd lost so much weight that I looked
like a six-foot snake standing on its tail. Some days I'd read the paper,
pretending like I was looking for a job.

Only I didn't want a job.

I wanted everything and nothing all at the same time. I wanted a
wild life that was totally normal. I wanted loving parents who stayed off
my back. And, I wanted something to do. Somewhere to be.

My mom was worse than me. Taking on every pound I'd lost,
mostly by eating whole bags of Doritos. Drinking her way through *The
Tonight Show* so that it felt like a different experience, like some crazy
show she'd never seen before instead of a tired show with changing
guests that always were the same. The most I saw her move was when
she threw all of Dad's things away, including his recliner. Just left them
right in the street. And I watched, laughing.

Because we were bonded in a lie. A secret.

We didn't tell J.J. about Dad. We decided we'd be feeling better if
we hadn't known, so why should we ruin his game of pretend?

We developed a ritual. The day was spent watching TV, primarily
soaps. If it was a big day we'd give ourselves a halfhearted manicure.
More TV. Then I'd run to the store and count out pennies while pay-

ing for a TV dinner and ice cream. We'd eat in front of the TV, barely talking but comfortable around each other. When Johnny Carson said good night, I'd help her to bed, making sure she'd put out her last cigarette (a new habit).

But one night, after I put her to bed, tenderly laying the covers over her, it hit me. This was the closest I'd ever felt to my mom. We were mother and daughter. Not resisting. Just being. Alike.

I spent that whole night awake, in bed, sweating.

The next day, after an hour-long shower, I took my mom's old car and met my dad at a truck stop in Alamo City (San Antonio). I didn't know what I would do. Really. I just knew I had to do something. He'd made Mom pathetic and me just like her. And us pretending he was gone was just making it easy on him, not us.

He agreed to meet me at Dixie's Diner, a place meant to look like the 1950s, which might have succeeded if it hadn't been so dirty inside. He ordered both of us a beer.

"I'm sorry, Taylor," he said. Sorry, Taylor.

"You said that on the phone," I told him.

"What do you want me to say?"

"I don't know." I couldn't think of anything he could say that would make this less fucked-up. "Mom made me buy a magazine," I said.

"What magazine?"

"A guys-fucking-guys one."

My dad said nothing, just scraped at a coffee ring on the table.

"She wanted to see what your new life was like," I said, then put Men of Iron on the table, which he quickly took and laid on the seat, facedown.

"If I'm like this magazine here, then I can assume that what you do with your spare time is something like what I see in the pages of Hustler."

"Mom's getting fat because of you. And she's drinking so much she doesn't even care what she's drinking anymore. I just thought you should know that."

"And how are you?"

"What do you care?"

He stared, silent, guilty, for what seemed like hours. "I know you can't understand this. But I got a life now, and it's . . . Taylor, you've always hated me anyhow, mostly." He put his head in his hands, not sure what he was doing, looking like he was going to break. "You're going to spin this day through your head a thousand times. I know you. You will. And you'll always come out with me being some sort of problem, but . . . Do you think I want to be like this?"

"Like I'd know."

"Well, I don't. I'm sorry for being this way. But I can't help it."

I looked at him, slouched in the booth, talking quietly in case anyone else could hear. His head down like a cowed dog. I mean, just looking at him, with his big forearms. His furry chest. His sausage hands. My stupid father. My only father, really. I'd seen better and worse. Mostly worse, I had to admit. He never hit me. He wasn't a drunk except some nights. He paid my life until now, mostly.

I looked down at my hands, my fingernails bitten to the nub. I took a deep breath and said what I'd hoped I'd be able to say. "I don't care, Dad," I said, and he raised his head to look at me, knowing what I meant. "I just don't care."

And then I went home, feeling relieved.

And wrote a letter to my mom.

And left.

Home.

For good.

If learning what restoring means is the first step in working with antique furniture, the second is surely learning when a piece of furniture is worth restoring. That decision depends on the purpose in saving the piece. If a person is restoring a piece of furniture because it is solid wood and can be used, then almost any solid wood piece is worth the effort. In most cases, it will be less expensive to restore an old piece than to buy a new one, and the old one will be of better quality.

"Rules and Tools for Restoration of Antique Furniture,"
Restoring Antique Furniture: A Complete Guide,
by Richard A. Lyons

Dear Mom,

I know you well enough by now to know that you're going to be pissed. But I also know you well enough to know that you'll forgive me, eventually. You told me the other day that you feel like all the world is sucking you dry. I know what you mean. You telling me all your regrets, all those things that keep you up at night. Those things that keep you looking at me as if my pathetic life were actually hopeful. Well it all sort of sank in, I guess. Which is what makes this so funny. See, you're going to be mad at me because I'm leaving home for good. With no good-bye (we both hate those anyway). But then I know you'll be happy when I tell you that I decided I'm going to change some things in my life. I'm going to give college a try. I decided to go to the University of Houston, at least for a year. I'm planning on still working and saving up some money. And I'm moving out. But for now, I can't really tell you where I'm going to live. I'm OK. And I'm not with Maria, so don't go bugging her about it. And I'm not knocked up or anything like that. Or drugged up for that matter. I'm just away, Mom. And I'm thinking of you just like you're thinking of me. And I can't wait to see you again when we're both a little more ourselves.

Love, Taylor

There are certain days that run like circles in your mind.

Monday at the Rooster.

It was February, but I was still wearing shorts. Shorts and a collared yellow shirt. My name, TAYLOR, emblazoned on my chest like a logo. A few food stains from months of working as a waitress, this time at the Rooster. Stains that made me keep my jacket on when I walked home from work, even if I was hot.

I felt like a working mother, only with no kids. So single I was alone. So broke I'd eat at work most days and take rolls from the restaurant (and the little butters) home for the nights. I was nineteen, the age of opportunity, and all I could focus on were the lifer waitresses I worked with, who'd been walking in and out of this synthetic strip-mall restaurant since it was constructed in the early eighties. And all the nighters at U of H, people who were getting degrees for pride only, so that they could work their secretarial jobs and not feel inferior. Or at least not feel inferior all the time.

I viewed myself as one of these people.

Someone who was overcoming circumstances.

Because I knew hard times. I was sure of it. I was on my own. My dad had left my family to give blow jobs to other truck drivers he'd never met before. My mom, who I hadn't spoken to since I'd left home six months before, now guzzled down anything that would give her a buzzlike feeling. *I've been tried,* I thought. *I know hard times.*

I was sure.

That Monday, I was sure.

The special of the day was red beans and rice. A man in my station ordered it. A black man with short hair that was just starting to gray. He was wearing a plaid shirt and a vest. And Red Wing boots. I decided that he was a construction worker.

"Red beans and rice. And a large iced tea. And, could you bring me some rolls?" he asked.

I brought him all of these things. And I watched him enjoy them. I watched the way he chewed. He didn't have a book or a magazine or anything, so I kept trying to figure out what he was looking at. What he was thinking. I imagined that he had a sick child somewhere. And a wife who he brought flowers to once a month.

He was a charming man, I decided.

Until he called me over to his table. "I just bit down, like so." He reenacted a hearty chew. "And a rock in these here red beans and rice . . . it broke my crown. Brand-new crown." He brought his hand to his cheek for effect.

I'd heard a story about rocks ending up in beans before. But I'd also heard of people who think that every customer is only one complaint away from a free dinner.

"I assume that I won't be expected to pay for this," he said. I told him I didn't have the authority to make those decisions. "Be right back" is what I said.

Clint, the manager, was behind the bar, flirting with the top-heavy bartendress he'd hired for those two very reasons. "Let me guess," he said, once I'd coaxed him away. "That nice black gentleman in the booth by the bar?"

I nodded.

"I tell you," he said. "A few years of this job and you can really pick out the winners."

Next thing I knew, Clint was at the table, trying his best to look official. Focused. Managerial. "Is there a problem, sir?" I was standing behind Clint, my arms folded across my chest, waiting for the prosecution to present his case. *This'll be good*, I was thinking, craving anything that might make one day feel different from the next.

Clint gave the man a long, dirty-feeling once-over. And the man spoke. "Your menu says red beans and rice, but it doesn't say anything about rocks." He said it like he was being witty.

"Probably because we don't serve rocks. Or can you read?" Clint was pretending to be witty, too.

The man reenacted the hearty chew, then explained the loss of his crown.

"Your crown?" Clint had this way of repeating everything the man said. "And let me guess. Was it gold?"

It was.

Clint wanted proof. "Well, if it fell out, you don't mind showing me the crown then, do you?"

The man explained he couldn't find it, then his head disappeared under the table.

"Taylor," Clint said. "Why don't you help this man find his gold tooth."

I disappeared under the table as well. I tried to get the black man to look at me, so I could squinch my eyes to say I was sorry. But he was focused on the ground. Sticking his fingers underneath the dirty table legs. I reached as far as I could underneath the benches, but still, nothing. Then I peeked out again and saw Clint investigating the man's near-empty bowl.

"Well, you certainly ate a fine meal before this mysterious incident," Clint said.

The man returned from underneath the table. I kept on looking. "If you think, sir," the man said, "that I wanted to lose my crown for a not-so-great bowl of red beans and rice, then you're a fool." I was still under the table, and wanted desperately to stay there, where I couldn't see what was going on. Trouble was, I could still hear it.

"I'm implying nothing," Clint said. "I'm simply letting you know that we can't give a free meal to *everyone* who claims to break a crown or whatever. I'm a businessman, and unless you can prove it to me, I can't pay for your meal or your fancy tooth."

I stuck my head out from under the table just as the man got up, threw down a ten-dollar bill, and walked out, right past Clint, right past Kendra, who locked eyes with the man as he opened the door.

I ducked back under the table to look some more until Clint told me to get the hell off the floor and go back to work.

One hour later I delivered my last check to my last table and started to wipe down my tables. I was in a bad mood, which wasn't unusual considering I was at work. But this was different. I was completely knotted up inside.

I was focusing on my rag. Thinking about how gross it was that I was cleaning the tables with a white rag that was clearly covered with brown spots from a day's wear. And, even more gross, I knew that when I was finished with my tables, I was just going to throw it back on the counter so another waitress could use it on her tables.

I threw the rag on the vinyl bench where the man had been sitting and began the catsup game—where you consolidate all the old catsups into a few bottles so that when you're done, it looks like you've got a few brand-new bottles filled to the top, instead of a bunch of half-filled ones with obvious signs of use. I picked up the emptiest catsup bottle and started pouring it into another one.

And there it was.

A gold crown that had never fallen on the floor but was wedged between the table and the wall behind the salt and pepper shakers. Right by the catsup bottle that I'd just picked up.

I brought the crown to Clint, holding it in the paper napkin I'd picked it up with, and he told me to throw it out. The situation had already been dealt with, he said.

So I brought the gross thing to the trash can. I threw it on top of the other garbage, and it fell out of the napkin and rolled into a take-out container. I sat there looking at it for a while, but I couldn't leave it there. I guess because it was gold.

So, when Clint wasn't looking, I picked it out of the trash with another napkin and put it in my pocket.

That night I tried to write a paper on the consequence of myth for my mythology class, but I couldn't think. Of anything. Except that tooth. I pulled out my spaghetti strainer and dumped the tooth in. Then I ran the water over it, hoping to get some of the junk off. I'd almost finished when the water forced the tooth over the edge and into the sink.

I stared at it. From close. From far away. I picked it up.

And my mind was racing.

Maybe I could track him down somehow and return it to him. Let him know that I knew he was right. That I hadn't doubted him. That I wasn't. White.

I imagined all the ways I might have intervened. "Clint, maybe if you weren't such a dumbass, you might have noticed the crown, right here." And I'd grab the tooth from where it was lodged. And this time the black man would be victorious.

And I would be the one who saved the day.

But I wasn't.

Which is why I kept the tooth.

Why I keep it with my rings, in my tigerwood jewelry box.

So that I see it every morning.

And remember.

That I didn't do anything.

And that I'm not anything.

Like him.

Or Kendra.

Or anybody on the outside for that matter.

the myth of the violet woman

He was about twenty-three, and his name was Reginald, or at least that's what his name tag at McDonald's said. I'd gotten into the habit of Egg McMuffins before my 9:00 A.M. mythology class, and Reginald was there at the counter every morning. Bright and early. He wasn't cheery, but other than that he was good at his job.

That job.

He was also a good librarian. I was working late one night in the library on campus, wandering the stacks, looking for a book on Melanesian creation myths, when I saw him there. He was kneeling with a pile of thick books on tribal rites. I stared a little too long, trying to place him. He looked right through me and said, "If you ask me to get you an Egg McMuffin, I'll whoop your ass."

I wasn't sure whether I was supposed to laugh. I decided not to, then proceeded to embarrass myself.

I said, "Do you do this every day? Work two jobs, I mean?"

"What of it?" he said, already returning to his reshelving.

"I just. Are you a student here?" I asked, trying to repair a damaged situation.

"What if I am?" was his response.

"Never mind," I said, even more embarrassed.

He spoke without looking up from his books, still kneeling beside me. "I'm getting my teacher's certificate," he said. "In elementary education."

"I'm anthropology," I said, then babbled. "But I'm starting to think that I'm living anthro, so why the hell am I majoring in it."

"How are you living anthro?"

I didn't have a clever response. "I don't know. People, I guess. I'm always studying people."

"Like me. Right now?" he said, his face so blank I couldn't tell what was going on inside of it.

I was staring at the bulge in his forearms. The little dimple in his chin. His thick, rounded lips. Anything to avoid his eyes. Then I spoke too slowly. "Like you. Right now." He glanced up at me so quickly that I'm not even sure he did, and then he looked away.

"Egg McMuffin with cheese." I'd been in every day since I'd talked to him in the library a week before. He still acted like he didn't know me.

"Bye," I said, to which he responded with a nod.

Because U of H is a commuter school, it wasn't like there were any events to help anybody along romantically. If I'd wanted to meet men, I could have gone to bars and met horny drunks, joined a sorority, or, I suppose I could have taken the offer of one of the random hecklers I passed on the walk home every day from class.

And then there was Reginald.

I went searching for him in the stacks one week later but couldn't find him. What I did find was Mary Jean, this fifty-year-old woman in mythology who asks too many questions and seems to care too much about college. She was driving herself nuts over which tribe to choose for our paper due next week. "That Romano is a real toughie of a teacher," she said. "That's why I like him so much. There aren't many people like him out there. I mean, he's focused, and dedicated, and so specialized." She paused a moment, leaning over to confide in me. "And handsome."

Mary Jean had decided to go to college after her divorce. "It is never too late to reinvent yourself," she'd been heard to say about a thousand times to near-strangers like myself. And from the way she caked on the makeup and loaded on the perfume, I'd say she'd been searching for a willing body to reinvent herself on.

I was thinking all this as she was going on about Professor Romano. And then I noticed that she was staring at my blank face. "Are you in there, Alisa?"

"My name is Taylor."

"Oh, I'm sorry. I must have mixed you up with someone in my study group. But I know how I'll remember next time. T for *tall*. T for *Taylor*."

"That's how I remember," I said, dying to get out of there.

"What was that?" she said. A great insult and she didn't even hear it.

I saw Reginald out of the corner of my eye, walking with a stack of books, his beautiful black arms flexing. "I've got to go," I told her.

Reginald and I ended up at IHOP. The preceding conversation in the stacks had gone something like this:

Taylor: Hi.
Reginald. Hey
Awkward pause. He looks at books. I look at ceiling.
Taylor: So, do you want to grab coffee or something?
Reginald: Not really.
Taylor: Oh.
Reginald: Sorry. It's just . . . I'm working.
Taylor: That's OK.
Reginald: Can you wait an hour?
Taylor: Sure. Where should I meet you?
Reginald: Out front, I guess.
Another awkward pause.
Reginald: Why do you want to have coffee with me?
I shrug.
Reginald: OK.
OK.

Coffee at midnight has "bad call" written all over it. And he was so tired by then that his eyes were starting to puff.

I asked him why he wanted to be a teacher, and he said, "Because education in this country is an embarrassment."

I asked him where he lived, and he said, "Why do you want to know that?"

I asked him how he liked U of H, and he just laughed. "Are you going to ask me how I like McDonald's?" he said.

I told him that I really liked anthropology. He pointed out that I was talking just like a white person. How amazing it is that white people study stuff that isn't practical at all because they're confident that there's a job at the other end of the tunnel.

"I didn't say that," I said. I hadn't. "But you have a point."

"I know."

I told him about how I almost didn't go to college. Because of money. And mostly because of Maria, who couldn't go, even though she was smarter than me.

"Smart," he said. "You mean in the grade way?"

"Yeah."

He laughed. "Where is she now?"

I told him that Maria ran away to Cincinnati to live with her boyfriend who drives a motorcycle and who calls her boobs Teta One and Teta Two. He said, "And you think she's smarter than you?"

I blushed.

We split the bill, and I followed him to the door.

"See you around," he said.

See you around.

In my mythology paper that week, I wrote about the Papuan Keraki in New Guinea.

Here is their myth explaining the origin of people: there was a palm tree in the land. One day Gainji, the Great Creator, heard voices coming from the palm tree. Mysterious voices, speaking constantly, but not in any coherent manner. Gainji the Great went inside the palm tree and there found many groups of babblers. He picked them out and separated them by their babbles, so that people who spoke the same language ended up together. And that is how people were separated to different parts of the world, speaking different languages, living different lives.

Here is why I like this myth: because in the world of this myth, people don't start different and end up becoming more similar later. They start together and are only separated because some god took it upon himself to figure out who belonged with whom. What made a group a group, in this case language.

B-.

Professor Romano asked me to meet him after class in his office.

"I enjoyed your paper," he said, then paused for effect, "immensely." He was sitting behind an old wooden desk in a spare but clean office, his strong, veined hands resting on my paper, his eyes looking unnervingly right into mine.

I noticed for the first time the few gray flecks in his hair. I was thinking, *He's probably forty-two, maybe forty-three. Definitely handsome.*

He stared at me, smug, as if expecting me to say something.

I said nothing, just shifted in my chair.

"Don't you want to know?" he asked.

"Know what?"

"How I can say that I liked your paper" — he paused again, grinning a disarming grin — "immensely, but . . ." He trailed off.

I imitated his tone. "But . . . what?"

"But only give you a B minus?"

I shrugged. "I've never been that good at papers."

He laughed, took off his little glasses, and rubbed his temples. Then he sat forward in his chair, leaning across his desk so far that for a moment I feared he'd leap right over and grab me. I could smell his clean, gingery breath, that's how close he was. Then he said it. "You need to take yourself seriously."

"Oh, I do?" I replied, which he claimed proved his point.

"Taylor, I look at you, and here's what I see." He paused as my face grew hot and I took a sudden interest in the patterned tiles on the floor. Blue octagons. White octagons. Neat.

I must have looked incredibly self-conscious, because he stopped himself short, saying, "Maybe you're not ready to know what I see."

I felt my lip shake nervously, almost like I was going to cry, although I couldn't begin to know why. "You can tell me," I said.

But he shook his head no. "Not yet," he said. "There's something I want you to do first."

• • •

My special "assignment" from Professor Romano was to write my own creation myth. If I were the head of a tribe, what mythology would I create to answer the most common questions in my people's lives: Who am I? How did I get here? How do I fit into society? How do I fit into nature? How should I live?

It was not a class assignment. It was to be reviewed with Professor Romano in one week in his office. Just me. And him. And we would have tea together and discuss.

I spent hours trying to write my myth. I didn't know whether I wanted to write a myth of forming or a myth of sacrifice. In a forming-type myth, there is some divine being who is in touch with holiness and chooses to craft people. After he literally constructs people out of something like clay, he sends them on their way, in the hope that they live according to his divine ways and teachings. In a sacrifice-type myth, the divine is less of a craftsman and more of a catalyst. The divine being creates life only through his own death. There is an emphasis on the ambiguity of life, where existing is a dual thing—from death comes life, and from life comes death, and so on.

I decided on this, a forming myth:

> During the time in which the earth was made only of brown, dusty dirt, Anesta was the only being who walked its surface. She, too, was brown like the dirt and brown like the sky was then.
>
> But she grew tired of brown. And she grew lonely in the empty space. So she spit on her large feet and walked the earth until beneath them sprouted orange flowers. Then violet fruits. Then radiant red trees, which were magnificent.
>
> But she soon grew bored of her flowers, bored of her fruit, bored of her radiant trees. Because nothing was alive like she was.
>
> So she spit on her hands and walked the earth upside down until beneath her hands sprouted people. Orange people. Violet people. Radiant red people. Stunning blue.

And she watched with pride as her colored people played in her colored garden.

But it took only two seasons before the colored people began to fight. The orange people were the shortest, so they needed to climb the trees to see far away. And they needed to eat the violets to stay alive. But the tall red people preferred to use the trees to build chairs to rest their tired, tall, heavy bodies, so they did not want the orange people to eat them. And they liked to pick the violets to put in their long red hair that draped to the ground.

And so on with the blue people and the violet people.

Everyone needed different things for different purposes.

So they fought and yelled and threw things and destroyed things. And the tall, brown Anesta, in a fit of fury, spit on the people and stomped on each of them until they became one with her being again, and no longer tainted her colored garden.

But again she grew lonely. Out of a pile of dried-up flowers, she constructed the first man who was brown like her. She allowed him to create the next person, and he made a small violet woman. But Anesta stomped the violet woman back into her feet, because Anesta had seen the violet people before and did not like them.

"I want a violet woman," the brown man said.

But all Anesta would allow was that he make a person of a color that did not yet appear anywhere in her garden.

And so he made a bland white woman, whom Anesta allowed him to keep.

And the garden spread to the ends of the earth.

And the white and brown people stemmed from these first beings.

And once every three thousand moons, a violet woman is born who lives only one moon before she disappears again into the feet of Anesta.

"You need to take yourself more seriously," he said for the second time.

"What?"

We were in his office discussing Anesta, eating stinky cheese with blue veins in it. "You heard me," he said as he fixed me a cracker with cheese on it. "Do you like Roquefort?"

I didn't know. "Yes," I said, grabbing the cracker, taking a bite, and quickly realizing I didn't.

"You have a gift for story, Taylor, but hardly a gift for self-examination."

"Oh."

"What is it that you're so afraid of?"

"Why do I need to be afraid of anything?"

"Spoken like a true child," he said, as I awkwardly poured myself a cup of tea.

I burned my tongue with the first sip, my mind racing with what I could say. What I should say. "You act like you know my life," I said.

"Maybe I do."

"I said that you *act* like you know it for a reason. You don't know my life."

"I know that you are of the tribe of people who are the most beautiful," he said. "You are your own violet woman."

I must have retreated a little in my chair, because he leaned back, away from me, and laughed. "All that I mean, Taylor, is that you're sort of ageless and timeless. It's a quality of the gods," he said. "It's a compliment. But something tells me you don't take those very well."

An uncomfortable silence hung in the air as I tried to figure out my role in this game he was playing. I looked him in the eye and he met my gaze without a flinch, daring me to look away. My eyes not moving from his, I asked, slowly, "What do you want from me?"

It was him who first averted his eyes, speaking casually again, relieving the tension in the room. "Taylor, it took me too many years to understand that there are few things on this planet that are worth my time. Most things I see, most people I meet every day are of flimsy construction. So, when I see something of value, I like to take the time to get to know it, maybe even understand it. Have you ever done that?"

"Done what?"

"Saw something you needed to understand so badly that you pursued it."

"I'm not that complicated," I said.

And he laughed.

After my meeting with Romano, I went to the library. "See you around." That's what Reginald and I had said to each other. But what does that mean? I decided it meant that we hoped to run in to each other. That we *would* run in to each other.

I searched the stacks, but all I found was Mary Jean. Again. "Taylor!" she shouted, too loudly. "*T* for *tall*. I remembered." She had highlighter all over her hands from her hours spent marking her books. "So," she said, as if it was any of her business, "I heard you're the teacher's pet."

"What?"

"Oh, you know what I mean," she said, not blinking, as if she could stare an answer out of me.

"Have you seen Reginald?"

"Who's Reginald?"

"Never mind," I said, and continued searching the stacks.

"How are you doing?" I said to Reginald at the McDonald's counter the next morning, ignoring the line of people behind me.

"Can I get you anything?"

"Egg McMuffin with cheese," I said.

"One fourteen," Reginald said, as if he'd never met me.

"Reginald?"

"Thank you," he said, his eyes moving to the guy behind me. "Welcome to McDonald's. May I take your order?"

Romano invited me to a dinner party that weekend. He said that I owed it to my mind to culture it a little bit. He explained that T. H. Thomas, the writing fellow that year, was going to be there, as well as a few other assorted journalists and writers and friends. "All you need to bring is yourself."

"I have to work on Friday."

"Well, if anything changes, you really should come." He wrote his address down on the back of his business card. I was staring at it in my hand: Dr. Jeff Romano, Department of Anthropology. The University of Houston logo was red in the corner. I was so absorbed in the card that I almost didn't hear him add, "And don't worry about what you wear. There'll be all sorts there."

That night, after work, I sat on my bed and stared at his card. I'd never had a business card given to me before. I wondered what my mom would think of my having a business card and eating cheese that smelled like old toes. I thought about calling her but decided I didn't have it in me. Not right now. So I called J.J.

"Taylor?" he said. "Where the hell are you?"

"I'm OK."

"I didn't ask if you were OK. I asked where the hell you are."

"Is Mom OK?"

"She never has been and she still isn't."

"I had to leave, J.J."

"Do you swear you're OK? You're not doing drugs or anything, are you?"

I couldn't help but laugh. "No," I said. "I'm living the life of a single mom."

"Oh my god."

"I'm not pregnant. It's just. I work at night. Go to school in the day. Go to the library in between. I like anthropology."

"Is that what you're studying?"

"Yeah."

"What the hell are you going to do with that?"

"Don't make me know everything right now," I said.

"So why'd you call?" he wanted to know.

"I got the guilts. About Mom."

"Have you talked to her?"

"No. I will. Just not now."

"And that's it?" he asked.

"Yeah. That's it."

"You're not calling so I can make up your mind about something?"

I was thinking about this lady who lived in the apartment next door for a while when I was about eleven, Miss Rocaine. She used to smell like a chemical garden and wear shoes so high that just watching her walk was suspenseful. According to our neighbor Al, for a whole year she screwed J.J. every day after school. I wondered if he regretted it.

"No. I just. Hi, I guess."

That night I took the bus to my mom's apartment. My old apartment. The first thing I noticed was how similar it looked to the apartment I was living in now. There was nothing homey about complexes like these. Nothing individual. Built specifically *not* to last, born out of the same do-it-yourself kit. For a minute I was worried that I wouldn't be able to remember which unit was hers.

But, of course, I remembered.

What was I doing? Why didn't I call beforehand? Why had I left her like that in the first place?

Because I had to. Because I had to. Because I had to.

I considered knocking but then worried that maybe she was drunk inside or something. So I decided to peek. The curtains were parted so I could see into the living room. A little sliver of her.

At first I thought she was vomiting.

She was on her knees in the middle of the floor. Was she dead? Drunk?

And then I saw the beads. She had her plastic blue rosary beads that she was clicking through as if her life depended on it. I was wondering what she was praying for. Probably for me. Or maybe for nothing. Maybe she was praying just so she could empty out her head for a while.

Either way, I left her alone, convincing myself it would be better to call instead, not to just show up like this.

When I got to my apartment, I did call her. She didn't answer. I felt first relieved, then guilty at being relieved. I left a message. "Mom, it's me. I was just checking in. OK? I'll try you again soon."

I thought how weird that was. Leaving a message. What would I have done if I lived in some time when they didn't have machines that let you take the easy way out?

I pretended that I would have knocked.

The next night I went to the library after work, smelling like fried okra, still wearing my uniform. Reginald hadn't been at McDonald's that morning. And I couldn't stop wondering what he was thinking about me. Did he hate me? Was he just shy or awkward like me? I had no idea.

I found him in the Civil War section, restacking books. The moment I came in, one of the books had caught his eye, and he was flipping through its pages.

"Hey," I said.

"I'm working."

"Why . . ." I trailed off. What in the hell was I doing here?

"Why what?"

"Why. Don't you. I just. Never mind."

"Why don't I grin every time I see your face at my counter in McDonald's?"

"Yeah."

"I had coffee with you. What more do you want?"

"I just thought that maybe . . ."

"Maybe what? We would date or something? I would take you out on a nice date and make nice with your family and nice with your friends and we'd be a happy little couple in your happy little white-girl world?"

"No. I just. I like you."

He leaned back against the shelves, then slid down to the floor. I slid down across from him as he started to speak. "I've been nothing but rude to you since we met. But you're just dying to get to know me. Dying for me to turn around your world or something. Well, I'm sure I

don't want that job. It's hard enough changing myself without changing the whole fucking world right along with me."

"I wasn't thinking any of those things," I said.

"That's because few people think what they're thinking. That's too
ugly. So instead they think one thing. And they tell themselves they
think another thing."

"I just wanted to get to know you better," I said and meant it, *hoped*
I meant it, feared I didn't mean it, that maybe my entire pursuit of him
had been some cheap, dumb attempt to right that wrong I hadn't been
able to fix. To prove whose side I was really on.

"Look, you seem like a nice girl. I just . . . I'm just not looking for
anything."

"Yeah," I said. I felt the edges of my lips quivering as he sighed, wiping his brow wearily with the back of his slender hand before darting
his eyes up at me one last time. "See you around," he said.

"Yeah," I said, my stomach sinking into my shoes, already feeling
like a wimp for letting him talk me out of what I was feeling. That in
him I'd found somebody else who had something to prove.

I traded shifts on Friday. Then I spent an hour trying to figure out what
to wear to the dinner party, until my bed was stacked high with out-
dated clothes. I vowed to throw them all away, knowing that the next
day they'd be right back in my closet. I settled on these fitted black stir-
rup pants and a tight shirt my mom had passed down to me. And a pair
of boots. And makeup.

I took the bus to his neighborhood. He lived in West U, a nice neighborhood near Rice University, in a small, two-story house that seemed
fitting for a professor. It wasn't like the overbearing houses in River
Oaks, with their boastful lawns. His house was something different. The
lawn wasn't angular and trimmed, the kind of lawn that is kept like a
crew cut. Instead, walking to the front door felt like walking through the
country, with uneven weeds poking out of the grass at my feet. And
there were four paned windows that weren't cluttered or doilyish. There
were no froufrou curtains trying too hard to make the windows seem

homey. The whole house was cozy on its own, with books and candles sitting on the windowsills, and the light from inside pouring out into the lawn. But the best part of it was the front door. It was a heavy oak door, with one inlaid panel at the bottom, and a thick center of glass above the brass knob. Surrounding this center piece of glass, almost like a picture frame, were small squares of colored glass. I could imagine the light shining through these squares during the day, making colored patterns on the floor that would move in time with the sun.

I took a deep breath, wishing I could just stay outside on the lawn and not have to deal with the people inside. Still I knocked, then heard the dreaded "Come in!" Slowly I opened that magnificent door, and entered.

Immediately I regretted my homemade makeover. The room was filled with men and women who looked like they'd walked right out of the TV show *thirtysomething*. And I looked more like I'd fallen out of the pages of *Teen Beat*. I realized immediately that I'd gotten dressed up in such a conscious manner that everything about me had become posed, unnatural. I had to maintain a certain posture just to fit in with my clothes. And, as a result, I was so stiff I couldn't even walk without looking awkward.

So I clomped down the long hallway, towards a room filled with people I didn't recognize. I stood at the door of the living room, just staring. The room grew quiet, and everyone stared back at me. I couldn't figure out why. I hadn't said anything. I wanted to ask them what they were looking at, but before I could Romano walked out of the kitchen, opening a bottle of wine. "Taylor, I'm so glad you came! So you've met everyone?"

"No," I said, talking directly to him, trying to ignore the rest of the group, hoping for help.

"Well, introduce yourself, then."

My eyes scanned the curious faces. I couldn't bear to look at anyone directly. "I'm Taylor," I said, and then sat down in the only chair I could find, one that was against the wall, away from the group. A tall man with a beard and silly round glasses scooted his chair over a bit to make room for me. "Do you want to squeeze in?"

I wedged in my chair and put all my effort towards keeping my fake smile from shaking at the edges. "I'm Tom," the glasses guy said. He reached out his right hand—I now know to shake mine, although it took me a moment to figure it out at the time.

There were eight people there all together, talking about Fitzgerald. I pretended to listen, fidgeting in my chair. *I shouldn't have come. I shouldn't have come. I shouldn't have come.* They had all just agreed to disagree on how Fitzgerald would have felt had he known that they'd published his last book he was still writing when he died, when Gwendolyn, the supersickly-skinny lady with a greenish complexion and an old-fashioned cardigan sweater, decided it was time to talk about me.

"So, what do you do, Taylor?"

Romano stepped in immediately. "Taylor is a student of mine at the university."

"A grad student?" she wanted to know.

I looked to Romano, who nodded as if to say, It's your turn to talk. "I'm studying anthropology. Professor Romano is my—"

Tom was laughing. "Professor Romano?"

"Well, he is her teacher," one of the other women chimed in. "I remember college. Such a wonderful time. You are so lucky to be so young."

"Thanks," I said dumbly.

"Taylor has never been outside of the state of Texas," Romano announced, as if I was the cutest little naïve thing he'd ever encountered. And it wasn't even true. But I didn't say that. I let the group guffaw collectively.

Then I asked where the bathroom was.

My mind was a blur of thoughts as I made my way to safety. I was thinking, *Who the hell was I to think I could ever fit in here?* As if I could put on a little more makeup and suddenly fit in with people who lived in houses like this one. I wanted to cry, and felt my eyes start to water as I walked into the bathroom.

But I didn't cry. I stayed in there for almost five minutes, staring at myself in the mirror mostly. I decided I didn't care if that whole group of hoity-toity people thought I was taking the dump of the century. I wasn't coming out of that bathroom. Not yet. Not until I was ready to go out there again, and prove to them that I wasn't just some stupid kid.

Just then there was a knock on the door. "Taylor?"

It was Romano. I opened the door, and he was standing in the hallway, his head dropped self-consciously, his hands tucked in his pockets, looking like a shamed child. Looking a lot like me just then. "Taylor," he said. "I shouldn't have said that. I'm sorry."

We were leaning on opposite sides of the hall, staring at each other. Really staring. Not looking away at all. Not saying anything. Until, finally, "I didn't mean to hurt you," he said, then leaned in and kissed me gently on the cheek. Then turned and walked down the hall. I followed him.

Dinner was already being served. Grilled chicken and vegetables. Homemade bread. Wine. I was seated next to him. Tom was talking about a trip he took to Mexico. About how San Miguel was beginning to look more like a retirement community than an artists' colony. This led to a discussion of the Ugly American, although it was beginning to seem like the ugliest Americans were all sitting right there at that very table. At a certain point, when Tom was accusing the skinny Gwendolyn of having a "ludicrous inability to think in a logical manner," Romano and I glanced at each other and I smirked. He reached under the table and squeezed my knee.

Afterwards Tom rolled a big joint and they all went outside to smoke it. I was about to follow the group outside when Romano called my name from the kitchen, where he was insisting on doing the dishes. "Taylor," he said. "Can you give me a hand here?" Tom flashed a grin, and Gwendolyn smirked. I walked back to the kitchen, embarrassed but happy to be away from the group for a little while.

I stepped in front of the sink, turned on the water, and picked up a plate, concentrating on the spots of sauce that had dried and stuck to it. I could feel his eyes on me as he dried. Then he put the towel down. Next thing I knew, he was wrapping his arms around me from behind, gently, his hands creeping under my shirt, then under my bra, as I kept doing the dishes, not sure what to do next. I felt him grow hard behind me before he turned me around and we began to kiss, feverishly, the way that I imagined people were supposed to kiss. I could feel his stubble burn against my skin. His hands running all over my back. He was breathing in my ear. "Taylor," he said, "you are the most fuckable creature I have ever met." He was pressing his body on me until we were rubbing against each other like animals. I felt my mind go blank and something else take over. Something wonderful and real. He lifted me up to sit on the counter, still kissing me, my legs wrapped around him. I was disappearing. I wasn't hearing. Anything. I wasn't thinking. Anything. And I was feeling. Everything.

Until I heard it.

"Professor Romano," a voice reprimanded, mocking. It was Gwendolyn, high, watching us, laughing. And then she left the kitchen as quietly as she had entered.

I told him that I couldn't go back out there. Not now. He told me that I was being ridiculous. "I'm . . . I'm going to go home," I told him.

He pulled me close one more time, wiped my hair away from my eyes, and kissed me tenderly on the cheek. "You do what you want to do, but . . . We can't avoid this."

"OK," I said.

OK.

Obviously I'll never sleep with Billy Talkington, since he died in that hunting accident. But if I *had* lost my virginity to Billy Talkington, the story would have been like this:

Billy took me camping. We packed a tent, canned food, and a case of beer, and drove his truck out to Lake Livingston. On the first night he was so scared he couldn't get it up. But on the second night, while the tent exploded with the sound of rain pounding the plastic, we got a little drunk, took off our clothes in our sleeping bags, and figured it out. Afterwards we were so embarrassed that we didn't even talk. He was worrying that, now that we'd done it, I'd make him tell his friends that we were seeing each other. And I was wondering why it felt so good for him, and not so good for me.

Losing my virginity to Charlie Simmons (the dorky guy I went out with after I set the shed on fire) would have been like this:

One day, when Charlie knew his mom was working late, he waited for me by my locker after the last bell. "My mom's not going to be home until six tonight," he said, so quietly that I could barely hear him. "Wanna, uh, come over?" he said. I told him I'd think about it, then ended up at his front door a few minutes early. Once we were inside his house, we ate cold macaroni and cheese and watched *Good Times*. When *Good Times* was done, he told me that he had a few condoms. We went into his mom's room, because she had a big bed.

Once I was in her bathroom, alone, I took off all my clothes. I came out in a towel, and he was waiting for me, naked, under the covers. He took off his glasses, and we kissed, our bodies barely touching. And then his hand grabbed my breast and he sort of rubbed himself against me, grunting like an animal. Finally he slipped the little guy in and we were done in a matter of about five seconds. (This virginity story I'm sure about, because it really did happen a few days after we made out on the generator, except that just after he rubbed against me, Charlie squirted all over himself and the sheets. He spent the next fifteen minutes worrying that he was going to get in trouble. Finally he decided to throw the sheets in the wash and pretend that he vomited on them while reading in his mom's bed. I went home and decided that I didn't want to see Charlie Simmons naked ever again.)

Luther would have been like this:

I went to visit him his junior year at A&M. He took me out for a nice dinner at a fancy French place, where they had tablecloths and linen napkins and waiters who spoke with thick accents. Afterwards, we drove back to his apartment. He took me to the roof, where he kept his telescope, and he showed me Orion and told the story of how the hunter Diana mistakenly killed her mortal lover Orion and dragged his dead body into the sky, that he might live on. We kissed for a long time on the roof until my legs were like noodles beneath me. In his bedroom, we drank wine and talked about his family and about how his last girlfriend broke his heart. And then we lay on his bed, on top of the covers, and he removed my clothes piece by piece, examining every curve. And I removed his clothes piece by piece. And then he began kissing me, everywhere, gently. And then he was on top of me, inside of me, staring deep into my eyes. And he said my name, just once, before I came, and then he came, collapsing on top of me. The next morning he cooked me breakfast, naked, and brought it to me in bed. And he brought me to the football game with him as his date. The next week I got a note in the mail: "I'm not sleeping well without you."

• • •

Carlos would have been the shortest of all the possible virginity stories:
I was drunk in a motel, in New Orleans, and I never saw him again.
It was painful and lasted too long.

This is how it would have been with Reginald:
I was up late studying for an exam, looking like a wreck, when I
heard a knock. It was Reginald, standing sheepishly at my door. I asked
him if everything was OK, and he said no. He told me that he saw me
with Professor Romano. "Why'd you have to hurry it and jump on
him?"
"Hurry what?"
"Couldn't you have waited a couple days at least?"
"What does it matter to you?" I asked.
"It matters because—" And he stopped talking, shaking his head.
"Tell me why it matters so much."
And then, without warning, he started to kiss me, strong and hard,
pressing me against the wall. He picked me up and carried me into my
bedroom. He laid me on the bed and proceeded to devour me.

This is the real story:
The day after the dinner party, Romano—who I now called Jeff—
told me that tonight was going to be my night. Would I maybe like to
go see an Athol Fugard play at the Alley Theatre? I'd never even been
to a real play before, but I told him that sounded perfect.
It was perfect. The play was amazing. It was called My Children!
My Africa! I always thought of movies as more moving than plays, because everything is more lifelike; but in this play the actors were just so
close. It was like real people going through a world of emotions right
in front of you. Right there. I was mesmerized, although a little distracted because he was holding my hand.
At intermission we went outside for some air. He led me into a dark

corner at the side of the building, pushed my hair off of my face, and began kissing me. "Taylor," he said. "We have to get out of here."

We were laughing as we raced to his car, holding hands, as a few people stared at us, trying to figure out if he was my father. Once we got to his house, he led me into his bedroom. He took off all of my clothes, kissing every part of my body. I must have been the only one naked for more than twenty minutes. And then he took off his clothes, eagerly turning out the light.

When he ripped inside of me, his eyes grew big and worried, then hungry. I was about to cry, it hurt so bad. But still he couldn't stop and I didn't want him to. I could see the pleasure take over his concern. And a few minutes later, he rolled off of me, satisfied.

We were lying side by side, not touching. "I had no idea," he said.

I was worried about the blood, but was afraid to look. "That's OK," I said.

"But I would have never—"

"It's OK," I said. "I wanted it, too." And it was true. I had wanted it. With somebody. In some way. I just hadn't quite imagined it like this.

the arms of antoinette

In the first months that Jeff and I were together, I assumed we were having an illicit affair. Something that would be fun for a while, as long as it didn't get in the way.

So I made sure it didn't get in the way.

At school I lied to Mary Jean, and anyone else who mentioned that Jeff and I spent a lot of time together, making up a story about how I was applying for a grant, and he was helping me with my application. And in class, I was business as usual. Every now and then, if we were taking a test or something like that, I'd go up to his desk and pretend to ask him a question but would really pass him a dirty note about what I wanted to do with him after class. And we'd also had sex in the empty classroom a few times (which was never very comfortable). But, mostly, being with Jeff wasn't a distraction for him, or for me. In truth, it had made me even more passionate about what I was studying. We would go out at night, and I could ask him about anything I wanted. And my work was showing that, for once, I had my heart behind something.

But even if my work was improving, and our time together was meaningful, that didn't mean I wasn't surprised—shocked—when he asked me to move in with him. His friends were also shocked, but not in a condescending way. More in a good-for-you way. Because it was well known among his friends that he hated people staying at his house. He was protective of it, almost.

When he'd bought the house, it was completely run-down. The plumbing was old. The roof was basically dangerous. There had been a termite problem. But still, Jeff knew that he wanted it. "I believe that houses have energies," he told me, "and the minute I walked in, I could feel that I was supposed to live here. It sounds crazy, I know," he said, embarrassed. But I told him that I knew what he meant. How the first time I came over, I wished that I could just stare at the door all night, instead of having to come inside.

"Really?" he said, excited, then went on to tell me how when his carpenter started doing work on the house, he had to break down one of the walls to get to the plumbing, and right there, inside the walls, he found the original door. He said the carpenter explained that all sorts of things are found in the walls of old houses. Money. Clothes. And occasionally things that previous workers didn't want to throw away. Or were too lazy to haul off. Like the front door.

That night, as if rewarding me for my interest, he gave me a tour of the house as he saw it. He showed me the curves in the walls that he said you rarely see anymore, not since the convenience of Sheetrock overtook the craft of plastering. He pulled up the Turkish rug in his office and showed me how the original wood was still there. It was inlaid, a mix of pine and cherry in square patterns. He couldn't bear to replace it with a newer floor, even though it was stained and splintered, clearly taken for granted at some point in its long life. He showed me the claw-foot tub in the guest bathroom. And then he made me feel the stairs. The deep dips in the wood from years of foot traffic. "Just think of all the people who walked up these stairs to make them like that."

That night we made up stories about the widow who used to live there. Because that was all Jeff knew about the lady who first lived in the house. We imagined that she was a playwright who was ahead of her time. Who used to have weekly readings of her plays in the living room, because none of the theaters would produce a woman's work. And that this is where her legacy lives on. Through the people who studied and learned from her, here in her own house.

Or maybe she was a dancer, back when Galveston used to be a big gambling town. A showgirl on one of the boats. Who was glad when her husband died, happy to have the house to herself.

We knew that our ideas were ridiculous, but this was a fascination we shared. Because how can you sit in a room, walk through a door, and not wonder who else has done the same?

"This house should have a name," I told him that night.

"Why?"

"Because"—I struggled for the right words—"she deserves one."

"She?" he said.

"She," I confirmed. "I definitely sense that this house is a she."

"Actually," he said, wrapping his arms around me, "she has a name already." He paused for dramatic effect. "Taylor, I'd like you to meet Antoinette."

I told the house hello. And the next morning he asked me if perhaps I would like to leave my little prefab junk hole and move in with him.

So many thoughts were running through my head. Like, what was my mother going to say? I was only twenty. He was over forty. She had already told me that she had no interest in meeting my pervert old boyfriend. What was she going to say now? What did I care? As long as he meant what he was saying. That he really wanted me that much.

I looked over at him, his eyes not meeting mine out of some sort of shyness or insecurity. He looked nervous, like a ten-year-old who'd just asked me to go steady and was awaiting my response. I took his hand and drew his eyes to mine. "Yes," I told him, then felt my eyes well up at the thought of waking up every day in the arms of Antoinette.

the myth of africa

My mother did not approve of my living with Jeff. I kept it secret for a few weeks, but after a while that just seemed ridiculous. So I told her.

"You're living with your teacher," she said, more as if to say, So, it's come to this.

"He's my mythology professor," I told her.

"It's immoral, and," she said, taking a dramatic pause, "I'm pretty sure it's illegal, since he's your teacher."

"It's a huge school, Mom. No one really knows."

I could hear her sigh on the phone. "How old is he?"

"He's forty-two," I told her, even though she already knew.

"And you are . . . ?"

"Mom, you know how old I am."

"It's perverted," she said.

"He's not a pervert," I told her. "We're just in love with each other."

"Maybe he's using you," she warned in a way that made me fear that *Why buy the cow . . . ?* was coming next.

"Maybe *I'm* using him."

"Oh, I see," she said. "Forgive me, then, for being so old-fashioned."

After that moment, she never brought up his name. I think she just blocked it out of her mind. She and I hadn't been that close lately anyway, and this just provided an excuse to give each other space. After that, our relationship consisted mostly of calling each other and talking about nothing. She got more into church, and I got more into Jeff.

• • •

After five months of living together, Jeff and I had developed a ritual. It
went something like this:

Mondays he went running in the morning. I went to school. In the
afternoon, I came back home and read for school, then went to work.
Jeff had tried to hook me up with a job in his department at the university, but it didn't work out, so he got me a job at Justine's, a fancy
restaurant with Continental-style food and high-end tips.

Tuesdays were always movie night. I admitted to him once that I'd
never seen a movie with Audrey Hepburn. So our first Tuesday-night
movie was *Breakfast at Tiffany's*. After that first Tuesday, I became well
versed in French New Wave directors and dead actors.

Wednesdays we had to have sex, more or less. That was our little
rule. Even if we didn't exactly feel like it. He said that relationships always slip if you don't have sex enough, so we made Wednesday manda-
tory sex night (with a few exceptions).

Thursdays were reserved for dinner parties with him and his friends.
Although I still didn't like Gwendolyn (the emaciated bitch who'd
made fun of me the first night I kissed Jeff), I'd become very good
friends with Tom. He called me Miss America. I think that nickname
started one night when we all got really high and Tom dared me to
sing "The Star-Spangled Banner" while standing on his picnic table
on one leg. Which I did. Well.

During the day on Friday I had no classes and no work, so I usually
attended a couple of the classes Jeff taught, because he liked to be able
to talk about his work with me. Friday nights were reserved for going
out to dinner. We had a map where he marked every country whose
cuisine I had tasted. He said that after three years, if there were any
blank spots on the map, we'd just have to travel there ourselves to eat
their food. By the looks of our map thus far, we were going to go to
Africa.

Saturdays we went running together, which I hated because I was a
little bit faster than him, and it always seemed to make him mad. And
half the time his legs would start cramping once we got home, so I'd

have to give him a massage, which I didn't mind, but he always seemed to complain that I was doing it too hard. Saturday nights I went to work at Justine's again. And he spoke to his ex-wife Teresa on the phone. We decided on that one together.

Sundays I slept until noon, usually exhausted from working Saturday. Jeff would get up at ten, drive to the store to buy *The New York Times*, which he claimed was the only worthwhile newspaper in the country. When he got back, he'd cook me breakfast (usually an omelette, turkey sausage, and coffee) and we'd eat it in bed. Afterwards he graded his papers while I wrote mine.

The reasons that I loved Jeff were much less organized and far more complicated than our routine. I loved Jeff because he always took me with him to parties, and never worried about what other people thought of me, or us. I loved Jeff because he couldn't resist working the tangles out of my hair when we watched movies. I loved Jeff because he was incapable of being surprised. No past was too dark. No story too horrendous, or too long. He could listen like no one I'd ever known.

And he could talk. So many people in this world (myself included) know a little about this and a little about that, which adds up to a lot of nothing, basically. But Jeff wasn't like that. If he knew something, he knew everything about it; whether it was a myth or a movie, he loved detail.

He also loved my details. I was never allowed to gloss over anything with Jeff. I couldn't just shrug an answer. I was always accountable. And it was terrifying. Terrifying and exhilarating.

Everything with Jeff was.

Then.

School was going pretty well, mostly because of Jeff. Whenever I'd write a paper, I would read it aloud to him so that we could discuss ways to improve it. The only bummer was that this occasionally led to fights. He was getting more and more pissed off at my professors. He said that most of my assignments were an utter waste of time, and some nights he'd confess that he really questioned the choices he'd made in his own life. Not just his ex-wife, but also his profession. "I should have been out in the field, making a difference, living a life that mattered. Academia is just exercise. Pure and simple. It's like running on a treadmill seven days a week in preparation for a marathon, only to find out that there *is* no marathon. So you're stuck inside a stinky gym. Running in circles."

Sometimes we'd talk about traveling to Tibet or moving to Zimbabwe. He even mentioned the Peace Corps a few times, but we never really did anything about it. Instead, we stuck to our rituals.

And then Maria came.

"Who's Maria?" Jeff wanted to know.

He also wanted to know where she was staying. It was well known among his friends that if you came from out of town to visit, you had to stay at a hotel. He was very particular about Antoinette.

I told him that Maria was my childhood friend and explained that money was tight for Maria and her fiancé (she was engaged to a cop named Richard). I didn't mention that she was pregnant; she was only two months, so he'd never know. I said Maria was really easy to be around and that he'd like her, which were both lies, but I didn't really have a choice. I wanted her to stay with us.

She arrived on a Thursday, which already threw things off. Thursday was Sam's night to host the dinner party, and Sam nights were always the most fun. There tended to be less philosophizing and more hanging out, listening to music, acting stupid. I wanted to just leave a key for Maria, so she could let herself in when she arrived, and Jeff and I could meet her after dinner, but he said there was no way he would let a stranger wander around his house. If I wanted my friend to stay with us, I'd have to be there to let her in.

It felt like forever that I was waiting for her, once Jeff had left for Sam's. What would she be like now? And how were she and Jeff going to get along? And would she be shocked that he was so old? Would he be shocked that she was so young? What would we all talk about? Why was I worrying?

When Maria showed up at eight-thirty that Thursday, I couldn't believe it was actually her. It wasn't like so much time had passed. But the last time I saw her she was high, riding away on the back of a motorcycle; now she was just beautiful. It wasn't her clothes, or her hair. She just seemed to glow. All over. She told me it was the baby.

I gave her a tour of Antoinette. I showed her all my favorite parts of it. Like the candles in the window. The heavy dresser in the bedroom. The claw-foot tub. The curved, plastered walls. The down comforters. The inlaid floor hidden beneath the Turkish rug. The painting on the wall that was given to him by his grandmother. The grooves in the wooden stairs. "Think of all the people who have walked up these stairs to make them worn like that," I said.

She ran her hands across the dips in the wood. "Wow," she said. "I never thought they'd be so smooth."

I made us a pot of chamomile tea and we talked nonstop. She told me about how she met Richard at the police station, when she was filing a complaint against Diego because he kept showing up drunk, and angry, at her cousin's house where she was staying. One night he even threw eight jars of mustard through her window.

But she told me Richard was like a dream. Not only did he beat the shit out of Diego one night when he was off duty but he also was the best guy she'd ever dated. She said he took great care of her, and from the way she beamed, I believed her.

I had just finished telling her about Jeff and our rituals when he walked in the door, half drunk. But well-behaved—more charming than irritable. The minute he saw Maria, I noticed him scratch his chin, which was usually what he did when he was sizing something up. "So, you're the infamous Maria."

"Yes, I am."

From the way he acted, you'd have thought he loved having strangers in the house. He showed her the bathroom and told her his joke about how the shower sings for you (the nozzle whistles). He even helped us make her bed in the guest room.

Watching him tuck the corners of the sheets the way he does (very tightly) made me want to cry. In a lot of ways, this was the first home I'd ever had. The first place I wasn't ashamed of. The first place where my food was in the cabinets, where my flowers (tulips) were in a vase on the kitchen table, where my T-shirts were draped over the wooden chair by the bed. Watching us make Maria's bed together was like opening up a storybook about family. There we were—husband and wife, mom and dad, the whole bit.

Later that night Jeff and I made love in a way that reminded me why we were so good together.

The next day, Friday, Maria and I went together to his graduate seminar on religion and myth. He was talking about Catholics, who he claimed are held captive by their mythology. According to him, they don't recognize their beliefs as myths but rather consider them truths. So instead of seeing religion as an attitude towards reality, they believe it to be a reality in and of itself. And thereby fail to see the hypocrisy in their criticism of other mythological religions. Prisoners of their own myths.

Halfway through the lecture, Maria leaned over to me. "Do you understand what the hell he's talking about?"

"Yeah," I said. "I do." Again I got chills. Just one year ago I would have spent the entire class fidgeting, not understanding, out of place. But Jeff had changed all that.

Which is why I surprised myself when I told him a lie after class.

I told him that Maria really wanted to see this band she'd heard a lot about. It was called Death Threat, a sort of punk thing.

"You'll miss Ethiopia," he said, referring to our previous plans for cuisine night.

I told him that "Ethiopians don't eat anyway," thinking I was being funny. According to his face, I wasn't. "Sorry," I said.

"You can't just say everything that comes to your mind, Taylor," he reprimanded.

"I said I was sorry."

"Just think, OK."

"OK."

"And have fun at Death Threat."

In truth I was the one who really wanted to go. I'd read a review of them in the *Houston Press*. It described them as "a psycho-billy version of Leonard Cohen on methamphetamines."

"I hate that kind of music," Maria said, but she pretended to Jeff anyway. "You haven't heard of Death Threat?" Maria said to him before we left. "Oh my god! Where have you been?"

While Jeff ate Ethiopia by himself, I was causing trouble for myself. Big trouble. The kind of trouble that comes from a couple of beers, loud music, and a lot of people pressing against one another.

It was the lead singer. Rock was his name.

He was tall and thin, wearing clothes that bagged just enough. His voice was something you could almost see, it was so thick and present. But what I liked most was that everything else about him was shy—the way he closed his eyes when he sang, the way he led the band with simple waves of his hand, the way he bowed at the end of the set. No jumping up and down. Just a simple, quick drop of his head.

And just before I left, when the show was over and Maria and I were standing by the bar, he looked at me. Checked me out, even.

"Didn't I meet you somewhere before?" Rock asked.

"Yeah," I lied.

"Where was it?" he asked again.

I scrambled and decided to make a joke. "Paris," I said. "Don't you remember?"

He froze for a second, then laughed. "You're pretty funny," he said, just as his manager pulled him aside for something. He turned and looked at me once more before he left. And he winked. Not the serious kind, but the joking kind. Very forcefully. Sarcastically. Like he was trying to tell me that he was funny too.

And I was hooked.

The next morning, Jeff wanted to go running. I was very hungover but feeling guilty about Rock, so I agreed. We made it through half of our six-mile route when his leg started cramping. He goddamned this and goddamned that, but in the end all we could do was walk, slowly, the rest of the way home. When we got back, Maria had cooked us some pancakes that were dry from sitting in the oven too long.

After a tense breakfast, I wanted to give Jeff some time alone, so Maria and I went for a walk around the neighborhood. We didn't say much, but it wasn't uncomfortable.

I pointed out to her my favorite house. It was this tiny one-story house with a deep, unkempt yard and a huge weeping willow that hung in front of the shuttered windows.

"I think it's spooky-looking," she said.

"Spooky? That's not spooky."

"It's so old," she said, then described to me the neat new subdivision where she and Richard were going to buy a house. "Just think," she said, "we'll be the first people to ever step inside," and she went on and on about the clean walls and working fireplace and its proximity to a new gym complex. But I wasn't really listening very well. I'd become distracted by something I saw in the garbage.

"Taylor!" she nearly shrieked. "What are you doing?"

Maria looked at me in horror from a distance as I rummaged through the garbage of the weeping willow house. A big pile of junk and lopsided plastic bags that had been left out on the sidewalk, waiting to be picked up.

"Girl, I had no idea things had gotten this bad for you," Maria joked as she walked over to me conspiratorially, sensing an adventure. "What the hell do you want out of the garbage?"

"Can you believe someone threw this away?" I said, then showed it to her. It was a wooden box—shaped like a small treasure chest, with a ship painted on the top. The paint had faded and cracked, but the ship was still there.

"Yes" was Maria's smart-aleck response, "I *can* believe someone threw that away."

It was actually nice to be teased again. "Well, I'm keeping it," I said. And hugged it to my chest and kept walking.

"What are you going to do with it?" she wanted to know.

"I'll fix it up, I guess," I said, then explained that this would be something that Jeff would appreciate. That maybe I would fix it up for him. And then I immediately felt guilty. Was I trying to buy him off or something because I felt like I was being a bad girlfriend?

"Can you believe," she said as we continued our walk, "that we both turned out so domestic?"

"I'm not domestic," I said.

"Please. You're playing house, aren't you? Dragging furniture from the garbage."

"I'm living with someone. That's all."

"So is he The One?" she wanted to know.

"Jeff?" I said, as we arrived at the house. I put down the chest in the grass and sat down beside it.

"No, who else would I be talking about?" she said, and I guess I blushed, because next thing I knew she was staring at me, her mouth agape. "Oh my god." She sat down, instinctively moving in beside me.

"I'm not seeing anybody else."

"You are trouble."

"I said I haven't seen anyone else. I've only ever been with Jeff." She watched me, silent, as my words really hit me. "Sounds pretty scary when you put it that way, doesn't it." I told Maria that every now and then, when I was being really impractical and ridiculous, I imagined what another man's skin would feel like. What I didn't tell her was that Jeff's skin felt different than that of any of the younger men I'd touched. It was looser. Not fat or flabby or anything like that. Just loose. As if with age it were separating from the bone.

"I love Richard" was Maria's response, as she proved again that she was in *that* phase. That phase where you think that life is perfect, that the whole world is revolving around you, just because you're so gosh dern in love.

"I thought you didn't want kids," I said, not thinking that maybe this wasn't the kindest thing to say.

"If I didn't want kids, I wouldn't be pregnant now, would I?"

"Sorry. I was just laughing like you were, you know. That we're so domestic."

• • •

Sunday and Maria was gone. Before she left she and I hugged for the first time ever as a good-bye, which made me feel weird and adult, all at once.

Jeff cooked breakfast and read the *Times* at the kitchen table. "Thanks for being so nice to Maria," I told him.

"I'm just glad to see you with a friend," he said. "You really should get some more friends, I think."

"Oh," I said. I thought I had friends. His friends.

It was as if he were reading my thoughts. "I'm not saying anything is wrong, sweetheart, I'm just glad that there are other people with whom you connect."

All that night I couldn't stop thinking about connecting with Rock. I imagined us making love outside, in a big field, daylight reflecting from his hair. I thought about this as I read the *Times*.

And I thought about this as I wrote my paper.

And unfortunately I thought about this when Jeff began rubbing my back that night.

"What's wrong?" he asked.

I told him it was nothing. That seeing Maria had just gotten me thinking about things I didn't want to think about anymore. That I was feeling guilty about my mom. Guilty about my dad. Really I was just feeling guilty.

He reminded me that I'd been talking to my mom more frequently now than I had six months ago. I rolled over and I looked at him. He was resting on his side under the covers, the chisels of his face more fantastic in the light. He smiled a little, as if he knew something else was going on in my head.

I could hear Maria telling me I was crazy to say this, but I knew I had to. I loved Jeff and he had to know. "Are you ever attracted to other people?"

"Of course I'm attracted to other people."

"Of course?" I said. "Like who?"

"Well, I was attracted to Maria. She's very pretty. But that doesn't mean I want to take my clothes off and do something about it."

"And that's supposed to make me feel better?" I said.

"Taylor, relationships don't fall apart because someone is attracted to someone else. They fall apart because people aren't honest about it. I mean, how ludicrous would marriage be if it meant that you were vowing never ever to be attracted to someone else? That's impossible. Marriage means you won't act on it. But attraction is inevitable."

"Maria?" I repeated.

"OK, I shouldn't have said that. I was just trying to make a point."

I was jealous until I noticed again the flecks of gray in his hair. I loved them because they matched his eyes. But I knew that Maria would never want to sleep with a gray-haired guy. Which made me feel better and worse all at the same time.

The smirk was back on his face. "So is that why you've been moping around all day, because you're attracted to someone else?"

"I didn't say that."

He took my hand, which was resting on his chest, and kissed it. "It's OK," he said.

I closed my eyes, finally feeling tired, when his voice snapped them open again. "So, who is it?" he asked.

"Why does that matter?"

"Is it Maria?"

"What?" I said.

"I'm just kidding," he said, although the disappointment on his face made it clear that he wasn't.

"No. Remember? Maria is who *you're* attracted to."

"Taylor, I was just making a point."

I rolled onto my stomach, retreating, but I was too mad to just sit there. So I turned to him and his smirky face. "His name is Rock. He's the lead singer of Death Threat. There. Do you feel better?"

He started laughing. "What does he play?"

"He's the lead singer."

"Have you met him yet? Or is this love from afar?" He said it in this awful tone of voice, like he was making fun of me.

"Yes, I've met him," I lied. "We're friends."

• • •

The next Saturday I lied a few more times. I told Sarah at work that
Jeff had surprised me with tickets to a play at the Alley, and would she
mind trading her afternoon shift with me just this once?

I told Jeff that I had to do some reading at the library, and would
work at Justine's after. So I borrowed his car and went to work the afternoon shift while he thought I was at the library. And then, when he
thought I was working, I went to Fitzgerald's, where Death Threat was
playing.

The minute Rock went onstage, I could feel everything in me race.
I was standing in the back, leaning against the wall, drinking cheap
beer. And he was sweeter than I remembered. It made me feel like
some animal looking at him, like some creature that needed to hump.
It was just so basic.

I imagined what he would be like off the stage. What he would be
like in bed. How he would look if he were curled up, sleeping beside
me in the morning. I imagined that he slept like a king, on his back,
his perfectly profiled face relaxed, gentle, not making a sound.

And that's when the girls came.

They were next to me, two girls who couldn't have been any older
than sixteen. They were smoking, dangerously, their ashy butts swinging closer and closer to my T-shirt. And they were chatting, incessantly.

About Rock. About how he was totally the cutest. About how she
heard so-and-so had slept with him once and said it was like the best
sex, ever. And so on and so on.

I was just about to tell them to shut up. If they liked Rock so much,
would they mind just shutting up so he could finish the set? And then
it hit me.

The obvious.

The only difference was that they were sixteen and shouldn't know
better, yet. And I was twenty and should.

I changed into my Justine's uniform before going home. And it was
home again, I decided. Jeff was home. Antoinette was home.

I took a shower and put on the negligee he'd given me for Valen-

tine's Day. It was simple, black with a V in the back. I'd put it on once
and it just made me feel stupid. Tonight I felt like an adult. A woman.

When he reached to turn the light off, I stopped his hand. "I want
to see you," I said, because I did. I did want to see him. He looked at
me, like an embarrassed child, and conceded. I took off his pajamas,
his boxers, as he took me out of my negligee. And we were like that,
naked, touching each other, staring at each other, long enough for me
to relearn his body.

And everything was different. Because in the light he knew. And I
knew. We both knew that I was younger. That my body was younger.
And still he offered himself to me. And still I accepted.

Monday, he insisted on picking me up from work. And he came early.
He talked to the hostess for a while as I closed my tables.

He was silent the whole drive home.

He waited until we were in the house, behind closed doors, to let
me have it.

"You should know that I blame myself for this. Even though I'm
mad, I blame myself. Because I should have known that if I dated a
child, I would get a child."

"What is that supposed to mean?"

"It means that I know you worked the early shift on Saturday. That
you weren't at the library."

"Why are you checking up on me?"

"And I know that you fucked your little musician friend."

"Oh, you do, do you?"

"Yes, I do."

I was so mad I could barely speak. I wasn't a child. "Why don't you
tell me about it then?"

"All I know is it must have really made you hot."

"Oh, yeah," I said. "I was really fucking hot."

"You go out and have some sort of crazy sex with some near-
stranger, and then come home and sleep with me in a totally different
way, and you expect me not to notice?"

"What the fuck are you talking about?"

"The negligee you haven't taken out of the box since I gave it to you. Making us leave the lights on. Taylor, having sex with other people changes you. And maybe if you'd been around a little more, you'd know how to hide it a little better. But. You make me sick."

"I make you sick?"

"Look, I know it's my fault. I should have known better."

"What's that supposed to mean?"

"You're just young, honey. That's all. This is all my fault."

By now I was crying, but he didn't care. He made up the guest room for me and said we'd talk about it in the morning.

Of course I couldn't sleep. I just kept thinking that he was being the child here. Not me. That he acted like I was untrustworthy because of my inexperience, but really it was him who'd been untrustworthy, him who had betrayed me.

So I went to his room. But the door was locked. I knocked.

There was no answer.

I banged.

Still he wouldn't say anything.

I yelled that he was a motherfucking asshole.

Still nothing.

I went into the garage to work on the chest. I had been planning on giving it to him. It had been my secret. But now, after this, there was no way.

I stared at it for a while, wondering who had painted the ship on it in the first place. Was it someone who was as frustrated then as I was now? Finally I got to work. I wanted to fix its broken hinge but didn't have anything to replace it with. Instead, I dusted it off with a rag, oiled it with Murphy's, and spent most of the time trying to remove the glue of a Smurfs sticker. As I scraped in vain with my fingernail, I thought of all the things I wanted to say to him. All the things I wished I'd said in the first place.

An hour later, after I finally removed the Smurf glue with the help of vegetable oil, I went inside and knocked again on his locked door.

Still no answer.

I woke up curled at the foot of his door like a dog, after he'd opened the door on me, then politely asked me to move because he had to go to work.

I followed him into the kitchen, glared at him as he poured his orange juice. And I told him the line that had kept me awake that night, in anticipation of being able to say it to him. "I never even met him, Jeff. But it looks like I'd never really met you before either."

"That doesn't make sense, Taylor," he said. "What is it that you're trying to say?"

My lip was shaking, but I didn't give in. I didn't want him to listen just because I was crying. "I'm trying to say two things. First, that not only did I never fuck Rock, I only talked to him once. And second, that last night I realized you're an asshole."

"What do you mean you just talked to him once?"

"What do you care? I mean, it seems like there are about a thousand other reasons not to be with me anyway."

"I was just— Are you telling me the truth?"

"Yeah. As a matter of fact I am."

"Why didn't you stop me, last night?"

"Just enjoying getting to know you better," I said.

For a week, we barely looked at each other. Until, finally, he woke me up in the guest room. "I'm sorry," he said. "I don't want to live like this." And he grabbed my hand and led me back into his bed.

And the next night we were entrenched in movie night, watching *Breathless*, the French one, acting as if nothing had changed between us.

Only something had changed since we fought. At least with me: I noticed everything.

I noticed the way he whistled when he breathed, the way his pale legs had little sock dents in them when he got home from work. The way he clipped his nose hair in front of me now, as if I wouldn't mind one bit. The way he called me sweetheart when he wanted something. The way he always asked me who I was talking to when I hung up the phone. The way his belly drooped over the top of his pants. The way he smelled like vitamins after we ran. After we had sex.

And I didn't have to say anything, but I knew he knew I was noticing him. He started running four times a week, not realizing that while that might change his little belly, it wouldn't change the way he kissed me on the head in the morning, more like a daughter than a lover.

But still I couldn't leave. Partly because I felt guilty. I felt like I was in the wrong. And I was hoping that this was just some phase of love or something. But also because this was my home. I mean, I was making two hundred bucks a week, enough to pay my tuition, but.

I thought about calling my mom. I did. But I couldn't.

And so I stayed.

Monday.

Tuesday.

Wednesday.

Thursday.

Friday.

Saturday.

Sunday.

Days didn't blur together anymore. In fact, each one was specific, precise, filled with thoughts I didn't want to think. Lies I didn't want to tell. Like "I love you" and "Nothing's wrong" and "I had to work late."

He knew I wasn't working late, although he didn't know that all I did instead was drive around.

At first I just drove around the neighborhood. Like one night I drove past the weeping willow house with the chest, now cleaned and with two new hinges. I left it at the front door, wondering if they'd take it back. And when I drove by the next night to check out the garbage, the chest wasn't in it. That day was the best I'd felt in weeks.

But still, I kept driving around and around at night. Every day it seemed like I went for longer and longer drives, farther and farther away. I would look at all the different neighborhoods, all the different people, and wonder what their lives were like, then obsess about what mine was becoming with Jeff. Sometimes driving around made me feel free, like I was getting away for a while. And other times I felt like I was just mapping out all of those things I would never do, would never be.

We went on like this for weeks.

And then Maria called.

• • •

I recounted it all to Jeff, sitting in his lap, wiping my nose on his shirt. I told him about how Maria lost the baby. How Richard left her and admitted that the pregnancy was the only reason he was sticking by her. Just fulfilling his duty. And how Maria was living with her cousin again, and Diego wanted to get back together with her. And how I thought that Maria would just disappear if that ever happened.

"It's OK, baby. Shhh," he said. Again and again. "I'm not going to leave you, Taylor. You're fine. We're fine."

That night we made love again, with the lights off, disappearing into the blackness of each other. Hiding in it.

The next night he took me to see *Ten Little Indians* at the Alley. The mystery was a welcome distraction, but when it was done, I was still depressed. And so was Jeff.

And after he bought me a hot fudge sundae, I was still depressed. And so was Jeff.

I assumed we were depressed for the same reasons. Because we'd watched our friend Maria hope for something and not get it. We'd watched her believe in something only to realize that everything she believed was false.

But once Jeff started talking in bed that night, I realized that I should have been feeling sorry for myself. Because now it was my turn.

"Why didn't you tell me Maria was pregnant?" he asked, curled up beside me naked as if nothing were on his mind. As if this were a casual, lying-in-bed question.

"Why would you want to know?"

"It's just—" He scrinched his forehead in that way usually reserved for academic stresses. He fumbled, searched for the words, stared at the ceiling. "It's just. I just worry . . . that . . . well . . . You're at that age where everything in the future seems exciting and important. And . . . well . . . You want children, don't you?"

I told him that we had never talked about that before, why should we talk about it now? He kissed my forehead and told me I was being naïve.

"Why does everything go back to me being young?" I wanted to know.

"Because it defines everything you do."

"When you act like an ass, I don't say it's because you're forty-three."

Jeff started to laugh. He kissed me on my forehead again, then my neck, and spoke to me in that tender voice that drew me to him in the first place. "I'm going to miss you, Taylor. I really am."

I pulled away. "What?"

He looked at me, steadily, unafraid. "Sweetheart, you couldn't have expected us to go on forever. I'm not that cruel," he added, as if it were a joke.

I sat there, still, vacant, trying to think of how to respond. I didn't expect us to go on forever, but. "You can't expect me to just forget . . . ," I said, incredulous, thinking about how just yesterday he'd told me he wouldn't leave me. And now. The way he was looking at me, as if this was what we knew all along. As if this was where we were always headed. As if this was why we'd played this little game. So that he could love with no pressure. So that I could get closer to anyone than I'd ever been, only to have him snatched away from me. Or, more accurately, run away from me.

"You can't expect me to just forget . . ." I tried again, but by now he couldn't bear to look at me. Not because he loved me, but because he didn't. And I was crying, quietly, not because I loved him, but because I didn't, yet still wanted desperately, more than anything, for him to let me stay there with him. Where everything was safe. Where every day was like the day before. And where we could always pretend that one day we would go to Africa.

from her tired, dirty skin

Three weeks after Jeff dumped me, I was at a doctor I couldn't afford having gravel removed from the palms of my hands.

The story went something like this: it was Friday night, day twenty-one after Jeff and I broke up. I was living with my mother again, because I'd exhausted my short list of friends and was too low on money to live anywhere on my own. She'd taken me in easily, mostly because my showing up at her door, freshly dumped, meant that she'd been right all along about Jeff and me.

Fortunately my mother had ended (or mostly ended) her liquor spree while I'd been away. Instead she'd taken to praying a lot and complaining about her various aches and pains even more, primarily the pain I gave her when I moved out and left her alone two years before, just like my no-good father and my brother who she hadn't heard from in months. She was complaining about all these things over dinner, a dinner that was far from cuisine night. Instead of eating whatever the fuck they eat in Zimbabwe, I was eating food straight from a factory in Kalamazoo. Some sort of meat loaf with a side of nonpotato potato. As I ate, she told me that if I went back to church again I'd at least meet someone who wasn't a pervert. There was a young adult group that met on Wednesdays . . .

I needed some air that night. I had to have some air.

And, sadly, that meant taking the bus to Jeff's neighborhood. And planting myself on the curb across the street from Antoinette, waiting for him to pass by her window. Once I'd sat down, I was immediately ashamed that I'd come out here. Gone to all this trouble for what?

Still, I waited, watched, remembered—all the usual pathetic things. I remembered how clean our sheets used to smell. And I watched the glow of the candle. The candle in the right window. I knew that candle. It was burnt down to the nub now, but the first part of that candle, the first time he lit it, I was there.

But not anymore.

By this time I was biting my fingernails ravenously, my brow so furrowed it was starting to give me a headache.

When Jeff came outside with Gwendolyn.

I was caught by surprise when his front door creaked open, and the next thing I knew I was kneeling on the gravel, hiding behind the tire of his car, which was parked in the street, next to where I had been sitting.

I crouched on all fours, my head looking underneath the car towards his front door, as she told him something that was so funny he laughed. He was able to laugh.

And I watched as she gave him a long, lingering hug that he relished. He was able to hug.

And I waited for the kiss that never came. Because after watching the hug I was fucking sure he was able to kiss again. Just three weeks after. Us. And just thinking about that possibility. It didn't matter that he didn't kiss Gwendolyn. Just thinking about him with someone else . . .

I was pushing my hands into the gravel, grinding them almost, not feeling anything except that this felt good. This felt better than what I'd been feeling for the last three weeks. This felt like.

Something.

But there had been other humiliating moments in these first twenty-one days after the breakup:

There was the day Jeff told me I had to leave. Day one.

I showed up at Tom's house with my bag of things. I could tell even then that Tom didn't really want his buddy's ex-girlfriend, twenty-year-old ex-girlfriend, staying with him, but still he let me.

The sofa was mine for six whole days before we had an exchange that went something like this:

Tom: *The real world doesn't work like this, Taylor.*
Taylor: *I thought you were my friend.*
Tom: *I am your friend. But that doesn't mean I'm your dad.*
Taylor: *What do you mean by that?*
Tom: *I mean it's time you made out on your own, OK?*
OK?

This was also the day that I moved back into my mom's apartment, right after Tom kicked me out. I locked myself into my old room and didn't come out except to go to the bathroom. After three days of this, Mom started leaving bags of vanilla wafers and cans of tuna in the hall where I could see them. She even slid a note under the door that said: "Taylor. Tell me what's wrong with you. I'm your mother. Love, Mom."

I called Jeff twice in these twenty-one days, although I must have considered calling him about a hundred times. The first time I actually called, I got his machine and hung up. The second time I left a message. I tried to be casual but came nowhere close. "Hi, Jeff. I just wanted to make sure you were OK." What the fuck does that mean?

I attended his class once, on day twelve. I glared at him the whole lecture. I even thought of passing him a note that said I thought he was a prick, but I didn't. And when the lecture was done, I couldn't stay. There were all these kids with all these questions about all this stuff I didn't care about anymore. Who the fuck cared about mythology? Mythology wasn't life. College wasn't life. Because college meant becoming more like Jeff every day, and I was sure I didn't want that. Which led to my dropping out of school. Just like that.

• • •

I tried calling Maria, but she was living with Diego again. And her cousin said their phone had been shut off, but she'd tell Maria to call me. Which, of course, she didn't, because I never heard from Maria.

In these three weeks, Jeff called me once. Just once. Over a year together, and one fucking phone call. "How are you doing?" he asked. I hung up.

And then there was that gravel incident. Day twenty-one. The day he stepped outside of his house with Gwendolyn and I had to hide behind the car. Trying to explain to the doctor how I dug gravel into my own hands because I enjoyed it. Trying to reassure him that the gravel incident, hurting myself, didn't mean that I was suicidal. That, in fact, the gravel incident was keeping me from being suicidal. It was letting me release it little by little instead of in one uncontrollable moment. And on top of that, the gravel incident had led me to a better place. Because as I knelt on all fours underneath a car like some psycho spying fugitive, it made me realize that perhaps I didn't want to be this low. In life. Ever. Again.

Which is how I finally accomplished something on day twenty-two. Maybe *accomplished* is too strong a word. But I did actively do something that felt like something at the time. I finished my assignment. My stupid fucking assignment that Jeff had used to canoodle me into his geriatric bed in the first place. My creation myth. Revised. I wrote it on a piece of paper that I slid under his door at the university on day twenty-three:

The world was not finished until Taylor died. From her heart came the mountains. From her skull came the dome of the sky.

From her blood came the oceans. From her tears came the rivers. Her face became the dirt in the fields. Her bones became the rocks. Her voice became the whistle of the wind. Her crying became the rain. Her yells became thunder. From her pain the sun was born. And when she thought that was over, she gave birth to the moon. Then from her tired, dirty skin came all of humanity, soiled before birth. And her eyes became the witness to all this mess that had been born through her.

And once I'd purged myself of that nonsense, I made my own fucking plans.

the way to somewhere

"I love the smell of gasoline," I told Milo, who I'd met one week before. A bit of gas had spilled onto him as he filled up the car, and he was wringing his hands in his ratty T-shirt, trying to rid them of the chemical stench. He responded to my comment by wiping his still-smelly hands on my jeans instead, which I didn't mind. I was sure the gas would make my jeans smell better, since laundry hadn't exactly been my strength lately. I used to do Jeff's laundry, and the smell of detergent still made me want to cry or hurl, usually both. So I avoided it.

But the smell of gasoline.

The car was an old Nissan Sentra. Brown. And we were going on a drive. A long one.

We each had one bag. Mine was a Houston Oilers duffel bag. His was a brownish athletic bag. It used to have his name on it, but all that was left now was the outline of the felt letters—M-I-L-O—where he'd probably pulled them off at whatever point *cool* entered his vocabulary. Also in the backseat was a six-pack of Bud cans and a painting he hoped to sell. It was of a naked woman with distortedly large fingers, no toes, and mismatched breasts. He called this painting *Choosy* but said the meaning part was up to me. He also brought one hundred condoms. "I always meet somebody," he said. "And they don't sell good ones there." My addition to the backseat was a paper grocery bag of snacks, including four boxes of Ding Dongs, which turned out to be his second favorite snack food after anything Little Debbie. We kept looking at each other, unable to contain our grins. Because we were going.

Somewhere.

The way to somewhere was the most amazing drive I'd ever taken. On the way to somewhere we had the windows rolled down. We had reggae playing on the radio. We had the beginnings of one-arm window tans by the time we'd reached Victoria, Texas. Because Victoria, and its Amoco, were on the way to somewhere.

Beeville was too. Or passing through Beeville. Because you have to pass through the barren roads of Beeville, Texas, to get to somewhere.

And under the sunset in Laredo. Because Laredo was on the way to somewhere.

We arrived at customs, which was staffed by men in uniform who looked like soldiers. But we weren't afraid. Because passing through this army of men was proof that we were on the way to somewhere. We weren't like the tourists in Nuevo Laredo, the people who were just visiting. We were adventurers going beyond the safety of the Zona Libra.

Where we were going required birth certificates.

It required getting past the men with guns.

It required a vehicle permit for Milo's car.

The backs of our legs were sticking to the vinyl seats with sweat, our one-arm tans had become one-arm burns, our bodies were feeling different. Because we were going to a place where not everyone had the balls to go.

You had to drive with a near-stranger for hours on end, awake on adrenaline, *speeding* on adrenaline, if you were on your way to somewhere.

You had to know exactly what you were doing, why you were doing it, but not have any idea of what "it" really was. It was just.

A future.

In somewhere.

You had to have legs that were so strapped down with ties that you suddenly felt that survival required the release of all of these ties.

At once.

You had to be young, I guess. Something in you had to be young. And unwise enough to feel wise all the time. Naïve enough to believe that you were going somewhere.

Or.

Had something.

You had to do.

In somewhere.

We never stopped for sleep. And we didn't stop *just* for food, or *just* for the bathroom. We only stopped for gas. If we could accomplish any of these other inconveniences while we were refueling, so be it.

the nativity makers

I'd met Milo about six months after Jeff made me leave. I was very drunk and working at El Cid, this dark and unfashionable bar on Westheimer, which is a main drag kind of street where you'll find one of the biggest shopping malls known to man, the Galleria, and a valley of strip malls with restaurants and stores and a variety of bars, mostly the kind that make frozen drinks with cutesy names. It was a Monday night, which is why I was drunk. So many old alcoholics come in on Mondays that you've got to be drunk not to want to kill yourself. The chatting and complaining, customer after customer. "Pour me another one, honey."

But Milo, of course, was different.

First off, he was young. Second, he was OK with his life, enthusiastic about it even. Third, he was funny. And fourth, he had no desire to kiss me, and I had no desire to kiss him. We shared an unattracted attractedness to one another.

Still, his good qualities were great ones.

He was a painter. Well, he wasn't really a paid painter yet, but he knew that was what he wanted to be, which was more than I could say for any of the other people in the place. I mean, I had no idea what I wanted to do. I liked bartending fine (oh, the privileges of turning twenty-one), but I couldn't see myself as some bitter barmaid forty years from now with corns on my feet and a dried-up womb. And so many tales to tell that I wouldn't be able to remember who'd heard what so I'd end up boring everybody equally.

But Milo was going to be a painter. A famous painter. He knew he might have to die first, but he planned to be famous. He also planned to do something every year that he hadn't conceived of the year before. "I know what I want, but part of what I want is stuff that I don't know yet, you know. You can plan to be reckless. A lot of people don't realize that. You can plan to be a drifter, even. It's the planning part that keeps you from losing all your teeth by the time you're thirty-five. You know, what keeps you sane. Like, if you say to yourself, 'Self, I'm gonna be a bum for a year,' then you won't be all fucked-up." He said this the first night we met, before we made plans to go out the next night.

It took just one more week together—a week that included three drunken nights with me behind the bar, one undersold Billy Bragg concert, and one afternoon driving around different neighborhoods and counting which one had the most McDonald's—for us to decide we wanted to make another plan together, and that the plan we needed to make was a moving plan.

We wanted to move because we shared one simple belief: that life here sucked.

The first reason life here sucked was because family life was as fake as a McDonald's commercial. People kill themselves trying to make their lunch, or their life, as special as the commercial; and it just isn't. I talked a lot about my mom, so unhappy, not so much because she was alone but because having a gay husband made her feel like she'd failed at living the commercial. Milo talked mostly about his ex-girlfriends. Three of the four had been sexually abused when they were kids. By relatives. Yet all of them were expected to attend family affairs—weddings, Christmases—their parents advised them to "move forward," but all that meant was "fuck yourself up so we can preserve this family." Or this family commercial.

The second reason life here sucked was because most people suck. We decided that most people we knew were little obedient worker bees who were more worried about fitting in and having a context than about their own passions. At first when we talked about this, I told Milo that, as much as I agreed with what he was saying, and as great as I thought it was that he was a painter, I didn't really have a passion. He

had long straight hair, which he flipped over his shoulder as he
laughed. He said I didn't *need* a passion. I *was* a passion. "You're an
artist, man." I never fully bought this line, but I hoped he was right.

Finally, because of points one and two of sucking above, we were
both in a rut. He'd been working at the Galleria in a record store. "I'm
working in a mall, man. And look at you. You can't shut up about
some loser you haven't seen in like six months. We're getting static,
you and me." I had no friends, and his friends were beginning to bore
him. I had nobody I wanted to touch (I'd fooled around with a couple
guys at bars since Jeff, but there was no one I wanted to see again), and
he was having a hard time getting rid of the two girls he'd been sleeping with. And then I had what he referred to as Jeff disease.

"For a cool girl, you sure are pathetic," he said, and I agreed. And
what better way to rid oneself of a pathetic, boring life than to move?
To plan to drift for a while. To reinvent. Everything.

The closest place we could think of that offered the most potential
for transformation was Mexico. And it was cheap. The bargain basement of dreams.

Leaving is strange when you're twenty-one because, technically, you're
supposed to leave. You're supposed to be out on your own. It's a sign of
maturity and life progression.

But somehow Mexico didn't count.

I told my mom I was moving. She said, "Next thing I know you'll be
a hooker or something."

"A hooker? Mom, please."

"Well, how are you getting to Mexico?"

"I'm driving."

"You don't have a car."

"My friend does."

"Let me guess. A guy?"

"Yes, Mom. A guy. A guy friend."

"A friend according to you, or according to him?"

"According to both of us. What's your problem?"

"I just know more than you do. It sounds great now, but next thing you know you'll be knocked up or strung out on drugs. Down the toilet like the rest of my life."

"Maybe," I said.

She took a long sip of her Scotch and soda (she was allowing herself one a day—maybe two). "Fine," she said. She had this annoying habit of transitioning immediately from bullheaded to emotional. I liked her better when she was being mean and pretended not to see that her eyes were tearing up.

I left and went to Jeff's. This time I knocked on the door. He answered. Alone.

"Hey," I said.

"Hi," he said, his voice tight, clearly displeased at my unannounced visit.

We stood that way for too long, awkwardly. I hadn't seen him in so long that I'd forgotten how weathered he was, how wrinkled.

"Did you need something, Taylor?" he finally asked, perturbed, breaking the silence.

"Sorry, yeah," I said. "I just. I'm moving. To Mexico."

"Let me guess. San Miguel," he responded, not quite meanly but accompanied by a fatherly chuckle.

"Are you trying to tell me I'm a cliché?"

"No, I'm just—"

"Come on," I said. "Tell me what you mean."

"Well, because you asked, there are so many cities in Mexico that are more . . ." He searched for the right term.

I decided to help. "Mexican?"

"Well." He shifted in his slippers, then nodded. "I suppose so. Look, forget I said anything. I'm sure it'll be a great experience."

Something about the way he said it made me mad. "You say that like you don't mean it."

"Why did you come here? Really? What do you want me to say?"

"Are you seeing Gwendolyn?" It came out of nowhere but I couldn't help myself.

A long pause.

"No," he said, slowly. "I'm not." He looked straight through me, engaging me in some while-we're-being-honest match I shouldn't have started in the first place. He said, "Did you really quit school so you could *move to Mexico*?" He said "move to Mexico" in this horrible tone that implied, mockingly, that I thought it was the most romantic place in the whole world.

"You don't even know what I'm planning to do in Mexico."

"OK. What are you planning to do?"

"A lot."

"I mean for money."

"I'm gonna teach English."

Another awkward pause.

"You're making a mistake," he said.

"No. You were the mistake."

He shook his head, clearly annoyed at the whole conversation, which only made me madder. He said, "Sweetheart, people who quit everything never get anywhere. Irresponsibility has its place when you're younger, but—"

"You know what I like best about our new 'relationship'?"

Reluctantly he fed me the next line. "What do you like best, Taylor?"

"I don't have to listen to what you think is best anymore."

"Whatever makes you happy," he said smugly. "Time for you to get to bed, rest up before you go and change your life."

"Fuck off," I said, as he disappeared into the house where we used to cook breakfast and say we loved each other. Into the bedroom where we'd stayed up late and imagined the people who might have lived there before us. Into that house that used to be my castle.

There are bulletin boards in various places near the center of San Miguel de Allende. Immediately they let you know that you are in a transient land. There's ad after ad after ad for roommates, apartments, sometimes even whole houses with servants and cooks.

The ad that Milo and I answered on our second day there was this:

"One bedroom in house. Couple OK. Cable TV. No phone. $150 US/month. Please stop by between 10 A.M. and noon."

The entrance was an iron gate off a side street. The walls were a beautiful shade of reddish orange with weeds poking through the cracks. Through the gate was a courtyard with a fountain that didn't have water in it. Instead it was filled with wood scraps.

A woman walked towards me and Milo. She had red curly hair that frizzed out of her ponytail. Her eyes seemed fixed in a squint, and her grin was only up on one half of her mouth. The other half of her mouth was stern, straight. She wiped blue paint from her hands onto her formerly white apron.

"You're American" was the first thing she said. And it was immediately clear from her accent that she was, too.

"Yeah," Milo said, looking at the ground.

"What brings you here?" she wanted to know.

"We came to see the apartment," Milo said, although I didn't know if I wanted to anymore. I wasn't sure if I liked her. Her appearance may have been domestic, but she was the kind of woman you could never interrupt. Not because she talked too much but because she made you fear you would say something stupid.

She smirked at Milo's reply. "Not *here* here. I mean why are you in San Miguel?"

"We drove here from Texas," I told her.

"Well, that's not much of an answer," she said.

Milo picked it up from there. "I'm a painter and we're just traveling."

"You might as well check out the room," she said, then she looked right into my face. Right in it. Way too close to be comfortable. "You're not a couple," she said, not like a question. More to say she knew.

"Is that a problem?" I asked.

She just shrugged, turned, and shuffled up the steps. She stopped halfway, and we almost bumped her in the butt. She turned around. "Do you have names?"

"I'm Taylor."

"I'm Milo."

"Ellen," she said, then continued to shuffle us up the stairs to what would become our room.

That night, Milo told me Ellen's life story. Or what he thought her life story was. He told me he'd guess that Ellen was a bitter woman who'd never married. Never had kids. When she was a schoolteacher, she'd told a boy student she loved him, and the impressionable young student told his parents; then everybody got so mad they ran Ellen out of town, and that's how she ended up here. She painted pictures of blue skulls. Skull painting after skull painting after skull painting.

"She's not that weird," I said.

"Maybe she's just a lesbian," he said, then raised his eyebrows in mock excitement.

The next day there was a note on our door. "Ellen and me we to eat supper at six. Please eat with us. Rosio."

"Rosio?" I repeated as I read the card aloud.

Milo, who was still half asleep in the twin bed next to mine, grabbed it out of my hand. "Who's this Rosio?" he said.

"I don't know."

"I knew it. We're living in lesbian heaven. I bet you we are."

"They're in their fifties," I pointed out.

"Lesbians always hang together. Find the old ones, and the young ones will come eventually," he said, mostly kidding.

"You have no idea what you're talking about," I said, and threw my pillow at him affectionately.

At dinner Rosio spoke very little but smiled constantly. She was a tiny Mexican woman with extremely short hair. She'd cooked an amazing spread of tortillas and chicken and vegetables and the hottest sauce I'd ever tasted, which everyone else ate as if it were as spiceless and mild as milk. Milo did most of the talking, and it was beginning to make me uncomfortable. Something about being so young and so sure of him-self seemed wrong. Like he was telling these women about life, and they were nodding just to be polite. He told them all of our philoso-phies on why life in Houston sucked, but all I could focus on was the word *suck*. When do you outgrow it? He'd just finished talking about his ex-girlfriends who'd been molested when Rosio placed her hand on his forearm, looking at him with that crazy smile of hers. "How nice to wear the wounds. So open on the skin. For all to see."

That night, when we were lying side by side in the twin beds, he was convinced. "I'm telling you, they're lesbos."

"So?"

"So. Nothing. It's cool with me. But I gotta state what's fact, you know."

I nodded halfheartedly, trying to show disinterest so he'd stop going on about his lesbian theory.

"What's your problem?" he wanted to know.

"Nothing."

"You missing Jeff?" he said in his fake, whiny, give-me-shit voice.

"No, I'm not missing Jeff."

"You homesick?"

I shook my head, not amused but also not angry. I had something on my mind. "Do you think I'll speak Spanish by the time I leave here?" I asked.

"You mean fluently?"

"Yeah."

"If you fall in love, yeah. That's the best way to learn the language, you know."

"And if I don't feel like falling in love?"

"When you least expect it, expect it," he said, which made me groan. I hate movie quotes.

Four days later and I still didn't have a job. It wasn't from not trying; I just wasn't having any luck. Instead I was sleeping late and wandering around the city a lot. Spending the days walking around, reading. I'd met a backpacker who'd given me his copy of *East of Eden*, which was reading like a dirty romance novel. I sent a postcard to J.J. one afternoon. And a few nights I went to the bar San Miguelito and drank a few beers, although I didn't like talking to other people that much. I may have met Milo in a bar, but traditionally I didn't take to talking to strangers. Only if they were exceptional people, and so far I hadn't seen anyone that exceptional. Just a lot of "artists" in roped sandals, and fanny-packed American tourists, and people like me who'd come here to reinvent themselves and still hadn't figured out exactly how that happens.

So instead they were bored.

And still the same.

Only Milo was changing. On our second night at Ellen and Rosio's he'd met Pixie. Her name was really Patricia, but she told him she changed her name to Pixie when she moved to San Miguel because it suited her more. Pixie was from Arkansas and she painted psychedelic landscapes which usually included packs of wolves. She was also crazy in bed (the first time Milo met her, he fucked her three times in the backyard of the hostel where she was staying—or so he told people). She had another lover who was a flamenco clapper guy, but Milo said that didn't matter. He was starting to think that monogamy wasn't natural.

Six days later he moved out of our apartment and into Pixie's hostel. It only took these six days before each of his dirty T-shirts, his magazines, his English-Spanish dictionary disappeared. He told me in town one night that he hoped I wasn't mad.

I wasn't. Frankly he'd started to get on my nerves. I mean, if he came here to change his life, why was he falling in love, the most boring, most predictable thing of all that is proven *not* to change you, except for the needy or for the worse? We'd talked about this a hundred times. About how love is a complement to life but not life itself.

"Give a man somebody to chase and he'll forget everything," Ellen told me my second week there. I'd gotten horribly drunk the night before, and some tourist with wraparound Oakleys that he kept on his head all night had tried to take me home. He was succeeding until the wife he hadn't bothered to mention came in and surprised him, and me. I left, amazed at how every bar in every country is the same thing.

So the next night I skipped the bar and stayed in with Ellen and Rosio.

We'd only been drinking wine for about ten minutes when they started to giggle like schoolgirls. We'd been talking about Milo moving out. "What?" I asked, self-conscious, certain they were laughing at me.

Finally, Ellen spoke up. "I had a son of my own, but I forget how boys are at that age. So sure of themselves. And so stupid."

Rosio chimed in. "He a bully to you."

"I'm sorry," Ellen said. "I know he's your friend."

"That's OK," I said. But I wasn't sure where I stood now, and feared that I was about to be the subject of more ridicule. Rosio said something in Spanish, and they both cracked up again. I was considering getting up from the table when Ellen spoke for her. "Milo asked Rosio if she was a lesbian."

I laughed, fakely, just sure the nervousness at the edges of my smile would give me away. But it didn't.

"I wish," said Rosio, which only led to more laughter.

That was the night that Ellen told me about her husband who left her, her children she rarely saw, her ugly divorce, her backpack.

After the divorce, Ellen wanted to be out of Milwaukee, away from her life, but didn't have much money. She'd heard of San Miguel. A place where old Americans go to retire because it's cheap.

When she moved here, she knew no one. Not a soul. She had only one backpack with her. She'd packed seven. But as she was loading her cab to the airport, she told the cabdriver, "Sometimes I wish I just lived out of a backpack."

And he said, "Well, that's up to you."

"Not really."

"Well," he told her, "if you only had a backpack, and wished instead that you had seven bags filled with 'stuff,' then you'd have a lot of shopping to do. But all you have to do if you have seven bags and want to live out of one backpack is leave six bags right here at the side of the road. And everything you own, voilà, is now in one bag."

That was Ellen's favorite story. She said she loved it because it was both the most exhilarating and the most depressing moment of her life. When she realized how easily everything could be dumped at the side of the road. Thrown away. Bags. People. Lives. Anything.

Ellen was lonely here at first, and was desperate for a job. But just when she was sure she would never find work, she met Rosio, who gave her a place to live and a job.

"I had bad divorce too. And in Mexico, divorce is real bad."

"So, what was the job?" I wanted to know, feeling like I was on their side again.

"I show you," Rosio said, then grabbed my hand.

I was concentrating on the sweat building in my hand as she took me to the back of the house. It was through a door at the side of the kitchen, which wasn't exactly secret, but I'd never been in there before. Inside was a narrow, tiled, spiraling staircase that took us to a room with a balcony that overlooked the street, its dim lights.

At first I was so taken with the view that I didn't notice what was staring at me from every corner of the room. Mary. The Virgin Mary. Mary with a half-shaped head. Mary before she's sanded. And Joseph with varying staffs, from carved pieces of wood to twigs. And sheep. And cows. And mangers. And hay. And, of course, the babies Jesus. All were carved with simple lines out of wood. The faces were not quite faces, more like silhouettes.

"We build Jesus here" is what Rosio said.

"Can you believe?" Ellen said. "I'm a goddamn Jew and I build nativity scenes for a living." She wasn't disappointed when she said this. She was more proud.

Because Mexico had changed her.

By the beginning of my third week in Mexico, I decided I was going to take flamenco lessons. I was running out of the money I'd come with, but Rosio assured me that if I couldn't pay the rent, I could work it off by building Jesus. Pixie told me that Herman (you say it "AIR-MON"), the flamenco clapper guy she used to sleep with, knew a guy who gave flamenco lessons and had a thing for American women, whom he described as "tough but easy."

I decided I'd meet this other guy. That I'd learn to dance, of all things. Because even though I really was just beginning my trip (I'd hoped to be there for at least a year), I hadn't changed yet. And maybe that was my fault for not trying harder.

Which is also why I started working for Rosio and Ellen. I figured it was better than walking around town reading American literature. Rosio started me off painting Joseph, who she said people paid less attention to. "If Mary have bad paint, no one buy the set. But Joseph, no one look so hard at him," she said.

Me and Rosio and Ellen had one more talk before I left Mexico. It was about me.

"Pretty girl like you must have the boyfriends," Rosio said.

I told them about Jeff. At one point Ellen wrinkled her nose. I asked her why, and her response was the following: "Don't waste any more time on saggy butts, because you'll reach a point sooner than you know when that'll be all you can get."

I told them that, as much as I knew it, I thought I'd loved Jeff.

"You no 'think' you love," Rosio said.

"I don't know," I said. "It's hard to have any perspective on it anymore."

I told them how strange (or maybe even sad) it was that I marked time in my life by the passage of men—Billy Talkington, Charlie Simmons, Luther, Carlos, Reginald, Jeff. If you asked me where I was three years ago, I'd have to track back in time on these chains of men. And I guessed the feelings had all sort of blurred.

They thought that blurring was impossible. That I was just blocking out what I felt. "Surely," Ellen said, "there must be someone who can still make you sick to your stomach."

"The good kind of sick to your stomach or the bad kind?"

"Both," she said.

"The bad kind of sick to your stomach is easy. Jeff. But the good kind. I don't know. I guess I don't really believe in all that romantic hoo-ha."

"A romantic ideal is a good thing. Keeps you young, hopeful."

"Hope is depressing," I told her. I told her about how every time I passed a store or a restaurant that was empty and struggling for business, I thought about the person who dreamed it up. The person who told their friends, "I'm opening this restaurant and it's going to be huge." And who sent out flyers for the opening and made spreadsheets on their computer calculating how much profit they were eventually going to make. And who ultimately had to watch their whole dream, all their hopes fall apart. And that's what happened to most hopes. They got crushed, usually in front of other people.

"Even I'm not that cynical," Ellen said. "And I actually have a reason to be."

"OK," I conceded. And then I told them that I'd thought of someone.

It was hard to believe that my love life would be of interest to anyone else. But Rosio and Ellen both sat forward in their chairs as if they hadn't heard any gossip in some time.

"There was this guy named Luther." I told them that he was the only person on my list who wasn't muddied, despite our awkward don't-tell-your-brother-we-kissed encounter. That we shared this weird moment. How he understood me at a time that I felt like nobody ever would. I explained that he wasn't my type at all. He was sort of conservative, more pure than I was. Kind of preppyish. Ambitious in traditional ways, wanting to be a doctor. But he had the magic of someone who dies young. Untainted. "But I guess," I said, "that's sort of cynical too. I mean, I think he's perfect, but that's basically because I never really got to know him."

"That not matter," said Rosio. "So long as you have a memory of that feeling."

We sat in silence for a few minutes. It wasn't weird. Just a nice quiet. I was thinking how strange it was, meeting these two women. I had wanted to have a night like tonight. A night when I felt like maybe I was growing up. Changing. "Did moving to Mexico change your life?"

I asked Ellen, hoping that maybe her answer would give me some clue as to what else I should be doing here.

"Everything changes your life."

Just days later, I got a FedEx from J.J. Inside it was a letter. This is what it said:

> *Taylor, you don't have to come home, but I thought you should know that Dad is dying. Call me. J.J.*

My eyes welled up when I read it. Mostly because my dad was dying. Also because J.J. didn't think to tell me what he was dying of, although I felt certain it was AIDS.

But a part of me was crying because I felt selfish.

Because reading the letter made me not just sad but mad.

Bitter.

Bitter that every time I tried to change myself, something changed me instead.

If an item is to be restored because it is an heirloom, nothing else about the piece has any bearing on the decision. Whether or not the piece has antique value does not matter because the prime purpose is to preserve a part of a family's history so that it can be enjoyed by future generations. Of all the reasons for restoring, this is probably the most noble — but here we may find our greatest challenges because some of these pieces may be in such poor condition that the owner is about to abandon them.

"Rules and Tools for Restoration of Antique Furniture,"
Restoring Antique Furniture: A Complete Guide,
by Richard A. Lyons

two hours a day

Two hours a day was all that was normal in my life once I got back to Houston. Because for two hours a day I pretended.

I took the bus to other parts of town and pretended that I did not still live at home.

I went to the movies and pretended that it was my work, that I was making movies for a living. Sometimes I even pretended that the movie theater was in Los Angeles.

I went to the bookstore and flipped through travel magazines and pretended that I was rich and going on vacation.

I went to bars and pretended that I was Miss Marple from the Agatha Christie books. When people tried to talk to me, I spoke in a phony accent and referred to mysteries whenever possible. The first time I did this, I expected the aging man who smelled like manure to tell me to go to hell. But he thought I was a real person. He asked me how long I'd been solving mysteries, if I could describe to him my hardest case. I told him about the blind man who'd been stealing nativity scenes all over Houston every Christmas. He grew quite concerned. When I then told him it was my hardest case because I'd never solved it, he vowed not to leave Jesus and Mary outside this year.

If I was stuck in my mom's apartment, then I pretended for two hours that I was a sociologist studying my mother's life instead of living in it.

Sometimes I would go on dates with men I'd met in bars, and I would pretend that I was interested in what they were saying, that I wasn't thinking about my dad.

I pretended, when I was with my dad, that he didn't have cancer. That he appeared healthy, instead of the way he looked now: his eyes sunk back in his head, his skin more purple than pink, covered with bruises. "You look great today," I'd say, sounding like a fucking salesman.

When I was wandering the halls of the hospital, I pretended that I was a medical student, and every now and then I'd think of one of Maria's and my predictions. That I would be living in River Oaks, married to a doctor (maybe even to Luther). Yeah, right.

And one night I went so far as to look up Luther's name in the phone book, pretending that I had a chance, that he would even remember me.

Another day I borrowed my mom's car and drove all over the city, pretending that I was looking for a house, for my own Antoinette. I drove through neighborhood after neighborhood, mostly the old ones, and wondered what it would be like to turn my car into one of these driveways every night.

And that's how I met Joe. He was in a more rural part of town, where there was a mix of old and new, Victorian houses one block away from trailer parks. And nobody seemed to mind. I was driving past a farmhouse with a barn-looking shed to the side of it. And a sign. CARPENTER'S HELPER WANTED, it said.

I pulled over just to stare at the sign, maybe pretend that I was going to call the number later and try to get a job. Then I practically jumped out of the car seat, startled by a voice behind me.

"Can I help you?" I heard, then turned around to see a white-haired man who looked like he hadn't shaved in a few days. He was wearing an old Astros T-shirt and worn jeans.

"No, I'm just—"

He cut me off. "I saw what you were doing. You were just looking at my sign."

It took everything in me to ask. To turn off that voice in my head that told me I had no business being here. But I did turn it off. And I asked what I really wanted to know. "You still need somebody?"

"Yeah," he said, then peeked into the car, like he was checking for a gun or something. Or maybe just to see if I was as tall as I looked.

"What do you do exactly?" I asked him.

"I build furniture. You want to take a look?"

I did.

As we walked towards the shed, I got a much better look at him. Joe was at least sixty. I supposed he would have been the sexy stereotype of a carpenter twenty-five years ago. But now all you could see were traces of that sexy guy—in the sunken wrinkles in his face that must have been dimples at one point, and in the way he stood, his hip half-cocked, his jeans worn just enough, with just enough paint to make him look like he was in touch with himself.

He led me into the barnlike shed, which was a spectacular room filled with wood and tools and sawdust and bookshelves and desks and even rocking chairs. I would later learn that he was known for his custom designs. His work was high-quality and simple, with clean lines. He had started off building Shaker reproductions in his twenties, because he thought this would be the best way for him to learn classic furniture form. Although he eventually began doing original works, he never strayed far from the Shaker philosophy. The Shakers had a tradition of furniture building that was based on utility—the idea that true beauty comes from function and form, not from decoration. And each piece is true to its purpose—whether that purpose is sitting or sewing. Later I would come to understand that this was the essence of Joe—where no word was wasted, and no gesture was without meaning.

As I walked around the shed, focusing on a corner cupboard, Joe told me that he didn't like people coming to his house. Instead, he'd go to his clients—who were usually gourmet-type people—and find out what they had in mind for him to make. He explained that if somebody wanted something ugly, he'd just tell them they'd found the wrong man for the job, because "Life's too long to make ugly."

He sat down in one of his rockers, and gestured to me to do the same. "So." He sighed, scratching his finger nervously on the chair's armrest. "Does this interest you?" he asked, as if referring simply to the room itself.

I nodded.

"You need work?"

I nodded again, still speechless from what was happening. I suddenly became conscious of the fact that he was rocking in his chair. Squeak. Squeak. Squeak.

"You talk?" he said.

"Yeah," I told him, laughing. "I talk."

"What do you know about wood?" he wanted to know.

At first I pretended I was qualified—I lied and told him that I'd built nativity scenes in Mexico. But when he asked me about what kinds of tools I used, I had to tell him that really I'd only painted Joseph. But I also told him that working with those two women, just for a few weeks, was the first time that work didn't feel like work but more like the passing of a day. And then I told him about that day that I took the chest out of the garbage. About how since then I'd been collecting things that were thrown away. Repairing them if they needed it. Like frames, ladders, chairs, whatever I found lying around. Usually chairs. For whatever reasons, that was what seemed to show up in the garbage most often.

"What do you do with all those pieces when you're done?" he wanted to know.

"I keep them until I find someone to give them to."

"Can I get you a beer?"

"Sure," I told him, thinking that he could get me anything so long as I didn't have to leave this place and go back to the hospital. Not yet.

After the beer he cooked me a burger, and just like that I had a job and somewhere to go every day. A way to move into my own place again. Maybe even get a car.

And Joe had someone to talk to, to teach, and to help him carry things from time to time.

I wrote a letter to Maria that night and told her that I had a new job. And I told her about Joe. I also mentioned my pretending and realized that it made me sound like a freaky child. I added the following explanation: "I wish I could pretend as well as I did when we were kids. Like when you really believed for an afternoon that you were an abandoned alien from the planet Bigstar, who ate only Ding Dongs and one day was going to take over the planet Earth."

Joe started me off learning about wood—grain, figure, texture, soft woods versus hard woods. This lesson also included a required day of rest in which we sat in lawn chairs, drank beer, and discussed conservation. After that I started measuring and sometimes cutting wood for whatever he was building at the time. Stripping some of his older pieces. Sanding some of the new ones. Initially I was only allowed to use hand tools, but after a few weeks he agreed to teach me how to use a router. But usually the days were short. He knew my dad was dying and told me I could take whatever time I needed.

"So," he asked, softly, as if he were afraid he might hurt me, "what's wrong with him, then?"

I told Joe that I'd assumed my dad had AIDS. But that I was wrong. It was cancer.

"What kind?"

I told him that he had it in his brain. All over his brain, really, like his skull had been wallpapered with it or something. We'd all been wallpapered with it. And nobody quite knew how to deal with it.

"'Deal with it'? That's a funny way to put it."

"What would you suggest?" I asked him.

"Just living through it, I guess," he said, then dismissed himself. "I don't really know. Got no business trying to know either. Just don't be too hard on yourself, all right?"

Back at the hospital, the pretending continued. J.J. and I pretended that the dozen unnaturally blue carnations for my dad were a sort of get-well-soon thing instead of a sorry-you're-dying thing.

Dad pretended to believe us.

Mom pretended none of this situation existed by never going to the hospital.

Mackie, my dad's boyfriend, was a small, younger man with womanish fingers and curly hair. He pretended that my dad was the love of his life. He cried daily. In the bathroom, in secret, but we could tell from his puffed-up eyes. I told J.J. about how Mackie was just kidding himself. "Dad was with Mom for twenty-seven years. And she's *just now* figured out he's not the love of her life." I explained to J.J. that the only way for you to know that someone is the love of your life is for them to die. That way nothing ever fucks up the image that you have of them.

He told me I didn't know shit about love. His girlfriend Nanette looked at him like he'd just said the sweetest thing she'd ever heard, and I could see her squeeze his hand extra tight.

Over two months, there were seven times when I thought my dad was going to die. Each time I asked Joe if I could leave and rushed to the hospital. And each time I pretended that everyone was there. My mother and J.J. and Mackie, even. I pretended my father looked right at us, and all the ways he ever hurt me or my mom or any of us just passed right through him.

And for a short while, each of the seven times he almost died, I was taken back to my favorite hours I ever spent with my father. The two hours when I was eight and he drove me to this tiny airport frequented by rich old pilots who owned their own planes. My dad and I hung over the chain-link fence and watched the teetering little planes come and go all day. As usual, he wasn't talking. But that day I remember seeing a lightness in his eyes. Like they were relaxed for once. And I knew then and now that he was pretending just like I was. Pretending that we were on one of the little planes going someplace exciting. Someplace different. Someplace else. And we knew without saying that in both of our dreams of flying away, we were each going away by ourselves. Alone. Without the other.

And that was fine.

spirituality sessions

I was twenty-two when I learned the real story of my parents' beginning:

My parents met at a hair goop factory in Kentucky when my mom was nineteen. Her dad had just died, so she had to support her mother, who drank too much and hated working, and her brother, who was a couple years younger. She got a job assisting Mr. Willensky, the head of the warehouse, making his appointments, keeping his secrets from his wife. He hired her because he thought she was cute and because she didn't say much. And one time he told her he liked the way she smelled.

My dad worked in the warehouse, packing orders. He was twenty-two, good-looking, and really quiet. My mom said she blushed the first time she saw him, and every time she walked into the warehouse after that. But he never did anything about it. "I was beginning to think he'd never notice me."

Finally one day, when they were both leaving at the whistle, she said, "I think maybe we should get together sometime." He said "Sure," and that was it.

They got married one year after their first date, when she took him to a church social. She said that first night he was gentle, not a great dancer, but a good singer, and made her laugh sometimes. They got married at the same church where she'd been confirmed. It was small, but she said that's what made the whole ceremony so perfect. Just them, their families, and God.

My mom quit the factory first, since my dad didn't want her working, and she was already pregnant with J.J. My dad quit a couple weeks
later. They decided to move out on their own. They'd been living for a
year with his mother, who was starting to get mean, according to my
mother, and who thought my mother was going to have too many babies, since she was Catholic.

One night, when they were alone in the house, my parents pulled
out an old map that had all the states. They said each one out loud,
just to see what it sounded like.

"Nevada."

"Washington."

"Idaho."

Two weeks later, they packed up the backseat of my dad's old Chevy
and drove to Texas.

My mom told me this story of their meeting when I announced that
J.J. and Nanette were getting married.

I was so stunned that she was talking about Dad that I didn't interrupt her as she babbled their story out, sipping her drink every now
and then. When she was finished, I had to know. "Why are you telling
me this now?" I asked.

"I think Nanette uses too much hair spray. I don't trust people who
wear so much hair spray" was her response.

"She's good for J.J.," I said, because she was. The only reason J.J.
had been so helpful with Dad was because Nanette had been func-
tioning as his conscience.

"So you think they should get married?" she asked.

"I do," I said.

"Marriage is not what it seems like."

"Mom, you don't need to lecture me. I'm not getting married, remember?"

"Ever."

"I didn't say that." I hadn't. But I had been thinking of it in those
terms lately.

"So are you or aren't you gonna get married?" she persisted.

"I can't predict that."

"So that means you want to, then. Doesn't it?" she said. Smiling like she'd caught me or something.

"I don't know."

She clinked the ice in her glass for a second, then looked inside expectantly, like a child, surprised she'd finished it already. "Romantic beginnings. Horrible ends. That's what marriage is."

"Not all the time."

"No" —she looked at me, grinning—"not all the time. But most. Who'd have thought my cynical little Taylor would be the dreamer?"

I ignored her comment. "I'm sure J.J. will be fine."

"I bet Nanette will plan a big wedding. She seems like a hoopla girl."

"I don't know," I said. I didn't even know Nanette, let alone what kind of wedding she would plan.

"Is my loving husband going to be there?"

"I don't think so, Mom," I said. "He's too busy dying."

Her face snapped into seriousness. "Don't you give me guilt about your father."

I don't know which was worse. Going on dates with people you never wanted to know, or that empty feeling that comes from spending an evening watching television alone.

At work I was fine. I could hang out with Joe, focus on specific tasks. Simple tasks that I could lose my mind in. Like sanding, or planing, or sweeping the floor. Or the more complicated lessons that were frustrating but absorbing for the same reason. He was teaching me more about building, getting me started on chairs. These days with Joe were my best moments during my father's illness.

But the nights, when I was by myself, weren't fun. Not at all.

I'd tried reading at first. Mythology books. Cheesy romances. Magazines. Anything. And no matter what I was trying to read, I couldn't concentrate even for the length of a paragraph.

So then I'd try cooking, only to find that I still didn't like to do it.
So then I'd flip on the TV.
And I'd watch several channels of nothing while I ate cereal for dinner.
Night after night. The same thing.
No one ever imagines their life will be like this.
For the first time in so long, I missed Jeff. Not because I wanted to get back together with him or anything. But because I needed perspective. A conscience. I needed someone to tell me I wasn't fucking up my life.

I was going to be a bridesmaid.
I told J.J. that, no offense, I didn't really want to be a bridesmaid. He told me he was cool with that, but Nanette insisted that sisters of the groom had to be bridesmaids, or it was bad luck. I think she also saw it as an opportunity to give me a makeover, since she'd mentioned to me before how nice my hair would look with a little body in it (translation: perm).

She had a bridesmaid shower, where I met her four bouncy friends from college. They all wanted me to tell them more about J.J. About what he was like in high school. About his job as a computer programmer. But every time I reluctantly opened my mouth, I'd be interrupted by some story that only they knew. About some college such-and-such who did whatever dumb thing. So, after a while, I just stopped making an effort.

After the bubbly, as they called it, Nanette brought out her drawings of the bridesmaid dress. Although she worked at Ann Taylor as a salesgirl, she fancied herself an aspiring designer and took every opportunity to act the part. She'd done a crayon sketch of what I can only describe as a lime green poof. There was a bow in the front and the back. And still more bows on the shoes, which were dyed to match. She then presented big bolts of the satiny lime material for the dress, which she let each of us touch, but only after we'd washed our hands.

She'd also drawn our hair plans, I think to break me into the idea of going on a hair adventure with her. Each of our hairdos, as drawn, was unique. All of them were poofy.

Next she pulled out her sketch of the dress she was making for her mother, a peachy number that had a simple rose embroidered into it in memory of her father, who had died.

I'd just about hit a proper champagne high when she pulled out the sketch of her bridal gown, which she was also going to make. I imagined the silkworms busy at work in her closet. It was a long off-white extravaganza with small bows across the chest. "I designed it myself," she said, and all the girls cooed.

Then it was time for the gifts. She got bath products and lingerie with snaps on the crotch, and, from me, a heart carved out of wood that I'd painted blue. Joe laughed at me the whole time I made it, knowing how much I hated anything girlie, hearts especially. But I told him I was making it because I thought she'd like it, simple as that. And she did. After she opened it, she told me about how she was going to glue some dried flowers on it so it would be even more beautiful.

Time alone with J.J. was becoming scarce. As much as I wanted to be happy for him, I found myself becoming jealous of the hyperactive lovebug who was always at his side.

But one night, at the hospital, Nanette excused herself early to do some wedding stuff.

And J.J. and I were alone.

He suggested we take a break and go down to the cafeteria. Dad was asleep and Mackie had just shown up, so it seemed like a good idea.

"So how was the bridesmaid thing?" he asked.

"Fine."

"Fine? You're such a liar," he said.

"Yeah. I would have never imagined you with someone like her, but she seems nice."

He shifted in his chair, uncomfortable. "Yeah," he said.

We sipped our coffee. Stared around at all the sickly greenish walls. I decided that if I didn't ask now, I'd probably never be able to ask him later. "How'd you know? You know, that you wanted to get married?" I asked him.

"She sort of decided."

"Oh."

"I don't mean that in a bad way. I just mean that I'm the kind of person who tends to float around. And she's the first person who told me I'd done that for long enough. That it was time to grow up, I guess."

"You're marrying her to be a grown-up?"

"You'd love to think that, wouldn't you? No, I'm marrying her because she's who I want to grow up with."

"Oh."

I told him again that I never thought he'd marry someone like her. And he said he never thought he'd meet someone in a spirituality session, but he did.

"A spirituality session?" I'd never heard this one. "What the fuck is that?"

"It's like a church thing, only there's no church. It's just people making themselves better."

"You're lying."

"No, I'm not."

"Why were you there?"

"Why do you think I'd go?" he said, gesturing to our hospital surroundings. "I guess I just thought it couldn't hurt."

"Why was she there?"

"She goes every year on these retreats. She calls them active life management."

"Why does she need to have her life actively managed?"

He looked at me, irritated that I could be so smug. "Her dad died of AIDS."

"Oh," I said.

"They didn't know he died of AIDS until he was already dead. So they never really knew how he got it."

"I had no idea."

"How would you? You never talk to her."

"Sorry, it's just—"

"I didn't come here to yell at you."

"I made Nanette a wooden heart."

"I know. I saw it. She really liked it."

"She did?"

"Yeah."

By now my styrofoam cup was empty, pieces of it in a pile in front of me like confetti.

"So. It's funny," I said.

"What's funny?"

"That. Well, I never thought you'd be the kind of guy to go on a spirit retreat, but it seems to work for you. I guess. I'm happy that one of us turned out OK."

"I haven't turned out yet, you know. It's pretty scary."

"You'll be fine."

"Do you think so?" As he said this, he ripped apart the last piece of my cup.

"Yeah," I said. "I do."

J.J. was piling up his tray to leave when I asked him. "So, is Luther coming to the wedding?"

"Who?" he asked.

"Luther. You know—" I said.

"From college?"

"Yeah."

"I haven't talked to him since I dropped out." He looked at me, his eyebrows scrunched in concern, curious. "Why do you remember Luther?"

"I don't know. I thought you two stayed friends." Awkward pause. "So do you know what he's doing now?"

By now he was irritated. "I don't know. I think he went to med school or something like that," he said, bitterness creeping into the edges of his voice. "He's in a different world, Tay. A totally different world."

• • •

A few nights later I was with my dad alone. I'd come in and sat with
him so many times by now. But still, every time, as soon as I sat down,
I had no idea what to do with myself. No idea how to approach this big
barrel of a man who'd had two lives, neither of which I ever understood. Neither of which took me into account. I remember always hoping that he was asleep. He usually was. Or, if he wasn't asleep, at least
the TV was on. Tonight there was no TV. Nothing but me and him.
Both awake. Never looking at each other directly.

"Do you want anything?" I tried.

"No," he said weakly.

"Do you want to play with the truck?" I asked, holding up the new
remote control truck I'd given him a week before.

He shook his head no.

"I can read you something," I suggested, remembering that I'd seen
that in a movie once.

He shifted his eyes as if to nod. I got up and searched for some reading material. And all I found was the newspaper.

"Sorry," I said, speaking too loudly. "There's only the newspaper.
Do you want to watch TV?" I hoped.

"No," he said. Then, "The scores."

"The scores?"

He nodded. I flipped through the paper, trying to figure out what
he was talking about, not wanting to ask him because I knew how hard
it was for him to talk. To do anything. I scanned the sections. Travel.
Style. Food. Metropolitan. Sports. Finally I understood. I flipped
through the pages of the Sports section, digging for what he wanted.
And then I started to read, relieved to be lost in the numbers.

"Astros seven, Mets two. Dodgers three, Braves one. Padres four,
Reds three." I looked up at him once as I read. His eyes were shut, relaxed, as if I were reading him poetry or something. "Cardinals four,
Giants one. Cubs eight, Brewers zero," and so on until the nurse came
in, telling me I had to go.

The wedding was still six months away when it actually happened.

Because this time my father was dying. Really dying.

And Nanette insisted that the wedding take place as soon as possible, regardless of the date she'd planned, so my father could be there. The wedding, she said, was for family as much as it was for her. And she said that she and J.J.'s wedding could make my father's death less painful, his passing more symbolic.

It started when each of us got a call from Mackie on Saturday at 9:00 A.M. The call that said, "This is it."

By 9:30 A.M. Nanette was sewing. She had to simplify the designs she had planned, but by 8:00 P.M. she'd made all four bridesmaid dresses while her mom was out getting the shoes dyed and buying flowers. Nanette then insisted that even though there was no time to make the peach dress for her mother, she could at least make her mother a peach shawl with the rose on it. And Nanette wore a white dress she'd made two years before, that she'd stopped wearing because it was out of fashion. She added on a few bows and pretended it was the gown of a queen.

My mother was mad. "Why in the hell does she want to have her wedding in a hospital?"

I had been on the brink of tears all morning, and this pushed me over the edge. "He's dying, Mom," I said. "He's really dying."

My mother locked herself in her room for the rest of the day.

Sunday morning she came out with her hair in an up-do. "I'm not going to let that man make me miss my son's wedding."

Then she saw me in my lime green dress. I'd spent an hour with my hair in hot rollers so I'd look a little more like Nanette's bridesmaid picture. And had succeeded. It was piled on top of my head, held together with pins and half a bottle of hair spray, and was bringing my height up to something like six feet four.

"You look ridiculous," my mom said, after taking in my getup.

"I know," I said. "But this is how she wants it."

"Well, you've got too much hair spray in. By the end of the night you're going to look like you have dandruff."

I met the other bridesmaids in the cafeteria as planned. I wasn't the only one a bit shell-shocked by Nanette's decision to have the wedding now.

"Is your dad contagious?" one of the bridesmaids wanted to know. I assured her he wasn't.

"Hospitals make me dizzy," said another. I joked that it was probably just the hair spray.

Finally Nanette joined us. She'd made up for her flat dress by ele-
vating her hair to an even higher level. And of course attaching to each
hair-sprayed clump an additional bow. Her mother came behind her,
quietly fixing anything she could get her hands on.

We walked as a group down the barren hallway. I held my head as
high as I could, knowing that Nanette would want it this way. A few patients wandering the hallway looked on in amazement. Or in oblivion,
depending on their condition.

My mom was waiting outside my dad's room, refusing to enter until
we arrived.

We walked in the door, and suddenly we were all there, together,
for the wedding. My mother and Mackie and a beaming J.J. and my
dad, barely able to move, but somehow taking it all in. Add to that a
nervous priest and three uncomfortable women who looked like
scoops of sherbet. We were all there as my brother and Nanette said
their vows, my brother tearing, Nanette warmed by the final outpour-
ing of our grief, a grief that she'd somehow made her own.

And we were all there for the first kiss of the bride and groom. My
dad was looking on, his eyes barely open. It was so weird that we were
doing this. Did he even know what was going on? He'd been in and
out of it so much, I couldn't tell. Then, he murmured a little "Thank
you." Everyone was sniffling, but it was as much out of discomfort as
out of pain or peace. We were crying because we knew that within the
next few hours he would be dead for real. And we were crying because
we were forever bound in this strange memory that could never fully
be explained to other people. That would never really have a context.
It was a group of desperate people trying for a moment not to be desperate.

It was our family commercial.

parting words

The day after my father died, I found myself again and again going through our last days together. Recounting every conversation. I had been so lucky to spend time with him before he'd died. But what did I do with those moments?

I kept searching for something, any exchange that we'd had, that would prove to me that my worst thoughts weren't true. But my worst thoughts *were* true.

I'd wasted the last days with him talking about nothing that mattered.

How was it that I managed to tell him the scores of all the baseball games but never mentioned that I didn't want him to die?

How did I sit with him and Mackie and talk about what he wanted inscribed on his tombstone and not tell them both how glad I was that they had each other?

How did I let my mother sit outside his room and cry, telling me that she had so much to say? Not even bad things. But that it was too hard. Too hard. Too hard. How could I let her do that? How could I not have made her go in there?

How did I give him a toy truck to play with in the room, and not tell him how sorry I was? For bringing that magazine to the diner. For not talking to him for so long. For lots of things.

It shouldn't have surprised me. Really. I mean, there are families on TV who talk about their feelings. Say that they love each other. All those things.

We were never one of those families. Not just my father. None of us were.

But it wasn't until he died, and all the words I could have said to him died with him, that it really hit me what I'd missed. All that sharing that we'd missed all along.

bending wood

The rocking chair was first built by Americans in the eighteenth century; they thought rocking was therapeutic. The Shakers even took this idea of rocking so far as to make adult cradles for the sick and the elderly.

Although Joe occasionally made the ladder-back rocking chair that the Shakers are most famous for, he preferred to make something more akin to the number 7 armed rocker, with a woven seat and back, and elongated egg-and-cup finials.

The steps to making this rocking chair are as follows:

Cut out all your parts.
Turn the legs, rungs, and stretchers.
Using a pattern, make the backrest and the rockers.
Bend the backrest and the back stretchers.
Drill the mortises in the legs and posts.
Put the frame together.
Apply the finishing.
Weave the seat and the back.

My favorite part was step four—bending the wood for the backrest and back stretchers. These parts, to me, seemed the most delicate, because these parts have to bend but cannot break.

To make wood bend like that you have to build a bending jig. A bending jig starts as a square block of wood. First, you cut it into two pieces, but the cut is curved, not straight, so that when you separate the two pieces just a little bit, it looks like a smile or a frown, depending on which way you look at it.

Then you steam the wood you are trying to bend, so that it becomes pliable.

And you sandwich that wood between the two pieces of the jig so that it's forced to bend into the smiley face. You then clamp the two pieces of the jig, with the strip of wood still in the smiley face, and leave it for two weeks to dry.

When you take the piece out, it will settle into a smaller smiley face than the one cut into the jig, but still it is curved.

And you've bent wood.

My new apartment was small, industrial-carpeted, and far from being "country," but my rocking chair was my favorite piece of furniture. It was the first rocking chair that I'd made myself. Joe had only helped me verbally, insisting that a carpenter has to feel his way around his work to get it right. My feeling was off, because it took me days and days. But finally, it was done. And sittable.

When I was homesick—not for home but for something that felt like home—when that pitted feeling crept into my stomach like pure craving, I would sit in my chair, and close my eyes and rock. And listen to the wood settle into place, and concentrate on the creaking. And I would pretend I was on the large wooden porch of my own house—my own Antoinette—somewhere with no humidity, surrounded by tall grass moving from a slight breeze, and I would creak and creak and creak.

The second rocking chair I ever made was a gift. I had given J.J. and Nanette a GRAVY BOAT WITH BOAT HOLDER: $67.50 for their wedding gift. What does that have to do with anything? It was six months later, and even though they hadn't registered for any of my handiwork, I decided I was going to make them a rocking chair. An extra wedding gift. A real wedding gift. I asked Joe if that would be OK with him.

"Of course. I'd rather you learn on your own stuff than trash mine," he said, lightly punching my shoulder.

Joe let me buy the pieces for J.J. and Nanette's rocking chair wholesale from him, and I was allowed to build it after work each day. So once we'd finished the cabinets and shelves and things that were on order, he'd run inside and reemerge with two cans of Bud. He had his own rocking chair that he sat in, so he'd nestle in and watch me make my chair like he was watching football on TV. He'd grin every time I screwed up. Occasionally he'd hand me a tool. But other than that I was on my own.

When I pulled out my backrest from the bending jig, I showed it to him, forcing a compliment, since it was the first time I'd ever done that on my own. He took my cue. "You're quite a bender," he said. "It's not so easy, if you ask me."

It is also not easy to bend in life. For example, one might think, having already lost my father, I would not concern myself anymore with the ordering of life, the ordering of death—that order having been thrown out the window already by a cancer I couldn't control. But this assumption would be only partly true.

True, the life part I've come to understand. I've finally adjusted to its variations from expectations.

Maybe I'll get married. Maybe I won't.

My father will never give me away.

This is a recent thing I had to accept. It is embarrassing to admit that, even when he was sick, I had always imagined my father giving me away. I'd even bent this idea to include Mackie. Like if I'd happened to meet someone who I wanted to marry, that I would want Mackie to be there with my father. In fact, the inclusion of Mackie made the whole tradition make more sense, in my mind. Tradition but in an untraditional way.

But without a dad, that didn't work anymore.

And now losing my father had changed over from something I worried about to something that happened, that I couldn't control.

My father would never be at my wedding. This I had come to accept.

Because I went through that experience, and I found where I bend, where I *have to* bend, where I was forced to bend.

But it isn't all about bending.

What if you were to die before me?

Out of order like that.

The child.

And then the mother.

I have spent my life bending, and it took you to make me realize exactly how I could break.

a t h o u s a n d l u l a s

I had spent twenty-three years hating Christmas. I hated it because I always felt I had to spend it with my mother, who hated it even more than I did. Even when my father was still with her, they both hated it equally, saying that having children had sucked all the Christmas spirit right out of them. Year after year of gimme gimme gimme was enough to make it feel like a day of high expectations that were never fulfilled.

This year my mom and her new boyfriend Hilton were going on a cruise. It was her decision. She said Christmas in Houston was so hot it didn't even feel like Christmas. There was no snow. Just the same old malls playing different music that was supposed to make you buy stuff you couldn't afford.

"You don't mind," Hilton said, in his thick drawl, "if I take her off yer hands this year, do ya?"

I told him no and meant it. Hilton was a beanpole of a man who had a mustache and still wore a cowboy hat to church. He didn't dwell on anything for more time than it took to make a joke about it and move on.

How my mother ever lucked out by finding him I'll never know. He said he saw her making a funny face at the priest during mass, reacting to something she didn't agree with. According to her, "The priest was reading that damn passage in the Bible that talks about the man serving the woman, which is fine, but then the whole point of the sermon became the problems with the new society, as he called it, where a woman is so independent that she doesn't feel the need to stick by her man, and I'm thinking, Who in the hell ever stuck by me?"

Hilton laughed as he told the story of approaching my mother at the free donut table after mass. He told me he walked up to her and said, "So, you didn't much care for that sermon now, did you?"

"No, I did not," she said, then went on to tell him just what she'd have loved to tell that stodgy old priest if only she'd had the courage. Hilton knew right then that she was for him. He had lost his wife in a motorcycle accident five years before, and said he hadn't met another honest woman until he met my mom. "I like a feisty lady" is what he said.

Well, now he had one.

And they were going on a cruise to Cancún to celebrate Christmas, and I had to decide how I'd spend mine.

I thought about Maria. She was still in New Mexico, only now she'd married a guy named Frankie who worked as an actuary. I called her to talk, and maybe see about visiting, but there were two babies screaming in the background so I decided I didn't want to visit just yet. There's that barrier that divides the kids and the kid-nots, where each side thinks they understand the other, and neither does. The woman without the baby thinks, *How can she stand having a kid screaming at her all day? How can she have any semblance of her own life when that kid's there all day demanding her whole self?* And the woman with the baby generally pities the babyless friend and worries about how she is coping with her empty life.

OK, so I'm exaggerating, but that didn't change the fact that I didn't want to spend Christmas with a family I didn't know that well.

Next I thought about Milo. I figured he must be back from Mexico by now. But when I called his old house, they said he'd moved to North Carolina to go to art school.

Nanette insisted that I spend it with her and J.J., but I'd grown more resistant to her insisting in the past several months. She was cooking dinner for J.J. and all her friends and her mom, and it sounded like a cocktail party instead of Christmas. And one of the few things I hated more than Christmas was cocktail parties. The mindless chatter that makes you feel like life would be easier if you just had an electronic button in your arm that said PLAY, so when people asked you the same tired questions again and again, you'd have your answer ready, instead of having to go through it a thousand times trying to change the phrasing until you finally give in to the rehearsed version, the one that's quick and to the point, that you think is funny, sort of.

Joe told me he'd spent the last fifteen Christmases by himself. "I like it that way," he said. "It's just a dumb day that makes everybody feel inadequate somehow."

So he'd created his own Christmas ritual, which to his mind was more in keeping with the intended holiday. After a little coaxing, he told me that his Christmas ritual went something like this:

Get up at 10:00 A.M. and go to Shipley's Donuts. Buy twice as many donuts as you usually eat and a cup of coffee. Spend extra time with the paper.

If you're feeling religious that year, like if you're worried about dying or if you're feeling like a bad person, go to the late mass, sit towards the back, and leave early to beat the traffic.

When you get home, build something for yourself. Something frivolous. Like a birdhouse or a wind chime. You're not allowed to mow the lawn on Christmas.

Watch a Clint Eastwood movie that you rented the day before.

Take a nap.

Cook a large meal that is 100 percent bad for you. Don't eat it in front of the TV. Set the table with the finest stuff you've got, and remember what it is like to enjoy your own company.

Eat ice cream in front of the TV.

Write something you still remember but never wrote down before.

Joe was afraid of forgetting everything, so years ago he'd built a wooden box he called his Memory Box, but he was always forgetting to write down his memories. So Christmas was the one day he was sure he'd write down something he still remembered, so he'd never forget it.

When I asked Joe if I could join in his ritual this year, he said he needed two days to think about it.

Exactly two days later he said yes, but I wasn't allowed to make fun of any part of it, and I couldn't just show up for the movie or for the ice cream. I had to do the whole thing.

I met him at his house as he was getting into his truck to go to Shipley's. Watching the way he walked, with the sway of a cowboy, I realized how incomplete he looked without a dog. I asked him why he didn't have one. He told me after he'd lost Choctaw, a chocolate Lab, buying another one would have been like betraying a lover. "I'm not a betrayer, Taylor."

He ordered four plain glazed donuts, and I ordered two chocolate filled. We ate them in silence as we read the paper. The woman behind the counter was staring at us with her little pity eyes that said, *Look how sad. It's Christmas Day and they're not even talking to each other. Just reading the paper.* But those were the rules. And I liked them. Not having to pretend that everything was significant.

We decided that since my father had died this year, it would be appropriate for us to attend church. It was the eleven o'clock mass and was filled with all the late sleepers in the church community who sang like they were hungover or depressed. I didn't sing, but Joe did, half-hearted and off-key. Once the mass hit the hour mark, Joe leaned over and complained that the Christmas masses went on for too long because the choirs felt it was their big chance to show off.

Afterwards we walked by all the people outside the church catching up with each other, wishing each other a merry Christmas. We didn't know anyone and passed right through without having to talk to anybody or shake hands with the priest.

At my suggestion, the building part of the ritual changed that year. I decided that we should make something for each other. "I don't need anything," he said. Finally, after I explained to him that *him* making himself something he didn't need was no different than *me* making him something he didn't need, he gave in.

First he showed me what he'd made last year. He walked with me out into his yard and pointed up into a tree at a birdhouse in the shape of a bird. "I thought it was funny," he said, then shrugged as if to say it

didn't seem as funny now. "I don't need anything," he said again.
"Too bad," I told him.

We drew an imaginary line in the middle of the shed. He had his side and I had mine. And we had three hours. We worked silently, just listening to the wind breaking against the walls of the shed. Every now and then he'd look up and laugh. Once he said, "I feel like I should have been in this place, like this, with you, about forty years ago."

I made him a thick pine jigsaw puzzle in the shape of a voluptuous woman. I painted her as a blonde in a red dress with eyes that were flirtatiously glancing sideways. The puzzle was only seven pieces:

2 *legs*
2 *arms*
1 *body*
1 *head*
1 *blond hairdo*

He named her Lula. At the time I thought he'd made it up.

He made me a small, square jewelry box out of a scrap of tigerwood. I recognized the striped pattern of the Brazilian hardwood immediately. He had shown me this scrap that day we'd discussed conservation, since this type of wood is now considered endangered. He'd kept the scrap for years, feeling guilty for having it but afraid to use it, opposed to selling it. He handed the exquisite box to me sheepishly. "I know it's stupid," he said, "since you never wear jewelry. But I thought someday you might."

And we brought our gifts inside the house and watched *Paint Your Wagon*, Joe in his armchair, me lying down on the stiff sofa.

We skipped the nap, each having taken one in bits and pieces during the movie. After we'd set the steaks to marinate in some bourbon, he showed me the bottle of wine he'd picked up special.

"Taylor," he said over dinner, "don't take this the wrong way, now. I'm a sixty-year-old man and I know I'm a sixty-year-old man. And I'm your boss and I know I'm your boss. And I'm your friend, flat out, but." He stopped, wiped his mouth with his napkin nervously before finding his words. "But having you here. I love my life, don't get me wrong, but it's funny to be sixty years old and have your dream girl sitting across the table from you. I keep trying to pretend, just for a sec, just for myself, that really this is forty years ago, and I've got a soulful, quiet lady I'm seducing with a nice dinner, but then I look down at my stupid old wrinkled hands and it's ruined for me."

"We wouldn't have gotten along when you were my age," I said.

"What makes you so sure of that?" he said, remembering how to flirt.

"Because you were a skirt chaser, remember?" I'd spent too many days hearing too many tales to have missed that one.

"Well, maybe we wouldn't have liked each other," he said. "But we would have had something."

I nodded, thinking how weird this was. Not what he was talking about, but how right he was.

He started talking about how he didn't know which was sadder: seeing people you'll never get to really know that way, or remembering people you might have known that way but never did, either because of circumstance or because you never did anything about it. He told me about Lula. She was a lounge singer he used to go see every time she played at this bar in Amarillo. And there was this one song, an original, called "Mr. Blue Eyes." He said it was a silly song, but he swore every time she sang it she was looking right at him. He thought about buying her a drink a million times and never did, figuring the illusion was better than the real thing.

"And now I think about it every month or so. Pathetic really." He explained that it wasn't so much that he thought he'd be with her now or anything, but more that he would have had some experience. Something would have happened to him had he been with her. She would have affected him somehow.

We ate our Blue Bell Cookies 'n' Cream ice cream ravenously before sitting down to write our memories.

"So, does this mean that this year you're going to share your memory?" I wanted to know.

"No way in hell," he said. "I'm not a good writer, and I still have to be able to look at you when you show up for work next week. I know better than to let a woman watch me whine for too long."

So I don't know what Joe wrote. He told me it was about Lula, but I think he was lying. I think it might have been about a thousand Lulas. This is what I wrote about:

> Age: 17
> I've been living with my family all my life, and there are still a few things they don't know about me. Like at night, when I can't sleep, I sit on the kitchen counter and eat cinnamon right out of the little jar. That's what I was doing when Luther came into the kitchen that night, wearing nothing but his boxers and a T shirt . . .

I didn't show my memory to Joe either. We just said good night and slept well knowing that another Christmas had passed in its own way.

Writing about that night—the night I kissed Luther—reminded me of a day, less than a year ago, when I didn't know what to do with myself and looked up Luther in the phone book. I was trying to find a reason not to call him. But in the end all I could think was *If he wants to see me, I'll see him. And if he doesn't, I won't. But if I don't call, then I definitely won't see him. So either I'll see him again, or everything will stay the same.* The only real drawback I could come up with was that it was a slightly crazy thing to do.

But I'd done crazier.

I.

Was sure.

In fact, some of my proudest moments were my craziest. Because at least, in those moments, I was doing. Something.

A woman answered when I called. In the few milliseconds immediately following, I thought of so many different things I could say or do, like hanging up, or asking to speak to her husband, just so I'd know he was married.

Or just asking if I could please speak with Luther.

"You mean big Luther or little Luther?" the woman said.

"Excuse me?"

"That's just my way of saying Junior or Senior, hon."

"Oh," I said. Frozen. About to hang up.

"Who's this?"

"I'm a friend. Of Luther's," I said.

"I see. Sounds like little Luther."

"The doctor one," I said.

"Honey, they are both doctors. But by the sounds of you I'd say you're looking for my son. He's the more handsome one anyway," she joked.

A long, dead pause.

"Are you there, sugar?"

"Yeah. Sorry. My phone was . . . having problems."

"So, he's coming over for dinner, but he's not here yet. Do you want me to have him call you back?"

"I was actually—Do you have his number? That would be fine for now."

"I always forget it," she said. Over the phone I could hear her fingernails drumming excitedly on the counter as she looked. "So, what did you say your name was again?"

Shit. Should I lie? Should I not lie? "Taylor," I said. Damn.

"Taylor! I remember you! Why, we were talking about you just the other day!"

"You were?"

"Sure we were. You know he's single now, don't you? That Rebecca. Bless her heart, she was terribly mean-spirited. I knew it from the minute I saw her. Never went anywhere without those big Dobermans."

"I don't think—"

"So, should I tell him you'll call him later, then?"

"I would love his number, if that's at all possible," I said.

"Sure. Sure. OK. OK. I can't wait to tell him you called." She paused and sighed, as if reminiscing. "Taylor Simone."

Taylor Simone? Who the hell is that?

It was like slow motion as I heard the sound of the door open. Of his mom telling him that Taylor Simone was on the phone for him. It was either hang up and wonder or stick it out and be embarrassed.

I stayed on the phone. I was definitely still crazy. But that was OK. You think and think and think about something, and all you have to do is admit you're a little nuts, and finally you can free yourself up to *do* something. Really do it. And then I heard his mother again.

"Taylor, I'm sorry, but"—she paused, clearly calculating a lie—"Luther just got called in to the hospital. It was really important."

"Could I get his number—"

Click.

And that was it.

I decided to tell Joe about it. "I once went after a Lula," I said.

I had his attention immediately. He stopped applying finish to a set of shelves and leaned over as if awaiting some insight into the mystical world. "I'll be. So what happened?"

"I don't think you're supposed to go after a Lula," I said.

"Married?"

I shook my head no.

"Fat or mean or something?"

No again. I explained that we were star-crossed by his parents, who'd moved to Houston recently, and who happened to be the only people listed under his name. "They think I'm someone else. And . . . It's someone he doesn't like, apparently. And . . . It's just too weird now, to call back. Besides, it passed, you know. That thought."

"I knew it," he said, as if there were some universal law of Lulas and their state of untouchability.

We worked side by side for about a half an hour before speaking again.

"Girl like you shouldn't need to track down Lulas."

"Thanks," I said.

Thanks.

I'd just gotten home and was eating an oversized bowl of Lucky Charms, watching an infomercial on acne. I'd become addicted to the infomercial, with its enthusiastic sense of purpose, and its before-and-after pictures. This was how I spent most nights. Infomercials followed by reading. Tonight I was reading Flannery O'Connor's *Wise Blood*, which seemed a nice follow-up to the infomercial—just a different set of grotesque characters with inflated causes.

And then the phone rang.

"Taylor, it's your mother."

"Hi."

"You're not drunk or anything are you?" she had the nerve to ask me.

"No."

"Are you dating that old Joe guy? Your boss?" She'd never quite forgiven me since Jeff, and made dating-old-men jokes at every opportunity.

"No."

"Somebody has been asking your brother about you."

I called J.J., since I'd promised my mom I would. He wasn't home, but Nanette filled me in quickly, eagerly.

Something like "J.J. has this friend at work who's a computer programmer and who's tall, six four I bet, and he's really quiet like you and he saw your picture and really wants to meet you."

"Based on a picture?"

"What do you want, a soul-o-meter?" she said in her corny Nanette way, laughing too loud at her own joke.

"Which picture was it?"

"Right before our wedding, when your hair's all pretty. Your mom said he sounds like just your type."

"Why is my mother in on this?"

"Oh, Taylor, you know how she is," Nanette said.

"Yeah, I do."

"Why don't you just try it?"

"I don't really like computers."

"You don't have to go to work with him, for goodness' sakes!" she said.

"Nanette, I sort of pride myself on never going on blind dates. Ever."

"Well, look where that's gotten you."

I was so in my head right then that I didn't react. I was just thinking,

I don't like being set up, yet I'll do something as unnatural as track down a guy I only kissed once. Didn't really even kiss.

I'm crazy.

"OK. OK," I said. "I'll do it."

His name was Robert, but everyone called him Bobbo (which I avoided). We spoke on the phone.

Me: Hey, how's it going?

Him: Good. Good. How are you?

Me: Fine.

Him: Cool. So. Crazy I haven't met you before but we're going out, isn't it? I mean, going on a date. Not going out out or anything.

Me: What do you want to do?

Him: I don't know. Do you feel like grabbing a drink? Thursday, maybe?

Me: Sure.

Him: Great. How about Sam's Boat? At six?

Me: Sure. OK. I'll see you there, then.

Him: Cool. See you there.

Hang up.

Phone rings again.

Me: Hello?

Him: So. I forgot. How am I going to know which one is you?

Me: I thought you knew what I looked like.

Him: How would I know that?

Me: From a picture?

Him: Well, I can ask J.J. to bring a picture to work.

Awkward pause.

Me: I'm six foot two.

Another awkward pause.

Him: OK. Well, I guess I'll be able to see that.

Me: So, what do you look like?

Him: I'm six four. Blond hair. I don't know. I'll wear a red shirt. How's that?

Me: I'm sure we can just figure it out.
Him: Probably. OK . . . Then . . . Taylor. Good to meet you and I'll
see you on Thursday . . . Then . . . OK . . . Gotcha.
Me (rolling eyes): Gotcha.

Nanette told me I had to go. "What does it matter whether he's seen
your picture or not?" she said, as she furiously squeezed lemons for her
famous homemade lemonade.

"Why did you lie to me?"

"Because," she said, "I'm starting to figure you out. I don't know
how to tell you this, but I don't go anywhere with you that people
aren't staring like you're a supermodel or something. But I know I've
gotta help you along to break you out of your shell."

"My shell?"

"Your shell, sweetie. You spend all your time with a sixty-year-old
man. And as much as I respect what you do—and you know how I
want you to make a tiled table for us and everything—I mean, you are
good at it. But if your work is going to keep you all holed up . . . Well,
then you just have to make an effort to get out. To be out. When was
the last time you kissed a boy?"

"A boy?"

"Oh, you know what I mean."

"Two months ago." I didn't tell her that it was a guy I'd met in a bar.
We kissed in the parking lot, but I gave him a fake number. He was
getting on my nerves already (he kept saying he wanted to take me
home and find my "special spot"), so why drag that out?

"That's no way to live," Nanette said. "My god if I looked like you
I'd have slept with every rich man in the state of Texas."

"Gross."

Nanette handed me my lemonade triumphantly, a smirk forming at
the edges of her mouth. "Don't tell your brother I said that."

"I won't."

"And just go out with Bobbo, will you?"

• • •

On Thursday I was so nervous about the stupid date that Joe noticed. I was sanding this table for him, furiously, as if I was in a race or something. Walking around and around the table as I went.

"You have to go to the bathroom or something?" Joe asked me.

I stopped what I was doing, wiped the sweat from my forehead. "What?"

"You're dancing around like Choctaw used to do, fidgeting in circles."

"Sorry," I said "I'm just nervous. I have a date," I explained, then started sanding away again.

Joe spoke louder. "Well, you're making me nervous, too. And I don't have a date."

I stopped again and flopped onto a rocking chair. "Sorry," I told him again.

"Why don't you just go home early if you're this shaken up?" he said, laughing at me. "God almighty, you're worse than a little kid," he said, then looked me right in the eye and added, "Don't let him know you're this nervous."

"I won't," I said. "I won't."

Being home was worse. I watched TV until I'd reached that state of lull that was thoroughly depressing.

And then I went for a run along the bayou.

I didn't bring my headphones, just so I could let out all the commotion that was going on in my head. I concentrated on all the other people running, wondering what each of them did for a living that allowed them to go jogging on a Thursday afternoon.

And then it happened.

Like when you learn a new word that you've never heard before, and from that point on you hear it every day, at least a couple of times. You're tuned in to something.

And I guess I was tuned in to Luther.

Because four miles into my run, as I was concluding that one blind date wasn't going to kill me, I saw Luther running towards me.

Or I thought it was Luther. It was hard to tell at first. A lot of people I've seen from far away have given me that glimmer of hope that maybe I was about to see my Lula.

My heart was racing. With every pace it looked more and more like him. The olive color of his skin. Still him. His barely curly hair. Still him. Deep dimples when he smiled. It was.

Luther.

Oh my god.

I just ran right past Luther.

And we'd exchanged a look.

First he'd given me the standard checkout glance. And then his expression, just as he was passing me, turned to the quizzical, as he tried to place me. Why did I look familiar? I imagined what he was thinking, what was racing through his head. Like, *Was I drunk one night and tried to pick her up?* Or, *Did we go to the same high school maybe?*

Just as he was probably shaking off the thought, I decided not that this was fate but that if I'd given him this much mental airtime recently, I should just let the ugly story of my Lula pursuit finish itself out.

I turned around and began to jog after him.

I pulled up beside him, just as a young, too-skinny teenage girl jogged past. My stomach was a big knot. He looked over at me, and I could see that now he was worried. Because if I'd turned around to run with him, he was supposed to remember me. But still he couldn't place my face.

"Hey," he said, trying to sound casual, hoping the memory request he'd put into his brain was going to be answered soon.

"Hey," I said.

"So, how've you been?" he said, searching for a hint.

"It's OK if you don't remember me."

We were still running, side by side, as he glanced over at me again and smiled. "How do I know you?"

"I'm J.J. Jessup's sister," I said. "Taylor."

He slowed down to a walk, stepping into the grass. I followed, still breathing heavy. He was wearing a faded Corona T-shirt that was drenched. He brought his hands to his hips as he regained his breath. Then he turned his head sideways, and his hair flopped into his eyes, which were squinting from the sun. "Wow." He laughed sheepishly. "It's been a long time."

He was looking right at me. Right into my eyes. So unflinchingly that I was conscious of it, thinking about where my eyes should look next. I had to look away. "Yeah. It has."

"You look great."

"Thanks," I said. Another awkward silence, as I thought to myself, *Is it really so hard just to talk? Why can't I just talk? Why am I incapable of making conversation?*

"So," he said. "How've you been?"

I laughed.

"What?" he said self-consciously, thinking I was making fun of him.

"Nothing. It's just . . . Six years. It's hard to know where to start."

"OK," he said, more like a question.

"I didn't mean that."

"What?" he said, confused.

"Sorry. I just . . . I didn't mean to be rude."

"You weren't rude," he said.

There was a long, strange pause, which he broke with a laugh. "Why is this so awkward?" He said it in that way that I remembered. That way of making anything seem fine. Making even me feel like I could state my mind.

"I used to have a huge crush on you," I said. "And I'm awkward. That's why. This. Is so awkward."

"Oh," he said, grinning. "So, you grew up well."

"Same," I said. "I heard you ended up being a doctor."

"Yeah. I'm about to start my residency. In, uh, emergency pediatric medicine. What about you?"

"I make things. Furniture, mostly. I like to make rocking chairs."

"Huh. That's great, actually. Simple."

"Simple?"

"That came out wrong," he said.

"I like it."

He wiped his brow with the inside of his shirtsleeve. Contemplated something. Then said it. "I hoped you'd turn out like this," he said.

"You didn't even remember who I was five minutes ago."

"I mean back then. When I first met you. I hoped you'd be just like you are right now."

I nodded, not sure what to say. And we just sat like that, like animals, taking each other in, sizing each other up.

"So, do you want to maybe grab a drink sometime, or . . ." He trailed off.

"Yeah. That'd be great," I said.

"I mean, I don't want to 'grab a drink sometime,'" he said, almost as if he were talking to himself. "I'd like to see you again."

"Me too."

"My schedule is nuts. What are you doing tonight?"

I told him about Bobbo. About how I had to go to Sam's Boat at six. He thought that was funny. "I really don't want to go," I told him.

"You probably should, though, right?" he said.

I thought about Nanette. About my brother. About how I'd feel if I'd gotten completely stood up. "Yeah, I have to go. But maybe after?" I said, then realized how desperate that sounded.

"No. You and Bobbo should have a good time without you worrying about me," he said. "I'll just get your number. But . . . you don't happen to run with a pen, do you?"

"No."

"Are you listed?" he asked.

"No," I said. I wasn't. And I was thinking that I just had my biggest opportunity ever with Luther and I blew it for some fuck-o Bob-o who I knew I wasn't going to like. What was wrong with me?

"I have a great memory," he said.

So I told him my number. And he repeated it to himself. Twice. And then we continued to run in opposite directions.

I was sitting at the bar with Bobbo, who was six one (not six four), blondish *gray*, and picked at his fingers the whole time we talked about nothing. And all I could think was that this was crazy. Why did I do this to myself? Luther had been right there. And now my ever seeing him again depended on his memory.

I am definitely crazy, I was thinking as Bobbo yabbered on and on about the time his buddy called a hooker to be with him and his girlfriend, and the hooker turned out to have a dick or something.

And then I heard someone say, "Taylor!" Was someone saying my name? I decided no. "Taylor," I heard again, and turned around.

And that's when I knew that, fortunately, everyone is crazy.

I was crazy enough to run after my Lula.

And my Lula was crazy enough to come find me.

Before I could figure out what was happening, Luther was introducing himself to Bobbo, pretending he was an old friend of mine. "I haven't seen Taylor since grade school. It's crazy seeing you all grown-up like this. She looks good, doesn't she?" he said to Bobbo, who was buying the whole act. As Bobbo went to the bar to buy another round, Luther leaned in to me. "I forgot your number."

I looked across the room, where Bobbo was slapping an old buddy of his on the back. "Do you still have the night off?" I asked.

"Yeah," he said as he found my hand and squeezed it.

"Let's get out of here," I said.

"You don't mean leave now, do you?" he said. I nodded. He laughed.

I didn't even look over my shoulder as we walked out of the bar. He still had me by the hand, and I followed him to his Jeep. He opened the door for me, then ran around to his side. And we sat there for one awkward moment. What had we just done?

"So," he said, turning the key. "Where do you want to go?"

"I feel like driving," I said.

"Driving?" He paused. "Could you be a little more specific?" he joked.

"Let's just get the hell out of here," I said.

We pulled into a gas station and I bought a "Best of Country" tape for a buck. And then we drove to Galveston. The hour drive passed like nothing. I kept looking over at him, and thinking that this was really me. I'd been talking like me all night. And I looked like me. I was wearing worn jeans with paint stains on them and a Bionic Man T-shirt. I'd thought about changing for Bobbo but decided that this was who I was.

And here I was, still me.

And Luther was there.

Still with me.

Once we got on the island, we stopped for a bucket of Kentucky Fried Chicken and went to one of the rest areas on the beach for a picnic.

We missed the sunset, but it didn't matter.

We talked about a lot of things. About my brother. About my dad.

"I'm really sorry," he said. "That must have been so hard."

I nodded.

"But at least you got to say good-bye, you know. Spend some time with him before he died."

Something about the way he said that, so earnest, made me want to laugh. "You really are trying to be nice, aren't you?" I asked him.

"What?" he said, confused.

"Nothing."

"What did you mean by that?" he said, really curious as to what I was thinking.

"I just mean . . . Thank you. That's very polite. And yes, it was hard. But what do you *really* want to know?"

He thought for a minute. "I want to know how you stop yourself from thinking about it all day."

I told him that I repressed it mostly, and that maybe that was why I kept having such weird dreams.

"What happens in them?"

I told him that in the dreams I went up the stairs to my parents' old apartment. And for a long time I would stand outside the front door, dreading what was inside. But then once I opened the door, it turned out that the inside of the apartment was huge, with more and more doors that kept leading to more and more rooms. And in the dream, my parents are giving me a tour. They're still together, and glance at each other like they really love each other, describing every detail of their big house. Right down to the trash compactor.

"Weird," he said.

"If I'd had it once it wouldn't be so bizarre. But it's a once-a-week occurrence."

He told me that he still had nightmares about his ex-girlfriend, who was named Taylor Simone. And so we talked about her, about my Jeff, about his Rebecca. Slowly we did what you're not supposed to do. Open up your bags. Pour their contents between you. And pick through to see if there is anything in there, any part of you, worth salvaging. As we sorted through each other's garbage, I began to feel lighter and lighter. And then I confessed that I'd called him once.

"Why'd you do that?" he said.

"Curiosity," I said.

"That makes it sound like I'm a freak or something."

"We're all freaks," I said, and meant it.

When we were done with our chicken, we went for a walk on the beach. And there was this moment when he picked me up and pretended he was going to throw me into the water. And then he put me down. I was laughing at the cheesy gesture until he pulled me close to him. The wind was blowing like crazy, and he put my hair behind my ear.

And then he laughed.

"I'm funny now?" I said.

"This is funny," he said. "Can't you see how funny this is?"

"It's sort of funny," I said, then whispered into his ear like he had done to me that first night that I felt something. "And it's sort of not." And then I kissed his neck, his cheek. And he grabbed my hand, gently, and felt each finger as he looked into me, through me. Through my freakishness. Through my inability to ever express anything. He knew.

Me.

Just like I thought he would.

And as we lay down on the beach, forgetting about the sand, forgetting about everything, I was thinking that I wasn't crazy after all. If going after a Lula meant feeling like this, I'd go after a thousand Lulas.

matched in spirit

I liked being giddy. Having that sort of excitement that comes from beginnings. Waking up happy, looking forward to something. To Luther. We'd been seeing each other pretty steadily since that first rush of a night together, as steadily as we could given his busy schedule at med school. It was funny, actually, trying to have a traditional relationship after such a crazy beginning. But somehow it was working.

He was much mellower than I would have thought. Someone who preferred a movie to a bar. Or a long run to a wild night out. But really, it didn't seem to matter what we were doing. I just loved to be with him at the end of the day, scratching his back to help him fall asleep.

And he wasn't the only thing that was falling into place. I guess you could say my family was falling into place as well. Luther kept saying that my family's relationships were changing for the better because of outside influences. Meaning that Nanette was great for J.J., really kept him centered. And that Hilton had all but saved my mother. She'd stopped drinking so much, and was now capable of having a conversation free from complaints. Sometimes even peppered with positives and compliments.

But I didn't attribute this to outside influences.

Unless you were talking about my father. Or, rather, about my father's death.

Once I'd gotten over the fact that I hadn't said all I wanted to while
he was alive, it was as if I'd discovered a more direct route to him than
the bedside—this weird feeling, like I had someone in the spiritual
world looking out for me. Someone who I could mutter to sometimes
when I was alone. It's hard to explain, but a part of me was sure that
my father knew everything I was doing now. How I really felt. How I
was growing. It wasn't about him being at my wedding anymore. It
wasn't about events or little moments. It was about everything. I felt
my father there for everything.

And I suspected that it was the same for J.J., and even my mother.

After my father's death—months after—Nanette and J.J. had the idea of
hosting a Sunday dinner once a month with the whole family. This Sunday was to be the first. I had wanted to give them something nice, as a
kickoff to the whole tradition. And that's how I got the idea for the table.
Almost a year before, I'd promised to make them a table. A long dinner
table with colorful tiles inlaid in the top. I'd helped make a plain-
looking one with terra-cotta tiles for a client of Joe's and wanted to do it
on my own this time. I decided to give it to them at our first dinner.

It was another after-hours project for me at Joe's. And, just like with
the rocking chair, he was ready to watch me struggle. He sat and
smirked all week, watching me cut my wood to shape with the miter
saw. I cut the outer trim pieces and the lip. Later I built the legs, and
bolted their supports. He got up from his chair at one point, thinking
that I was going to need his help, but I didn't. The next night I var-
nished the table and left it to dry. And I warned Joe that we were going
shopping for tiles in the morning.

"Shopping?" he said. "I don't think so."

Still, the next day he shaved, the usual sign that he expected to be
out at some point during the day. We went to a tile store and looked
through all of the different designs. I narrowed it down to three and
made him pick from there, reminding him that Nanette liked vibrant
colors. He pointed to a bright blue tile, with a slight pattern in it. "That
ought to suit a loud girl," he said.

After work that night, I mortared the tile to the table. And the next day, after it had dried, I laid down the grout, pushing it into the spaces between the tiles.

By then it was Friday. I told Joe I was going to pick up the table on Sunday. That I'd wipe the extra grout off the tiles then. "I'll do that for you tomorrow," he said. I told him not to bother, but knew he'd do it anyway.

"What are you going to do with the chairs?" he wanted to know. He was referring to a corner of the shed where I'd stored about ten chairs I'd taken out of the garbage in the past year and fixed up. Most of them were the bentwood chairs—the ones with the swirly backs that I always associate with ice-cream parlors—since those seemed to be the most popular things to throw out. My theory was that it was because they were so light. It was like throwing away a candy wrapper to most people. But there were also other kinds. Stray stacking chairs, with no matching chairs to be stacked on. Ladder-back stick chairs with wounded, ripping seats. Even the occasional wooden folding chair. "You got anything planned for them?" Joe wanted to know.

"I do now," I told him, thinking I could give Nanette six of the chairs, too. He liked the idea. Together we dug through the pile of fixed-up chairs. I selected my favorite six. Of course, none of the chairs technically matched. But when you put them together, beside the colorful table, it just worked. Joe called it matching in spirit, which surprised me, since this mess of color and styles couldn't be further from the work that he did.

Luther met me at Joe's that Sunday to help me load everything into his truck. He loved the table. He thought it was such a nice, heavy piece. He was just sure that this was something I could do for a living. That a lot of people would want tables like this. I shrugged off the suggestion. First things first. I wanted to see Nanette's face when I gave it to her.

Once we'd secured the table in the truck bed, I went to collect the chairs. Joe was there, arms crossed on his chest, as if he were supervising. At first I thought he was just bored, until I figured out that he was up to something.

I'd just picked up this one stick chair that had a lasso carved in the back. It was painted burnt orange, with a woven seat. It had a sort of antique look to it. I'd found it thrown out with a teddy bear so worn it barely had any hair left. I'd guessed it had once been a part of a kid's desk set, although the chair itself was full-size. I'd had to strip it, repaint it, and replace the seat. But I was pleased when it ended up looking like a newer, cleaner version of itself. Joe might have been thinking the same thing. His face never breaking from seriousness, Joe said, "How much you want for that one?"

"This one?" I said, holding up the cowboy chair that he was clearly staring at.

"That one."

"Nothing," I told him, gladly handing it over. "Why didn't you just tell me you wanted it?" I laughed. "It's been sitting in here for over a month."

" 'Cause I knew you'd give it to me," he said.

"Well, that wasn't so bad, was it?" I kidded, then went to the remaining four to find a replacement for Nanette and J.J.'s set.

By the time we got to J.J. and Nanette's house, my mother and Hilton had already arrived. They were all sitting in the living room, with Hilton and Nanette doing most of the talking. I laughed to myself, thinking that once Luther got in there, it'd be all of the Jessup "significant others" keeping up the appearance of normality, of casual conversation, better than any of us original Jessups had ever managed before by ourselves.

Once we'd sat down for about an hour, all of our catching up done, J.J. and Luther having rehashed enough college stories to keep them happy for a while, I announced that I had a surprise.

Everybody went out to the truck parked in front of the house.

Luther and I crouched into the camper shell and pulled out the tiled table first, as Hilton continually repeated how impressed he was with my work, and how worried he was about me carrying something so heavy. I assured him that Luther and I had it under control, pointing out that I was bigger than Hilton was anyway. But still he hovered at the table's edge, waiting to catch it if I happened to let go.

Surprising no one, Nanette gushed once we'd set it in the kitchen. "It's just, so thoughtful," she said again and again.

Then, eagerly, I told her that I had something else. Another surprise.

"No, you don't!" she exclaimed. "This is too much."

"Taylor, when did you become such a little giver?" my mom asked matter-of-factly, although I was sure she'd already decided that the answer was Luther.

Everybody went out to the truck again.

As we all stood huddled together by the back of the truck, I told them the story of the chairs, sort of. I told Nanette that the surprise was that I'd gotten them some chairs for the table, too. Then I added that she didn't have to keep them unless she liked them.

"Of course I'll like them," Nanette said. "You made them."

I told her not exactly. That, really, it wouldn't hurt my feelings if she thought them too weird. But that I couldn't bear it if everyone pretended to like them, only to throw them into the garbage again.

"Again?" said Nanette. "What do you mean by that?"

"Taylor," Luther said, shaking his head. He said I had a way of getting into messes when it wasn't necessary. But I didn't want to pretend that I'd made these, or that I'd bought them at the store. I wanted them to know the truth and be comfortable with it. Appreciate it, even. Or else I'd wait for someone else who did.

I explained that the chairs were from the garbage. I told her the tale behind each one as I pulled them out of the truck. And then I eagerly showed her what I'd done to fix them. I showed her the green chair with the tall back that had been thrown out of an elementary school library, along with some bookshelves. I told her about the gum that I picked off the bottom, the hours I'd spent removing the old varnish, and then showed her the initials that had been carved on the inside of one of the legs, which I'd decided to leave.

"Oh, Taylor," she said, bringing her hands to her face. "I love them! J.J., aren't these just amazing?"

J.J. seemed a little more puzzled but went along with it anyway, as expected.

And then each of us grabbed a chair and carried it into the house. Once inside, we would set the mismatched chairs around the table, then eventually sit in them and share a meal together, as different as ever, yet matching in spirit.

4

If a piece is being considered for restoration because of its possible antique value, the decision becomes more complicated. One important factor here is the overall condition. That is, if as much as one-fourth of the principal parts is missing, the true value is lost. However, if excellent craftsmanship can be employed and the part replaced with old wood, then the piece should be restored. Obviously, this course of action will enable future generations to enjoy the piece, and if the work is done well enough, it may not even be detectable by the inexperienced eye

"Rules and Tools for Restoration of Antique Furniture,"
Restoring Antique Furniture: A Complete Guide,
by Richard A. Lyons

i would have moved

I might have moved to become an anthropologist. Like after I'd graduated from college, maybe I would have moved to Africa and discovered
a remote tribe that lived off the land and had never heard of war.

Or maybe my carpentry would have led me to move somewhere.
Maybe to Florida, where people have a larger need for patio furniture
and rocking chairs.

Or let's just say I was Mrs. Jeff Romano. I'd have moved for the sake
of my family. I might have strapped up the kids and all their things into
our little VW and next thing you know we'd have been a happy family
in Kansas City. Whatever's best for the kids, after all.

Most likely, I later learned, I would move consciously as an adventure. A way to shake up my life. As if people in Montana were really so
much different than people in Texas, once you boiled away their accents and got down to the basic character types: greedy, giving, irre-
sponsible, holy, et cetera.

All of these.

Were ways to move.

Reasons to move.

Reasons I had imagined.

But I ended up moving for a reason I'd written off a long time ago
as a terrible idea.

I moved for a man.

Not for a job, not for a husband, not for the kids, not for the lust of
life.

But for lust, flat-out.

You could put it that way.

There were different ways of looking at it, ways I'd run and run and run in my mind countless times.

You could say I moved for a man.

Or you could say I moved because I was starting to understand the way that I loved.

You could say I moved for a man.

Or you could say I moved because I'd just begun to figure out what my personality was like when I was happy.

You could say I moved for a man.

Or you could say I moved because I didn't want to spend my life what-iffing, living in that overpopulated land of regret.

Luther and I had taken trips together before. Before we moved to New York together. Before he told me he loved me.

The first trip we took was to New Hampshire in the White Mountains. It was in our third month. We had to go to one of his med-school friends' weddings in Concord on a Saturday, so we flew out a few days ahead to go camping.

"You've never been on a plane?" Luther asked me the night we finalized our plans. "Wow."

"Wow yourself," I said, reaching that point where I could be mad or not mad, depending on the next words to come out of his mouth.

"You're so lucky," he said.

Not mad. I asked him to explain what he meant.

He said that I was lucky because I was going to be able to remember the first time I ever was on a plane. Whereas his first time was wasted. Done. Gone. And unremembered.

The minute we got on the plane, he was watching me, wide-eyed, waiting for each of my reactions.

To the overcompensating flight attendants.

To the vibrating overhead compartments when we took off.

To the annoyed dispositions of all the passengers.

Luther kept asking me to tell him what I was thinking.

"What are you thinking now?" he asked, as we passed over the grid of the city.

"I had no idea that Houston was so ordered," I said.

"How about this?" he asked, when we entered our first cloud.

"I don't like it. But. They feel so close," I said.

"You have to tell me what you're thinking, right now. Tell me quick, quick, before you think too much," he said, as we soared above our first mountain range.

"Oh my god" was all I could mutter, as I pressed my nose against the smudgy window.

Luther was looking over my shoulder, trying to see what I was seeing. "It's amazing that no one looks anymore," he said.

I turned around to examine the plane filled with people reading, napping, staring at the stains on the backs of their tray tables. Passengers. He was right. We then vowed that we would never be that way. No matter how many flights we'd taken. And in what direction.

When I first told my mom that I was moving with Luther to New York, she told me this: "Your father and me, we just picked up and moved to Texas. Just because the word Texas sounded good, if you can believe that. But moving is uprooting. And you pay a price each time. Don't ever forget that."

I reminded her of the time she told me that their moving on a whim was the most romantic thing she and my dad ever did. That moving was how they got away from his mother and their old lives. Their old selves.

She said, "Maybe I grew bigger or taller or something, but my little baby roots, they're still in the grass someplace else. I gave up my baby roots."

This is the reason I was willing to give up my baby roots:

The first day of our camping trip in New Hampshire, Luther and I hiked five miles up to find a place to camp. I carried my own back-pack. I even had half the food we were going to need for the trip.

But Luther was moving so much more quickly.

He had to wait for me sometimes. Never for more than a few minutes.

But still.

He had to wait.

Because I was behind.

The first few times I made excuses. Not big excuses or bad excuses. More like "I'm sorry. I'm not used to the altitude." Or "I'm sorry. I feel like such a rookie." Or "I'm sorry I keep apologizing. I just hate anyone having to wait for me."

He couldn't have cared less. Time he was waiting for me was time he could spend examining little bugs, or drinking water, or just listening to the anti-sound of the forest.

And then I'd catch up. And we'd hike along once more.

But before I knew it, I'd be just that bit behind again. Pushing myself where he was just lollygagging along. And all the while my mind was racing with a new discovery I couldn't make sense of.

Finally, in staccato, broken speech as we hiked a steeper section of the narrow path, I said, "I can't win."

"No one wins at camping, Tay."

"I don't mean literally. I just . . . In my right ear I can hear my brother telling me to stop being such a girl. Like I should be keeping up. Leading us or something."

"I don't care if we have to stop every now and then. Relax, will ya?" He stopped long enough to turn around and roll his eyes at me in a way that was sometimes annoying. Usually adorable. Or annoyingly adorable.

I tried to explain to him what was frustrating me. How strange it was sometimes being a girl. How hiking in some ways could never be fun with him. Because I always wanted to at least keep up, preferably be in the lead, but then, as I told him, "At the same time, I don't want to sleep with any guy I can beat in a race. It's a lose-lose." In my mind it was sort of a funny thing to say. He didn't smile but instead frowned with worry.

We walked for a few minutes just to the sound of our feet crunching twigs, weeds, rocks. He stopped to pick up a stone, which he handed to me. He'd promised me earlier that he'd find me a worry rock on this trip that was so smooth I'd never want to bite my fingernails again. I took the smooth black stone without saying a word.

"This isn't a race," he said.

"I know," I said. I know.

It was in our fifth month that Luther found out he was going to NYU for his residency. He drove up to Joe's place and stuck his head into the shed.

"So," he said, finally, "I matched."

"Where?" I asked.

"NYU."

I felt everything change at once. To just be living your life, like so, having an amazing time, and all of a sudden you have to assess everything. I was assessing what this meant for us. It meant that we were done. Over. We were still in that blissful stage, before you figure out what you're really like together. We were in the midst of the good stuff, and there was no way we could pretend we knew where we were going. Yeah, I decided in that split second. It was over. I was only twenty-four. We'd been dating for only four months. We didn't know each other well enough. It was over.

Joe felt it too. He left the shed quickly, without feigning an excuse.

And Luther and I took each other in, although I knew I felt more upset than he looked.

Then he said it. "I want you to come with me." He was at my side, kissing my neck. "I mean it."

"Why?" was all I could think to say.

"I guess . . . If I can ask you to move, then—" He stopped himself.

"What?"

"Because I love you, OK. I love you."

I waited, stunned, then spoke. "I want to say, 'I love you, too,' but that always sounds so dumb."

"Just say you'll move to New York with me."

And my mind was racing.

Don't ever shape your life around a man's.

This is not a race.

People will say you moved for a man.

You have to stay focused on yourself, because in the end, nobody else will.

Don't ever move for a man.

Maria moved for a man.

Stop pretending that this is going to last.

What about Sunday dinners?

This is your own life.

This is something real.

Don't be a passenger.

How do I know it won't last?

This is something real.

Who cares if it lasts?

This is not a race.

Don't be a passenger.

I'm not pretending. I'm not. It's real.

"I'm in," I said, thinking, *You could say I moved for a man.*

Or you could say I moved for me.

Or you could say that I thought I was moving again.

leaving joe

Before we left Joe's place that day, Luther and I went in to say good night to him. I didn't have to tell him anything. I guess he read it in my face, or in the way that Luther and I were just standing there, grinning like idiots. As soon as we came in, he just nodded, and smiled a smile that hurt to look at. Like he was trying his hardest to fake being glad.

"You two look like you've got news," he said.

"We do," Luther replied, as I wished that I'd told Joe by myself. Not like this.

"I'm moving to New York," I told him, hurrying to say it before Luther said it for both of us.

"I'll be," Joe said, then got up from his chair to get us each a beer. As he walked past us, I caught him looking at me. It wouldn't have seemed strange if he hadn't looked away the minute his eyes met mine.

The next day when I got to work, there was a box waiting for me. I gave Joe a look, as if to say he didn't need to do this. He shrugged. "You didn't tell me when you were leaving. And you never know these days. People are across continents in just hours anymore." He shrugged his shoulders again.

I opened the box, hungry to see what was inside. It was a set of his old books. They were all about restoration. And they were all clearly

Joe's. Not a stain on them, but they were dog-eared and underlined with notes in the margin. "I can't take these," I told him. "They're yours."

"I know everything already," he said, then gave a smug little smile.

"They're all about restoration," I said, as I opened up a book that was filled with pictures of antique doors.

"Not much gets by you, does it," he replied, making fun.

I opened another one to the first page, and read out loud. "Restoring, as the name implies, is the act of bringing something to its original condition."

Joe was embarrassed. "I didn't want you to read them now. I just thought you'd like them." He explained that he'd liked reading the restoration books from the beginning. The fact that there were so many ways to do the jobs. And so many questions that had to be answered along the way. Should he modernize his process, using the advanced tools and gadgets that are available today? Or should he be more of a purist and use only the tools that were around when the piece was first created? He said he'd been thinking that I would like this type of work. "It's kind of what you do anyway, with all those chairs of yours," he said. "These are just all the ways you can do it well."

We said our final good-bye days later. But this is the moment I'll always remember. This moment when I looked into his eyes and understood that he was giving me everything that lay behind them. And was expecting nothing back except that I use what I was being given.

do you want to hold?

New York was the only city I'd ever encountered that moved more than I did. Nothing sat still. Nothing rested. Not even the dogs were allowed to be lazy. Instead they were shuffled outside for "walks" by anxious owners wielding plastic bags, waiting impatiently for their precious pups to poop so they could move on to that meeting they always seemed to be late for.

And the smell was amazing. Everything had a distinct aroma. Walking down the street was like being bombarded with smells. Of car exhaust. Fresh baking bread. Garbage trucks. Italian food. Beer. Vomit. Everything. Though there were some smells I didn't care for, I couldn't help but admire the stench as a whole. It just smelled. Alive.

And finding an apartment was like high-stakes gambling in a Vegas casino. "Do you want to hold? Or do you want to try for something better?" There are so many people in Manhattan that the only hope we had to find an apartment without an expensive broker was to know someone personally who was moving. Or dying. People pounced on these tiny apartments like animals on prey. When Luther and I first worked out the details of my moving to New York, I told him that I wanted to hold off on living together for a while and find my own place.

He laughed. "Do you know how much it costs to live there?"

Once he told me that I'd be spending upwards of ten thousand bucks a year, at least, just to rent, I had a change of heart.

So Luther and I found a real estate agent named Nickie who took us to five cramped apartments—with kitchens the size of bathrooms, bathrooms the size of bathtubs. And as we looked at each one, Nickie would quickly explain how lucky we were that this place was still available. "Are you sure you want to pass this up? I don't know if I would," she'd say. And then we'd have to make the decision on the spot, because, chances were, it wouldn't be available in two hours.

"Do you want to take this one? Or do you want to try for something better?"

I joked with Luther that this was like *Let's Make a Deal* from hell. Spending all day deciding between door number 1 and door number 2. By the end of the day, we'd done nothing but try for something better. Either plaster was falling from the ceiling, or the bathroom sink was in the kitchen, or it was a basement apartment with no windows and a roach (or rat) problem. There was one that we'd both liked, that had exposed brick walls and a fireplace (nonworking, but still charming) and just overflowed with the energy of history. But, of course, it was over $2,000 a month, which, even if we could afford, I'd have had a hard time with it on principle. We could buy a house in Texas for that. Luther agreed.

And so we were homeless, or at least hotel bound, for another night.

The next day we got a call in the morning, early, from Nickie saying that she'd just gotten word of an apartment that was available, but that if we didn't come see it before 9:00 A.M. there was no way it would still be available by ten. That was how good it was.

Luther and I had just ordered room service, a little treat to celebrate our new city. Neither of us wanted to see the place. Because we knew it was probably just another run-down closet-sized space with a funky construction.

But the gambling itch got to us. What if this, the apartment behind door number 6, was the one? And we'd passed it up? We rho-shamboed to see who was going to have to check it out. I beat him paper-to-rock, then rock-to-scissors, and the best two out of three was done. I was left like a princess in bed, a remote and a pot of coffee at my side, while he went to find out what was behind door number 6.

He came back to our hotel three hours later with a key in his hand, which he dangled in front of me as he hopped onto the bed.

"No way!" I said.

"You're going to love it" was his response. "So, get dressed!"

We decided to take the subway there. I know now that we could have easily walked, but at the time it was a great adventure, trying to figure out which colored lines went where. And it felt good to be going through this whole culture shock with each other. Something about being away together intensified our relationship. It wasn't about anybody but us right now.

The apartment was in midtown, in what's called Hell's Kitchen. The place had a long, skinny hallway that led to a tiny living room with one little window. And in the back was a decent-sized bedroom. We'd seen some places where our tall mattress would have fit only if the bottom of the mattress continued into the sliding-door closet. But this one had room for our oversized bed, a dresser, and maybe even a TV.

I loved it. Mostly because it had the energy of something that has been lived in. Not in a used way, but more in a historical way. I was aware that Hell's Kitchen had a history of gangs, stink, and slum living. Around the time of the Civil War, it was mostly tenements, factories, and slaughterhouses. This part of town was generally considered architecturally cheap. The original construction of the tenements had been hasty. And some of the later renovations of them even hastier. Still, this building, this apartment, seemed to have a sense of itself. I wondered who had lived here before. What their lives were like. I imagined that maybe a writer or a musician used to toil away within our new walls or, before that, maybe a factory worker. I gave Luther a big hug, relieved that we had a place to unload our things.

"But you haven't even noticed the best part," he said.

"What's that?"

I followed him to the corner of the bedroom, where there was another door. He swung it open. "A walk-in closet," he said.

It was the strangest room I'd ever seen, although I would soon learn that it wasn't unusual in Manhattan. It was half of a room. You could see where the windowpane in the corner had only three sides. A wall had been built right in the middle of the room. I wanted to knock on the wall and see who I was going to be sharing a room with. It was such a strange, impractical little thing. "This isn't a closet, exactly," I said, still amused.

"It is now," he said. "But the people who lived here before us, they used this as a bedroom." He laughed. I walked inside. It was just big enough to fit a mattress and maybe a side table. "It's all yours," he said, still excited. "I can use the closet in the hallway."

"But I don't need this much closet space," I said, thinking to myself how cute it was that Luther didn't realize he had more clothes than I did.

"Nope. I dragged you all the way out here. The very least I can do is give the lady a closet."

"Wouldn't it be better as a study for you or something?" I said, thinking that this wasn't something I really needed. At least not for clothes. But he wouldn't hear of it.

"Look, I just want one part of your new life to be glamorous," he said, half-kidding. I imagined me with a closet filled with expensive shoes and shiny shirts. It just didn't work.

"Maybe I could keep my books in here," I said. "Or my tools."

"Just say thank you," he replied.

"Thanks," I said, and meant it.

That night we went to a French place in the West Village that was recommended by our Zagat guide. And I was introduced to another amusing thing about New York. People here seem so impatient. Like if you talk too slow, you can feel them tense up with a sense of time wasted. Yet, when it comes to food, they'll wait forever.

When we arrived at the French place (that didn't take reservations), a straight-faced hostess told us that the wait looked like about two hours. And all of these New Yorkers were actually waiting as if it was nothing special. That's when I knew that, as much as I'd observed this place and the people in it in the few days I'd been there, in no way did I understand the psyche of its inhabitants.

We ended up skipping out on the French waiting game and instead went for a burger at Corner Bistro, where people seemed a little less fancy—although, worth noting, we did end up waiting about an hour for a booth.

That night Luther and I got really drunk. And we made plans.

"It's so weird," I told him, "that all of our energy was so focused on the move, that we didn't quite talk through what was going to happen once we got here."

"I know," he said. "Lucky for you, you don't have to worry about too much."

"I want to find a job," I said.

"I know. I know," he said. "I'm just saying that there's no rush."

I was still in awe of the bustling around me. "Did you ever think you'd end up here?"

"In New York?"

"Yeah."

He thought about it for a minute. "Not really. I always knew my residency would probably take me out of Houston for a while. But I didn't dwell on it, if that's what you mean."

I told him about how Maria and I used to talk about where we'd be in the future. And how often New York would come up. "It's just such an amazing opportunity, really," I told him. "I mean, my mother said she dreamed of coming to New York when she was little. And she never did."

"It's sort of a cliché, though, don't you think?" he said.

"Maybe," I replied. "But I aim to find out by taking in as much of this place as possible."

"That's my girl," he said. Then he grabbed my hand in that slow-the-moment-down Luther sort of way. "I'm glad you're here with me. Really."

"Cheers," I said.

Our first week in the city was busy, fun. We went on a pub crawl in the East Village, to museums. Walks around our neighborhood. A trip to Central Park. We even went on the cheesy boat that goes in circles around the island.

But most of our time was spent getting the apartment in order. First we painted all the walls. Then I treated the wooden floors, which were so thirsty they looked like they were about to crack. And

I spent a lot of my time unsticking a transom that someone had painted shut. I tried to picture the person who would cover the baby window so it would better blend with the bland walls. No one I would like to meet. I imagined that the transom was relieved at my allowing it to breathe again.

Once we'd cleaned up the place, we unpacked all of our boxes. As I organized my clothes, I tried to make my closet look as full as possible. I couldn't bear the thought of hurting Luther's feelings. But, in the end, I filled it with my tools, three of my chairs, and a side table that wouldn't fit anywhere else.

I had no idea at that time how I should have cherished this first week we spent together. Because I probably saw Luther more in that one week than in the next six months, given his schedule at the hospital. I'd expected it to be bad, but I suppose the reality of just *how bad* had been beyond my understanding.

The first few days after Luther started his residency, he was gone during all of my waking hours. The only thing that was regular in his schedule was his Sunday night call to his mother. But with me, nothing was regular. Sometimes the only memory I'd have of him being there was feeling him curl up next to me in bed in the middle of the night and sigh. I missed him terribly and wasn't quite sure what to do with myself. How to deal with this huge letdown I felt every time that Luther walked out the door. I tried to fill my time. At first it was with all the easy (lazy) choices.

Here is what I learned that first lazy week on my own:

I learned that anything can be delivered to you at any time — groceries, dinner, laundry — so that leaving the apartment becomes unnecessary.

I learned that I can still get sucked into talk shows. Even though sometimes I have to change channels because I get too embarrassed for the people on TV, who think they've made it because the world is listening to their problems.

At night, I learned that New York cable TV is in a world all its own, with its own set of morals. There's a channel on *basic* cable that has gnarly porno all the time. It's mostly this disgusting lady with a chap-red face and bloated breasts who invites on porn star guests—girls dancing in cheap-looking G-strings, men swinging their genitals like lassos. It just proves that people in this world are so much weirder than you could ever imagine. I mean, this is airing because it turns people on.

I learned that the telephone, while great for casual conversation about nothing, is a tough way to keep up with people. I called each member of my family, and they all wanted to know the same things. How's *the Big Apple*? Where are you living? How's Luther? What's it really like? What have you been doing? Blah, blah, blah as I recounted the same stories again and again.

And, finally, I learned that staying at home by yourself in a small apartment is really, really depressing.

I didn't want to complain to Luther. I knew it wasn't his fault. But I vowed to make the most of the time that we spent together. I found out that he was going to have Saturday night off. I must have looked through Zagat about a hundred times trying to find the perfect restaurant. I decided on a Cuban place in the East Village. I made a reservation, put on the sexiest getup I had—cool jeans I'd gotten at a vintage store and a black tank—and waited for him to come home.

It had been so long since we'd been awake together that we ended up dealing with first things first. The minute he stepped out of the shower I grabbed him and pulled him into the bed. It was quick for both of us. When we were done, I rolled over to talk to him, and he was already asleep. Dead asleep. The kind of sleep that would be cruel to interrupt.

And so I put on my robe and went back into the living room to watch more TV. I couldn't stop my eyes from tearing up. Not because I was angry with him. It wasn't his fault he was so exhausted. But I just felt so alone, then. And not even in control of it. I realized that usually the times I most liked to be alone were when I was choosing it, instead of it choosing me. Like, in Houston, I was fine staying home on a Saturday as long as I knew that there was something else I *could* be doing, if I wanted.

But here it was just me. Bored and depressed.

And I knew I'd better do something about it real quick.

• • •

On my first trip out, I learned that, no matter what city you are in, people are always intrigued when a six-foot-two girl walks into a lumberyard. Even in New York, someone will inevitably try his best to figure
out what your story is.

"What can I get for the lady?" I heard, in a little accented voice. It
came from one of a number of guys who were standing in front of the
counter, not behind it, and talking about the Mets. This guy had broken off from the rest of the group, partly to do his job, and partly to figure out what I was doing there.

I told him that I thought this was a lumberyard, but maybe I was
mistaken. Because from everything I could tell, I was in a cramped
hardware store. Gadgets hanging from as high up as the ceiling. Aisles
so tight together that I barely fit through. He guided me to a section
where prepackaged veneers and moldings hung from pegs in the wall.
"Are you fixing up your apartment?" he asked, taking his first guess.

I shook my head no. "Do you sell wood scraps?"

"What are you going to make?" he asked.

"It depends on what kind of scraps I get," I said.

He brought me through a door that led to a warehouse that was
about three stories tall, piled high with wood in separate metal compartments attached to the wall. Walking by on the street, you would
never know that this was what was inside. "You need big wood?" he
continued.

"Just something small for now," I told him.

I ended up with a few scraps of yellow birch, not really sure what I
was going to do with them. Probably make another heart for Nanette
or something, since she never seemed to tire of them.

As I carried my pile to the counter, he pointed at my arms. "You're
a big lady."

I didn't know what to say, so I said nothing, just sort of raised my
eyebrows.

"I mean, you must do work with your hands," he continued.

"I'm a carpenter," I said, for the first time in my life.

"A lady carpenter," he said, raising his eyebrows. "I like that."

"Uh, thanks," I said, then waved as I went out.

"My name is Ernesto," he called after me. "I'll see you next time, OK," he said hurriedly. "I'll see you next time."

The next day I walked the city. I figured that was the best way for me to feel my way around, figure out where I stood relative to all these people and neighborhoods.

I walked a full loop south—from my apartment to the southern tip of Manhattan and back—which took the whole day. I wandered down through Chelsea, the West Village, Soho, Tribeca. All the way to the bottom of the island, where the Statue of Liberty is, then back up on the East Side, through Chinatown and Little Italy. Through the East Village. Gramercy. And then I crossed back over to my side of town through the base of Central Park.

Along the way I took in the people around me:

The people in suits.

The people in grunge wear.

The slicked-back people in their hipster gear.

The van drivers who loaded and unloaded their goods all day

And the homeless people on the street, who were mostly mentally ill, and almost always ignored. Because after a while the number of them becomes too overwhelming. It was truly awful. I wasn't surprised, exactly. I'd heard about this before. Even still, I would never have thought I could walk right by such awful things. But what would I do if I stopped? What would I say? How could I change anything? I gave each of them some money anyway, which only made me feel worse. Sometimes I couldn't even tell if they noticed I'd left change in front of them.

I was having these awful thoughts, but they'd no sooner enter my head than I would become distracted by something else. Some cute kid or a dog or a building that seemed to rise out of nowhere. I guessed that I was approaching the head of a New Yorker, where the mind is so stimulated that few things sink in completely.

That day I gave in to every distraction. I stopped in at any place that
caught my interest. Bookstores. Lingerie stores. Toy stores. Bars. Li-
braries.

And I soaked in the architecture. I was beginning to appreciate our
apartment hunt. At first I'd been frustrated that a place to live was so
hard to find. But that day walking around Manhattan, I realized that in
a city this small, on an island that is contained by definition, the inhabitants have no choice but to be resourceful about space. This was
no Texas, where strip malls are built out of card stock, used for a year
to supply a neighborhood with stuff, then run out of business because
yet another strip mall, made with newer, shinier card stock, has just
been erected across the street. This isn't the land of "your first month
free!" apartment complexes that have poor people picking up all their
things and moving every three months, ever in search of the deal. New
York is forced to renew itself every day. Today's dumps are tomorrow's
lofts. And most old apartments are regarded as treasures. Expensive
treasures, but they are treasured nonetheless.

In Soho, I stopped at a church. It caught my eye because, in the
middle of an everyday street, this huge church just comes out of
nowhere. It is surrounded by a brick wall, and at its side is a small
cemetery, which butts up to the apartment building next door. I let
myself in the wrought-iron gates and stared up at the magnificence.
Three sets of thick oak double doors were in front of me. Written
above them in crackling paint it read, ST. PATRICK'S OLD CATHEDRAL,
ERECTED 1809. It was the original St. Patrick's, before they built another, bigger one midtown. I went to the huge, heavy door, felt its
knocker, then pushed it open.

I've never been much of a prayer person, but in a building like that
you can't help but sense some sort of God. It's confusing, almost, because in some ways it seems that the building itself is the thing to be
worshiped, with its stained glass, carved statues, thick and sturdy pews.
I sat in one of the pews and bowed my head, as much to hide from the
eyes of the other people in the church as to meditate for a few minutes.
It was funny how much I'd forgotten how to pray. The first things to
come back to my mind were the words themselves. "Our father, who

art in heaven . . ." I even remembered the Spanish words, which were drilled into our heads in grade school. *"Padre nuestro, que Estás en el cielo."* This is what I was thinking as I tried to pray. I was comparing the versions, seeing if I could remember them. And then I'd try to shut out that thought and meditate. Just let everything in. And then I'd start thinking about what I *should* be thinking about and I'd have to stop myself again.

Finally I just focused on my heartbeat. Because it was so quiet in the church that I could hear the slight beat through my head.

At first I was thinking about how good it felt to be out today. How glad I was to be here. And how scared I was to be so far away from everything I knew. True, I had Luther, but being here with just him, I was aware of how there was a lot I didn't know about him, that I *couldn't* know about him. Yet. This thought both thrilled and terrified me.

And then I was thinking about my dad. I wanted to pray for him, I did. But then, how do you do that? Do you ask for things? Like "God, please watch out for my dad up there. And for Mackie down here." Or "Dad, please bless me in these trying times in New York." Definitely neither of those. Instead I muttered an "I love you and I miss you," and got up to light a candle at the feet of the Virgin Mary, only to realize that they no longer had candles. Instead, at the feet of the fifteen or so statues in the church were sets of electric "candles," in red holders with lights that only appeared to flicker. I paid my twenty-five cents anyway and gave the plastic red case of the semicandle a little tap on its top.

I decided as I left that I was no good at praying, but felt better all the same.

And then I continued my walk towards home.

three new things a week

One month after we'd moved to New York, I got a job at a place
called The Corner. It was an antique shop in the West Village run by an
old lady named Rosalind. I'd wandered in there looking for a desk for
Luther. I'd found just the one I wanted, when she told me the price.

"Oh, that's too bad," I said, as politely as I could. Then, more tenta-
tively, I asked what was on my mind. "Does that price ever change?"

She shook her head no. "I don't like to play bargain games. I find
them stressful," she said, then began to polish the piece furiously, as if
demonstrating her stress for me.

"It really is a lovely piece," I said.

And then we talked about the desk and the beauty of dovetail joints,
and next thing I knew, I was leaving without the desk but with a job. I
thought it would be the perfect work for me, at least until I'd gotten
the city a little more figured out.

Although Rosalind was quiet, she paced the store all day, compul-
sively straightening the furniture, shining pieces so repeatedly I was
sure she was going to wear holes in them. She was almost three times
my age but moved about three times as fast as I did. And she was strong.
The store was stuffed so tight with furniture that every day she would
move some of it out into the street, just to make room to walk around.
And on rainy days, when she couldn't leave it outside, she would busily
squeeze through the maze of furniture and knickknacks, as if her body
had memorized the layout of the store.

For my part, when I wasn't helping the few nonbrowsing customers that came in each day, I fixed whatever pieces Rosalind would let me touch, which weren't many. I reglued dovetails, polished brass, fixed runners. It was good, easy work. I liked to think I was helping Rosalind in some way, although she couldn't have seemed to care less that I was there. I think she hired me just so she wouldn't have to talk to any customers. We could pass entire days talking only once, usually about what we were going to eat for lunch.

It was starting to seem, too, that Luther wasn't noticing me anymore.

Admittedly, I wasn't paying much attention to him either, mostly because he was gone so much. But also because I was keeping so busy. I'd promised myself that I would do three new things a week. I did everything from tourist sites, like the Empire State Building, to the IMAX, to the Museum of Natural History, to free chamber music at the Frick museum. Just anything I could get my hands on, particularly if it was cheap or free. And what was most amazing was that, once I started getting out so much, and seeing all the different things, I started to learn about more places to explore. Smaller jazz clubs. Out-of-the-way theaters. Unmarked bars.

I really felt like I was getting to know not just my neighborhood but also this city, which had seemed like such a long shot in my life until now. But as much as the city was speaking to me, Luther wasn't.

"Who do you talk to when you go out?" he wanted to know one night as we lay in bed.

"I stick to myself, mostly," I said, which was true. New York was a great place for being by yourself. I told him that I mostly felt anonymous, unobserved. Then I told him a few more details about where I'd been. But he was still focused on the fact that I was doing all of this by myself.

"Don't you ever get tired of running around so much?" he asked.

"If I get tired of something, then I try something else" was my reply.

This, for some reason, seemed to satisfy him. "I like that you're like you are," he said.

I curled up next to his shoulder and took in that smell I never tired
of. "And how am I?" I wanted to know.

"You approach things in such a simple way. It's refreshing."

Refreshing. I kept running this word again and again in my head.
Because it confirmed something I'd been feeling. *Refreshing* wasn't exactly the kind of word you use to describe someone you know very
well. And the truth was, I didn't feel like I knew Luther that well. In
fact, I was starting to feel like I knew him less than when we'd first
moved here. Or maybe I was just overthinking everything.

"Luther?" I said.

"What, honey?" From the tone of his voice, I could tell he was tired.

"Tell me something."

"Tell you what?"

"I don't know," I said. "Tell me anything. Tell me about your first
bicycle. Or your first kiss."

"Taylor, go to bed," he said, then tackled me with a hug, which I accepted.

And there was a third person who didn't notice me.

The woman across the hall. Sarah Anne Hoecker, it said on her mail-
box. Apartment 9. She seemed to have the exact same schedule as me. I
saw her in the morning when she went to work, usually wearing jeans
and some sort of funky hat. And I saw her when she came back from
work, listening to music with her headphones on. And we usually passed
each other when we went running on the West Side Highway. We had
this uncanny knack of running at the same time, whether it was in the
morning before work or on the weekend. And at night, through our
walls, I could hear her singing, and sometimes talking on the phone.

And she never, ever said hello.

From what I could tell, she was my age, with close-cropped hair
and almond eyes. She also had a much more exuberant personality
than me, I would guess, from the way she always sang loudly to herself,
even in the hallway. More than that, she seemed like someone I would
like. Someone who would like me.

At first I regarded her as a curiosity of sorts.

But one day, after I tried for an hour to get Rosalind to agree to go to a free concert at MoMA with me (she never did), something in me clicked.

I became hell-bent on meeting Sarah Anne Hoecker.

I tried a few tricks. I looked forward to them like experiments. Little things, like digging through my backpack as if I couldn't find my keys so I could stall and mutter something about how I just had to get a new backpack. To which she'd respond with a nod and a quick turn of her own key.

Then I even went so far as to borrow an egg for a cake that I wasn't making. I knocked on her door. She answered still in her running clothes.

This is what we said:

Me: Hey.
SAH: Hey.
Me: Sorry to bug you. I don't think we've met officially. I'm Taylor.
SAH: Sarah Anne.
Me: Cool.
Awkward pause.
Me: I'm your neighbor.
SAH (chuckling a little): I know. You live with that big guy.
Me: Yeah. So. I was just wondering. I'm baking this cake. And. You don't happen to have an extra egg lying around, do you?
SAH: Sure. Hold on.
SAH runs into kitchen. Comes back with egg, smiling.
SAH: There you go.
Me: Thanks.
Door shuts. End of encounter with SAH.

Thanksgiving was fast approaching, and I wasn't going anywhere. I'd thought about going to Houston for the holiday, but by the time I made up my mind that Houston would be more fun than sitting around wondering if Luther would get off work, the ticket prices had already reached a level of ridiculous.

We were ending our second month here, and my three-adventures-a-week plan was falling short occasionally. I was getting tired of being out all the time. I wanted to be in. But I wanted to be in sharing time with *real* people. Not TV people, or people over the phone. Real people.

At first I thought about crying and being depressed. I know that sounds dumb, but when you're by yourself so much, you really can make a choice to cry. You may not be able to make a choice *not* to cry. But a little cry becomes an option of the day when you're home alone bored—Like: "What do I want to do? Should I go get a snack? Or I could cry, maybe?" *pause* "Nah. Maybe later." And then you resume TV or a video game or whatever way you are passing the time.

I opted out of the little cry.

And I started to fiddle with my little scraps of wood, trying to shape them into something. Finally I gave up. I took two small, crappy blocks of plywood and pulled out a pencil. On one block I wrote, "Why I am sad." On the other, "What I'm going to do about it." On the first, I scribbled a few words about loneliness. About not having friends. About feeling distant from Luther. But having no one to blame. The second block remained blank for a good hour. These weren't the days of elementary school, where a teacher could walk in and make two people talk to each other, or make up, or what have you. This was life.

This is what I decided to do about each of these people:

I decided that even if Rosalind hated talking, I was going to talk. I'd turn her into another experiment. See what, if anything, could make her react.

I started my communication project on a Monday, when the store was so slow that Rosalind had been polishing one table for over an hour. I hated watching her work so hard at her age. But whenever I tried to help her polish and clean, she shooed me away. I was relieved when a small man with mismatched shoes walked in to check out clocks. But fifteen minutes later and he was gone. Rosalind was still polishing the same table. I returned to my stool and watched. Then spoke.

What I spoke about surprised even me.

I told her that I missed Texas. That even the act of rolling down a car window made me crave home. "It's not so much that I miss the people there, I just . . . I miss familiar turns in the highway. I miss dogs on my running path who know me. Or driving past places I used to go to with my brother. Or my dad."

I glanced over to see if she was listening. She was leaning forward, looking up through the store's front window at a little sliver of sky. "It's going to rain," she said. I was thinking to myself just then that she didn't hear a word I'd said, when she looked right at me. "I heard that there's nothing else in this world like a Texas rainstorm."

"Indeed," I said, considering the day a victory.

Sarah Anne Hoecker was next. But she was more of an accident.

Luther was working overnight, and I didn't feel like seeing a movie by myself, or going to a smoky bar. I made up my mind to work on one of the chairs in my closet. There was one that was completely stripped. I figured I'd try to paint it. I wasn't much of an artist, but I could at least make some cool designs.

I went back to the lumber-hardware store. Ernesto was there. I waved a quick hello, then went to get some paints. And some more brushes.

When I dropped my pile of odds and ends on the counter, Ernesto was looking at me with a big smile. "You're a painter, too, carpenter lady?"

"Sometimes," I said, then laughed, thinking that he probably paid more attention to me than anyone else at this point in my life.

"I'll see you next time, OK," he said, the exact same way he'd said it before. "I'll see you next time."

When I got home, I looked for a place to work. The lack of space wasn't my biggest problem. I was worried about the smell. There wasn't a lot of ventilation in that apartment.

So I opened my front door, thinking I'd split the fumes fifty-fifty

with the hallway and nobody would get hurt in the meantime. I
propped the door, opened the hall window, sat on a little footstool, and
got to work.

I stared at the chair for some time. It was one of those ice-cream-
parlor-type bentwood chairs. With a round vinyl seat, and a wood back
that circled around, approaching the shape of a heart. Since I find
hearts sort of heinous (unless they're for Nanette), I figured I'd have
my fun with painting it, then hand it off to someone. Rosalind? No.
Maybe the Salvation Army? I found that thought pretty funny. And
vowed that if I couldn't give it away in a week, I'd just donate my handiwork.

I was surprising even myself with the froufrou design. I'd painted
the chair deep blue and was trying my best to put flowers on the back.

And that's when Sarah Anne Hoecker arrived, back from a date.
Who was still with her. I tried to be as small as possible. It didn't seem
like they knew each other too well, and I didn't want to get stuck in the
middle of some awkward thing.

They got to her door (mine was a few more feet down the hall).
He'd just put his hand on her shoulder when she pretended that she'd
caught my eye.

"Taylor!" she exclaimed. "I have got to see what you're making this
time!"

Confused, I shrugged my shoulders, not sure why she was taking
this sudden interest in me. "I'm painting," I said.

She dragged the poor guy to check out my doilylike creation. And
she wouldn't stop talking. "Taylor is just so creative. She paints out
here all the time," she lied. "Do you mind if we just sit here and watch
you for a while?"

"Um, no," I said.

And they both sat down in the hallway. And watched me paint these
tacky flowers on the back of the chair. "I'm not very good at this," I   •
said, embarrassed. *I do good work,* I was thinking, *but this isn't it.*

"Nonsense!" she said, and I was thinking she was a nut job.

We sat like a little show-and-tell circle for about five long minutes.

And then Mr. Date spoke up. "You know, I hate to break up the fun, but" — he got up stiffly from his spot — "I have a meeting really early to-morrow."

"OK!" the new, bouncy Sarah Anne said, waving her hand above her head. "Well, I'll e-mail you this week!"

And Mr. Date walked down the hallway, confused.

Sarah Anne sat still, listening, until she heard the door slam shut on the bottom floor. Then she turned to me and scrinched her eyes shut, as if to say she was really embarrassed. I was just looking at her, waiting for her to speak.

"Damn. I am so sorry," she said in her normal voice, then started to laugh.

"What in the hell was that about?" I said.

"All the way up the stairs I was thinking to myself, *Why in the hell did I ask him up?* Just the thought of kissing him made me want to scream."

"Then why'd you invite him up?" I asked.

"You're going to think I'm terrible."

"What?" I said, assuming it was money or some other unspeakable motive.

"I felt sorry for him. He's so shy. And he seemed to like me. And, oh my god. What is my problem?" she said, then lay back on the floor, laughing, not worrying about how dirty it was.

"At least it's over," I said, tritely. Thinking that now is the time she'll get up, same as always, and head into her little kingdom across the hall.

But she didn't.

"Do you want a beer?" she asked, looking at me sideways.

"Sure."

"I want to check out what you're doing. That's pretty cool. I like it."

She leaned over and smoothed her hand across the vinyl seat, want-ing to touch the paint but not touching it, since it was still wet.

"Do you want it?" I asked.

"What do you mean?"

"I mean, would you like to keep this chair? I don't really have space for it."

"But you're not even done."

"I'll be finished with it tonight."

"I can really have it?" she said, not hiding her excitement. She examined it more closely, the way someone eyes something for sale.

"You can really have it," I repeated.

"Wow," she said, disappearing just long enough to bring me back a beer.

I was proud of myself. I'd moved here knowing no one, and I'd made a friend. I called Maria and told her. She just laughed at me. "You're such a weirdo, Tay. You make friends all the time." I told her that this was different, harder. But in the end it was too hard to explain my little victory.

I thought some more about how easy it would be to disappear in this city. And I hadn't.

But still, I felt like I was disappearing at home. It seemed like all Luther and I ever talked about lately was logistics. He'd want to know what I did for the day, and I'd tell him. And then he'd tell me a little about the hospital, but not much. Just a list of the cases, with none of the details. And then we'd talk about what was on TV, or what restaurant we wanted to get takeout from. And that would be it.

Some days it bothered me more than others. It was just so strange. Like there would be lulls in the conversation, or something. I knew that he was tired and all of that, but I found myself wondering what we used to talk about when we were in Houston. I knew we'd gone out to bars. Restaurants. Parties. But what did we talk about?

I was thinking this on Thanksgiving. Luther had the day off, and we'd slept in. I'd made him breakfast, which we'd just finished, and we were lying in bed, my head resting in his lap as he braided my hair into clumsy little braids.

"Tell me something," I said.

"I hate it when you say that," he said, not in a mean way.

"I just want to talk about something."

"OK," he said obligingly. "What do you want to do today? I was thinking maybe a movie."

"No, I don't want to talk about that," I said, sort of teasing, and sort of not.

"What do you want to talk about?" he said, irritated.

"I just . . . Don't you wonder sometimes what we talk about?"

"No," he said. "I don't."

"I guess I just . . . I feel like we talk about stuff, you know. Like TV. Or dinner. Or whatever, but I don't really know what goes on in your head."

"Taylor, you're being silly."

"I know I am. But just indulge me. Tell me one thing."

"I really don't want to play this game. This is dumb."

"Tell me more about work."

"I already told you about work."

"No you didn't. You just mentioned that you had three cases or something like that."

"What do you want me to say?" he said. "I went to work, and now I'm here, with you. And all you want to talk about is how we don't talk about the right things." Now he was getting mad. I'm embarrassed to say it, but I was actually glad. It was great to be fighting. To have at least roused a little something out of him beyond this superficial plane we'd been living on.

"I'm sorry," I said, not really meaning it.

"You really want to know about work?" he said, anger creeping into his voice.

"Sure," I said, no longer knowing how to react.

"OK. Here's what I did at work," Luther said, with no emotion in his voice as he recounted what had happened. He spoke his story like he was reading a list. "A man came in with his little kid who had cerebral palsy. His wife had been out of town, so he was taking care of the kid, who was maybe eight years old, and weighed only about fifty pounds. And he brought the kid in because he'd beat the shit out of him. First the dad said the kid had fallen out of his wheelchair. But part of my job is to get him to admit what he's done. So I had to go tell the dad how hard it is to take care of such needy kids. And I had to act like I was on his side, so he'd feel OK about telling me he'd beat the crap out of this kid. And so he confesses, and supposedly that means that our side won out. Except that now the kid is just going to go to the state for a while, which is hardly what you'd want for a kid like this either. So you know that the kid's going to end up right back with his dad. And that's what I did today. There," he said. "Do you feel better now?"

"Oh my god," I said. "That's terrible."

"Exactly," he said. "There's a reason that I leave work at work, Taylor. Life's too short to talk about awful stuff."

I was thinking to myself that I couldn't disagree more. That there was something about the baring of souls that I found essential. And beautiful. To bring all those weaknesses and frailties to the surface and split the burden between you and the person you loved.

It was funny how he reacted to my silence. He started to scratch my back, as if he were comforting me. As if it were easier for him to focus on me than on himself.

He kissed my shoulder, letting out a little groan. "Come on," he said, master of changing the subject. "Let's get out of here for a while. I'm sorry I yelled at you," he said, rolling out of bed. "Let's get up. It's turkey day!"

And then we took a quick shower together so that we wouldn't miss any of the movie.

keeping in touch

This is a conversation that my mother and I had about once a month on the telephone:

Mom: And things with Luther are good?
Me: Yeah. Things are fine.
Mom: Still working all the time?
Me: He has to.
Mom: I still can't believe you're in New York!
Me: Yeah.
Mom: You know, I always wanted to move to New York. But I never did.
Me: I know.
Mom: I mean, I've never even been there.
Me: Yeah.
Mom: You know, I really should visit.
Me: You should. I think you'd get a kick out of it.
Mom: But I wouldn't want to be in the way or anything.
Me: Really, Mom. You should visit.
Mom: Do you think so?
Me: Yes, I think so.
Mom: I'm just trying to think of when I could get away for a while.
Me: Well, my schedule's not crazy at all. So just let me know and I'll look into a hotel or something for you. Maybe get tickets to a show or something.

Mom: *Oh, that'd be so great! OK. OK. I'm going to check on my schedule. It's about time we do this, don't you think?*
Me: *Just keep me posted.*
Mom: *I will. I will.*

the god of still and silence

"What do you mean this is the first time you've seen snow?" Luther said, as I sat at the edge of the bed, my nose pressed against the window.

"You know I've lived in Houston all my life," I said.

"So you've never been skiing?"

"Nope."

"Or snowshoeing?"

"That would be hard without snow," I said, teasing him.

"Oh my god," he said, flopping back on the bed. "So, tell me what you see." He turned on his side to watch my reactions.

And I told him how white everything looked. How there was a thickness in the sky. And even through the window, it *looked* quiet.

"Cool," he said. Then, "Well, the first tradition during a snowfall is to spend a few extra hours in bed." He laughed and pulled me on top of him.

An hour later, his beeper went off.

"I hate when you have to leave," I said, wrapping my arms around his neck, trying my best not to make him feel guilty.

"Me too."

It was still snowing outside. And it was my day off. And I had nothing to do. Determined not to opt for the little cry, I knocked on Sarah Anne's door.

She opened it about a minute later, just roused from her Saturday sleep-in.

"Hey," she said, as I followed her into her living room. She lay down again on the sofa, clearly wanting to drift back to sleep.

"Wake up," I said.

"What's going on?" she replied halfheartedly.

"I've never been out in snow before."

"What?"

"I've never really seen snow before. I'm that girl from Houston, remember? The one who's never been anywhere?"

Her eyes opened with delight. "No way," she said.

"Way," I replied, raising my eyebrows.

"But it's snowing right now."

"I know it is," I said.

"So go get out of your pajamas, Taylor!" she said, trying to wake up enough to be enthused for me. "Jesus, I need some coffee."

First she made me stand in the middle of the street. It was snowing so hard that there were no cars in sight. It was like the city had been kidnapped by the god of still and silence.

"Good, we're in time," Sarah Anne said. Then she explained that the best time for snow on the streets is when it's first falling. Before it gets all muddy. "See how white it is!"

I saw. The wind was blowing the snow up, so that you couldn't really tell which direction it was coming from. It was like the whole street was a fishbowl. And I was in the middle of it, watching all the bubbles rise to the top of the tank.

"And listen to how it crunches underneath your feet," she said. "It's really awesome." And Sarah Anne took a few steps and stopped. And I took a few steps and stopped. And then I took a few more steps, still soaking in the sound.

"OK," she said. "Now we have one of two choices. We can either go to Central Park so you can see what *a lot* of snow looks like. Or we can go to a pub and get drunk and watch it all out the window."

I opted for the park, then the pub.

"Good answer," said my guide.

And we went to the park and built a little snowman.

We were sitting beside it, taking a rest, as the snow continued to fall down around us. I was still amazed at how clean and white everything looked. "Does the city look cleaner once it's melted?" I asked her.

She shook her head no. "Not really. Maybe once it's *all* melted. But while it's melting, after about a day, it gets all brownish. And then you can start to see where dogs and drunks have stopped for a piss. And you can see trash or dots of dog doo frozen inside. Really, it's best out in the country," she said. And she told me about the farm where she grew up in upstate New York. And the games they used to play in the snow.

"Do you ever miss all that?" I asked.

"No," she said, without even thinking. "My whole life I knew I belonged on the stage. And there was nothing that was going to keep me from being an actress." And then she sighed, probably because she'd reminded herself that she wasn't quite there yet. That right now she was more of a waitress than an actress.

I told her that I knew it was going to work out for her.

"How would you know?" she said, making fun of me. "You haven't even seen snow before, and I'm supposed to gain wisdom from your life experience?"

I'd been playing with a wad of snow in my lap, which I threw at her. "This city is starting to make me feel like I'm some caged-up animal," I admitted.

"But you love it here!" she said. "I mean, you've done more stuff here in under a year than I have in my three."

"Yeah, but."

"Well," she said practically, "where else would you want to live?"

I paused for a minute. "Don't you think it's weird?" I said.

"What's weird?"

"That we throw around places to live as easy as that."

"It's the modern age, Taylor. Get a grip."

"Yeah, I guess so."

"Besides, aren't you the one who hates Texas?"

"I don't hate it."

"What about your little monologue about strip mall culture?" she said.

"I just miss my baby roots."

"Your what?" she said.

"It's an expression."

"It's a creepy one, if you ask me. Baby roots? You're just homesick, silly."

I knew I was, and said so. But what was I homesick for? It was more that I felt that by moving I'd given up. On what I'd left behind.

"You think too much" was her reply.

A few hours later, damp and cold, we headed back from the pub towards home, tired from a day of playing.

And that's when I noticed it.

This time it was a door sandwiched between two black plastic bags on the sidewalk, waiting for a pickup that wouldn't come today, given the weather. It looked so pathetic. A huge door. Getting completely covered by snow.

I walked over to check it out. Sarah Anne followed to see if I'd found anything good. In Texas, picking trash is regarded with one perked eyebrow. In New York, the sidewalks are viewed as the city's own bargain furniture store. Not that I'd minded the stigma before, but it was fun just to walk right into the garbage and check out the door while Sarah Anne casually assessed my find, maybe even wishing that she'd found it first.

"It's huge," she said.

"I know."

It was the biggest door I'd ever seen that wasn't attached to a building. It was oak, about eight feet high and five feet wide. It came to a point at the top and had huge, ornate iron hinges. I brushed off the snow to see the details. The back of the door was covered with little square panels. About four across and seven up. And it had an old sliding lock, which was missing a piece. I pulled off my glove to feel the lock for myself.

From what I could tell, I told her, it was a Gothic church door.

"What's it doing here?" she wanted to know. I looked over to see what building this garbage belonged to, expecting to see a church. I didn't. What I saw was a nightclub called the Dungeon.

Sarah Anne was examining a few scratches at the top. "It's in pretty sad shape," she said.

"But look how beautiful it is."

"It must be really old."

I pulled it out a little more so I could get a better look at it. "The lock is just missing a few pieces," I said, as Sarah let out a little "Oh, bummer."

I saw what she was talking about. Spray-painted across the bottom in hot pink was the word MARTIN.

"Martin," Sarah Anne said.

And I repeated. "Martin."

"What do you think it means?" she asked.

"I think it means that Martin is an asshole."

"Well, so much for that," Sarah Anne said.

"Wait," I said. "I think I want to keep it."

"What are you going to do with Martin's door?"

"A Christmas present?"

"You going to paint it or something?" she asked.

"This is way too nice to cover with paint."

"Tell Martin that," she said.

It took us almost five minutes to separate it from the pile.

"How strong are you feeling?" I asked her.

"A little drunk, but mighty strong," she said, circling her arms as if she were preparing for a fight.

We did a little test lift, to see just what we were in for. Sarah Anne immediately let out a groan. "Oh my god, this is heavy," she said. It was too heavy. The thing weighed over a hundred pounds. But by now she didn't want to give up either. We dug around in the garbage until we came across a huge piece of cardboard, probably from a refrigerator. We laid the cardboard in the snow, then lifted the door just long enough to lay it sideways on it. And then we dragged it around the block.

"Now what are we going to do?" Sarah Anne asked, sweat dripping down her face. We were at the entrance of our building, with stairs to climb, and no way in hell we could get the door up them by ourselves.

So we waited and found that this was one of those rare but telling situations in this big city where people are friendlier than usual. Maybe it was the snow, how quiet the streets were. Or maybe it was Sarah Anne looking like a damsel in distress, left with a door and no big man to help her. As if on cue, two guys showed up. They introduced themselves as Tim and Doug. There was remarkably little chitchat. They asked if we were in over our heads and we admitted, yes, we were. And then we each grabbed one corner of the door and turned it on its side. And walked, trading off who had to be backwards, until we'd carried it safely up the stairs to begin its next life.

b o o . c o m

I wrote this on one of those free postcards that they leave near rest rooms in restaurants. Typed on the front of the postcard in yellow letters, it said: BOO.COM. Just like that. As if BOO.COM was a message you'd want to send somebody. I thought Joe would get a kick out of it.

Dear Joe,
Started working on restoring a door. A gothic church door, of all things. Also am hungry right now for something, anything, off of your grill. Miss you.
Taylor

That same day I told Rosalind about Joe. I told her about the house where he lived, with the shed next door. "It's not a bad life," I told her.

"Neither is this," she said defensively.

Then I asked her about furniture. What did she like about it? What did she like about antiques?

"I've been doing this all my life," she said, as if that were actually an answer.

Christmas was taking over the city. You could see it in the countless trees and buildings strung with lights. And you could smell it from the nut vendors in the streets. And you could hear it everywhere, since Christmas carols had been playing in every store in the city since Thanksgiving. Still, I hadn't tired of it. Christmas in New York is as good as billed.

And the little rituals are even better. Like going shopping for a Christmas tree in the street, then dragging it home, leaving a trail of needles behind you.

Or ice skating in Central Park.

And we also went shopping together, learning the hard way that the last place you want to shop at Christmastime is Macy's.

It was going to be our first Christmas together. Alone in New York. We'd thought about going to Texas, but he had to work until noon on Christmas Day anyway, so going elsewhere was just impractical. So we decided to enjoy our time in New York, which wasn't difficult for me.

Because I had my door to work on.

It was like the countdown to Christmas that I remember feeling as a kid. Only this time I was counting down to giving my gift, instead of the other way around.

In order to make room for working on the door, I cleared out my walk-in closet. I went through all my things—and they were just that, things—

and decided that maybe I could do without a few items. I donated what I could to a shelter a few blocks away. And then I managed to squeeze everything else into my dresser, with the exception of the two dresses I owned, which I moved into Luther's little closet in the hall.

Then I went to visit Ernesto, who had learned my real name by now.

"Taylor," he said. "Taylor, my friend. What does the lady carpenter need today?" I told him that I needed sawhorses.

"We don't sell those here," he said, then told me to wait. Next I heard a burst of Spanish coming from the back. And some laughing. When Ernesto came back, he had a sawhorse under each arm. "These too old for you?" he asked.

They were definitely old. And worn. And wobbly. But they'd do. I bought some braces from him and thanked him for his trouble.

"No trouble for you," he said. "I'll see you next time, OK. I'll see you next time."

When I got home, I put the sawhorses in the closet, then went over to fetch the door from Sarah Anne's apartment, where I'd been keeping it. She helped me slide it in on a makeshift dolly and set it on its side. The huge door kissed both walls.

"What happened in here?" Luther wanted to know that night. He'd opened up his own closet to find my dresses, which he now held on hangers.

"It's a surprise," I said.

"A surprise, huh," he joked. "And just what do I get to *do* with these dresses?"

"That's not the surprise."

"What is it, then?"

"I'm doing something in my closet."

He hung the dresses back in his own closet again and sat beside me on the couch. "What are you doing in your closet?" he asked, continuing the game.

"I'm making your Christmas present."

"What is it?"

"It's a *surprise.*"

"I see," he said. "So you won't tell me?"

"I won't tell you."

"Well, then, can you at least take a break tonight?" he asked. "From your *big surprise?*"

"Of course," I said. Then I told him about a movie that was playing at the Ziegfeld that I thought he'd like.

"I was thinking instead we'd just have a nice long dinner. And talk." Ever since that night when I told him that we never really talked anymore, he'd been making efforts. They were completely transparent, but I appreciated them anyway. They reminded me of his weekly calls to his mom. These calls were more a symbol to her that he cared than they were caring in and of itself (sometimes he watched TV with closed captions while he talked to her). But still, I told myself, he had listened to my silly complaint and was making a logical effort to do the right thing. It was at least a step in the right direction.

"Sure," I said. "Sounds great."

I told Rosalind about the door. That day she seemed in better spirits, maybe because business was picking up as Christmas neared. "Do you know the kind of door I'm talking about?" I asked.

"Of course I do" was her response. "Although I've only seen them on churches. Never just standing there, useless. But I guess that's a matter of taste."

What did she mean by that? It was hard to tell. Rosalind was one of those people who, no matter what they say, there always seems to be some current of negativity running underneath.

"I sure am glad I work here," I told her, just to see what her reaction would be. Whether she would opt for the easy way out, the polite "I am too, dear." Or whether she'd just ignore me completely. What she did was something in between. She looked at me quizzically, then returned to the task at hand, which at the time was replacing the roll of receipt paper in the register.

• • •

When I started working on the door, I realized how much I'd missed wood. I mean really missed it. I missed being organized in my mind for a few hours every day. Not vacant-minded. Just organized.

I'd been working furiously. First I took off all of the hinges, removing a bit of the rust with steel wool. And then I researched the missing part of the lock, finally finding it at my third antique fair.

Next, I bought some gloves and aprons and invited Sarah Anne over; she thought that helping me with this door could be good research for her acting at some point. So we soaked our steel wool in spirits and rubbed the surface until we'd cut through the old finish. But still Martin remained. In the end, I had to scrape off a thin layer of the wood so that I could replace Martin's name with the clean wood underneath.

As we worked, I told Sarah Anne that this door was the last of great craftsmanship. I explained how, once machines arrived, most of the crafts requiring patience, exactness, or attention to detail were scrapped in exchange for efficiency. Joints became inferior; the mortise-and-tenon was replaced by the dowel joint. The wood became thinner. More furniture was made, but the more efficient we became, the more every piece of furniture looked like every other piece of furniture.

She took in every word, feeling the door's edges. "It really does say something, doesn't it?"

Luther was growing increasingly curious, especially since our apartment smelled like a chemical factory most days.

"That can't be good for you, being all cooped up in there."

I agreed but told him that I worked out in the hallway whenever I had to do something that was going to have fumes.

"The neighbors must love that," he said, sort of joking.

"It's just Sarah Anne," I told him. "And it has that big window." And then I told him about my plan. I was thinking that, after Christmas, I'd leave The Corner and try to work somewhere else. "I've been looking into it," I told him, "and I think there are some really good restorers in Queens."

"Queens?"

"It's not like Egypt or anything," I told him.

"That's just a long way to go."

"Yeah, well, I can't take much more of Rosalind. Of doing so little every day."

"And this doesn't have anything to do with that stinky surprise you've got in the closet?"

"It has everything to do with that," I said, then reminded him that I was not going to tell him what it was. He was just going to have to wait.

I think I sanded with my little palm sander for ten years. That's what it felt like. I tried to convince Sarah Anne that it was a great workout, but she only fell for it once, and she lasted only an hour. And she kept complaining that the sanding paper we were using was too fine, that it was taking too long. I tried to explain that if you sand it with a paper that's too coarse, you only create more rough edges and scratches to sand, but she remained unconvinced.

I left a few little cracks in the wood, but there was one split that was way too big to leave. This task of fixing the split was completely ridiculous in that tiny space. Once I'd put glue along the split, I had to maneuver in a yogalike fashion just to get my clamps around the pieces. Once I'd clamped it, finally, I tightened it until a bead of glue oozed from the split; I wiped it off, then left the door overnight to dry.

The next part required Joe's help. I'd never called him before because he hated the telephone. I'd heard him talk on the phone before, and he was terrible at it. All of a sudden he stiffened up and spoke only in complete sentences. Really it was the weirdest thing. But this was an emergency.

"How do you know what's a good scratch and what's a bad scratch?" I asked him.

"I'm sorry," he said, loudly, "but I don't think I follow you."

I told him that I was at the point where I was trying to fix scratches and scrapes on the door. But then I explained that I didn't want to remove *all* of them, because I wanted it to still look old when I was done. But then, if I wasn't going to remove *all* of them, how would I choose which ones were good, and which ones were bad?

"Well," he said, after a long pause, "do any of the scratches *spell* anything, like, say, for example, 'Fuck you'?"

"Funny guy," I said.

"Funny guy," he repeated.

I told him about how there was a name on the door before, Martin, but that I'd already removed that.

"Well, then. As far as I know, they're all good," he said. "So long as you want to keep them, that's all that matters."

It sounds ridiculous, but I picked a select few that I wanted to keep just as they were. For the rest of the grooves, I "raised the grain." I took a paintbrush and painted over the grooves with water repeatedly. Eventually this swelled the wood fibers so that they raised back up again, and the grooves were gone.

Two weeks later, it was time for the final stage. Applying the finish. I'd decided not to stain it, since I liked to see the wood in its original state. I ended up using what's called yacht varnish, a polyurethane varnish that can take a beating from the weather, just in case this door was allowed to live outside at some point in its life. I ended up putting four coats of finishing on. It took days of waiting in between coats for it to dry.

Then, finally, I put all of the hinges back on. And the lock.

And I was done. Two days before Christmas.

The next day I wished that I hadn't rushed through the work, so excited. Because I was missing it already. I tried to think if there was something else I could work on, but there wasn't.

That night I couldn't sleep. I went out into the living room to watch TV and ended up in the closet, hanging out with my door. Luther's door. I wondered about the door's past life. Where it had come from. It may seem strange, I know, to be sentimental about a door. But to me it was more than that. It was a symbol to me of work in its purest sense,

work as a form of worship almost. This was the most effort and care I'd
put into a single piece yet. And it was by far the most beautiful. And
also the most strange.

And the only thing that excited me more than the piece itself was
the thought of giving it away. It was like the chairs. An odd gift, maybe.
But you couldn't give them to just anybody. It was only fun if people
were coming from the same place. If they could see the effort and the
history that went into each piece.

I ached when Luther left for the hospital on Christmas Eve to work
overnight. He didn't even know how long he'd be able to stay home
Christmas Day, if he'd have to go back. But he promised me that even
if we had to prop his eyes open with toothpicks, he'd stay awake long
enough for us to celebrate our little Christmas.

Luckily I had a distraction that night. Sarah Anne had an all-night
party. It was a rowdy bunch, mostly actors. The highlight of the
evening was the drunken rounds of carol-oke. She'd borrowed a
karaoke machine, and we were only allowed to sing Christmas carols,
which no one did well. But it was fun anyway.

Once her place had cleared out at around three in the morning, I
helped Sarah Anne clean up. Or, rather, I cleaned up while Sarah
Anne made out in her bedroom with some dude dressed like Santa.
But I didn't mind. It was sort of peaceful, sorting through all the empty
mugs and wrappings. Tidying up the tree. And by the time I was done,
I was so exhausted that I had no problem falling asleep.

The next morning, when I got up, I immediately called Joe to wish
him a Merry Christmas before he went out for his donuts. The conversation went like this:

Me: Merry Christmas!
Him: Merry Christmas to you. How's your scratchy door?
Me: It's done.
Him: That's it. It's just done?
Me: It's pretty cool, actually. I think you'd dig it.

Him: I'm sure I would like it. OK. I guess you'd better go. You have a
Merry Christmas, now.
Me: You, too.
Him: OK. Bye.
Me: Bye.

I hung up the phone, cursing its shortcomings. Its inability to bring
me back to the *real* Joe, not phone Joe. But then, opting out of the little cry, I decided that nothing would make Joe madder than knowing
that, right then, I was feeling sorry for him. And me.

So I set to work preparing our apartment. I'd gotten enough lights to
make our whole living room look like a winter wonderland. I strung
them on the ceiling. On the walls. Over the furniture. Until the whole
room glowed.

I must have checked on the door about fifty times before Luther
came home. There were definitely a few spots that I could have done a
better job with, that I *would* do a better job with next time. But still, it
made me remember what my dad had said that day when I was helping him with his model cars. "Just think," he told me, "when this
thing's done, I will have touched every piece."

When Luther came home, he buzzed the buzzer before coming up.
Which is what we'd agreed on, so that I could set up my "surprise." In
the minute that it took him to climb the stairs, I lit my strings of lights
and turned on a little Chet Baker, who is especially good at Christmastime.

He opened the door, weary, but delight still spreading across his
face. "Come here, baby," he said, and gave me a huge hug. "The place
looks great!"

We curled into the sofa together, not saying anything. Just relaxing.
"I missed you," I said.

"Me to. What'd you do?" he asked. And I told him about carol-oke
and hanging lights. And about how I'd looked into baking a turkey but
picked up a take-out dinner instead, so that dinner wouldn't suck.

Luther walked into the bedroom and started changing his clothes. I
followed him. Watching him dress was one of my favorite things to do.
Luther appeared, from the outside, to have such a casually fashionable
way about him. But to watch him dress was to see beyond that. Usually
he tried on several things, scrutinizing even T-shirts in the mirror to
see if they looked right, selecting socks from his drawer that actually
matched, although you'd never notice it. Or, if you did notice his
socks, you'd think they matched by accident. Finally, after trying on
two button-downs, almost identical blue, he gave me a kiss on the
cheek. "So, when do we get to open the presents?"

I've always been terrible at surprises. I was amazed, really, that I'd
made it even this long without telling him. "Now?" I offered.

"Now, huh?"

"Now."

"OK," he said. He went into his own closet and returned with two
boxes. "Which one do you want first?"

"The big one," I said.

I ripped away the paper. "You wrapped it yourself, eh?" I said, kidding. It had obviously been wrapped by a very practiced wrapping spe-
cialist at the store, with designer paper and not a crease to be seen.
Inside was pink tissue paper. I broke the tape, trying not to tear the tissue. I pulled out its contents, feeling the fabric. It was a black leather
skirt. Very nice.

"No offense," he said, "but I saw those two dresses that are in my
closet. I figured you could use a change." I might have been offended,
had I not agreed. Those two dresses were hideous. As were most
dresses and skirts, if you asked me, but still. This was nice. "I thought
maybe you could show off those legs a little more," he said.

"You're next," I told him, then grabbed his hand and brought him
to the closet.

"So, what do I do?" he wanted to know. "Do I open the door and it's
in there? Or do I close my eyes?"

"Just open the door," I said.

He opened the closet door and peeked inside. It was lying on top of
the sawhorses. With one of those little plastic stick-'em bows on it.

"This is it?" he said. "Oh my god, it's huge." He looked at it for a long time, almost as if he was afraid to touch it. Then he ran his finger along one of the hinges. I told him that some nightclub was just throwing it away. "A nightclub?" he said. "Really?" Really, I told him. Then he walked out of the closet and gave me a big hug. "Thanks a lot."

"So, where should we put it?" I asked him.

"Well, I don't think it'll fit on our front door," he joked.

"I was thinking maybe we could put it over there," I said, pointing to the corner by the sofa. "Or maybe I could make a table out of it. Or a headboard. Or we could build a dungeon," I kidded, but he didn't laugh.

"Whatever you want," he said, as he handed me the smaller gift. "Your turn."

I looked at the box in my lap for a second. I'd been looking forward to giving him that door for so long. And now it was done. I don't think he even noticed all the work that went into it. I told myself to be reasonable. That not everyone gets as excited about wood as I do. And then I just felt embarrassed, thinking that maybe I'd given him an impractical gift. I focused on the box in my lap. It was wrapped with *The New York Times*, clearly his handiwork this time.

I ripped open the little box. Inside was an index card. On it was written, "Two tickets to that August Wilson play you've been wanting to see."

"It's a certificate!" I said, half-joking, as if I'd been waiting for a certificate my entire life. Still, it was nice. And practical, I told myself.

"I didn't know what my work schedule would be like," he explained.

"Thank you!" I said, then leaned in for the little kiss on the lips.

And then we sat back on the sofa. And said nothing.

Enjoying the quiet until this weird sort of sadness took over.

I found myself longing for my Christmas with Joe. This was what I hated about holidays. Having to measure everything up. I felt disappointed. Really disappointed. But I wasn't sure why. Yes, I'd hoped for more of a reaction to the door. But that wasn't the only thing. It was as if I'd felt closer to Joe, reading the newspaper across from each other as we ate double our usual dose of donuts, than I did right now to Luther.

"Taylor," Luther said, squeezing my knee, flashing his dimples. "I, uh, forgot to tell you what your last gift is."

"What's that?"

He grinned. Then leaned over to whisper in my ear.

"Me," he said.

"You?" I said, hating to admit that I was not, right now, in the mood for sex.

Luther was enjoying my squirm but thought it was out of anticipation of his next words, instead of any fear of what they might be. "I have off until New Year's Day."

"Oh my god, you do!" In truth, there was nothing I could have wanted more. Nothing. Not just because I didn't have to work then, either. But because somewhere I was thinking that this was all I needed. To spend more time with him. To remind me why we were so good together.

sand stuck between your toes

I remember Maria once telling me that she dumped a guy because he insisted on wearing shoes at the beach.

It was the year after high school, and she'd been seeing Peter for a couple months. She decided she wanted to go all the way with him, so she planned a weekend in Galveston, where they would stay in a motel near the water.

But their first day there, when they went on the beach, Peter said that, even though he loved the beach, he couldn't stand the feeling of sand between his toes. It really bothered him. Would she mind if he kept on his shoes?

"No, of course not," she said.

And then not only did she not sleep with him, she dumped him as soon as they got back. "My whole life is like having sand stuck between your toes," she told me.

But as disappointed as she was, she also said she wished all breakups were that efficient, with some emblematic experience that told you right then and there that this coupling was never going to work.

Luther and I ended up spending Christmas Day in bed, mostly. In and out of sleep. In and out of clothes. We ate our take-out meal, split a bottle of wine, watched TV, and went to bed by 10:00 P.M. I was surprised he even made it that late, since he'd barely slept in the last forty-eight hours.

• • •

The next day it was snowing outside. I brought him some coffee, thrilled that we would have so many days together.

"So," I said. "I have a few ideas."

"About what?"

"What we're going to do today."

"Shoot."

I gave him the options. Make a snowman in Central Park. Do another pub crawl. Go to the CD store, buy three CDs, come home, maybe get high, and listen to them. Go skating in Rockefeller Center. Buy a few board games and have a tournament.

"Well, which would *you* rather do?" he asked.

I told him that I would like to build a snowman, then do the CD plan.

"Sounds good to me," he agreed.

He was a hell of a snowman builder, determined to make the biggest. And he'd even thought to buy a carrot for the nose and limes for the eyes at the local deli before we'd left.

Then we went to the megastore in search of good CDs. We agreed on three: Stan Getz with João Gilberto, Nick Drake, and Rush (my idea, as an homage to the old days). At first we put them on shuffle, but they didn't shuffle that well. So we went with Rush first, so that we could mellow out from there.

"What do you miss most about Texas?" I wanted to know.

"That's easy. You."

"But I'm here."

"Oh, yeah," he said, thinking he was being funny. "I guess I miss my car. And living in a nice, big place."

"I miss driving, too." I was thinking about how long it had been since I'd driven. Would I still remember how to do it? Of course I would. And there was a trade-off, I told him. "I mean, that subway thing is damn handy."

"Damn handy," he repeated.

"Do you like it here?" I asked.

"I *have* to like it here" was his response.

"No, you don't."

"Well, what good is living in a place if you don't at least pretend to like it?"

The next day I told him all the planning of the day was on his shoulders.

"You're not going to be happy with this one," he said.

"What?"

He wanted to spend the day at home. I guess I couldn't blame him, since he never got to stay in. So he disappeared into the TV. I snuggled with him for a while, then I got bored and went over to Sarah Anne's.

"How's the love nest?" she exclaimed.

"It's all right."

"It better be more than all right, the way you've been complaining about never getting to see him."

"It's good," I said.

"Then what are you doing over at my apartment?"

"Do you want to go for a run?"

In the next three days, Luther and I had sex four times, saw two movies, and went to one nice dinner. We had a poker tournament, but opted out of ice skating. We tried to decide on a place for the door but couldn't. Because we were both being stubborn. I wanted him to decide where he wanted it. And he wanted to leave it up to me. We also tried one yoga class (I'd always wanted to) and went for one run together.

But mostly, we were bored. Or rather, I was bored.

And, of course, that worried me.

I remember reading somewhere that there is no such thing as other people being boring. That if you find yourself bored with someone, then you're just as guilty as the person you are accusing of being boring.

But I went so far as to make plans, I told myself defensively. I went out *of my way to avoid boredom.* Again, I started thinking. *What did we used to talk about? What do Sarah Anne and I talk about? Am I just being hard on him?* I had no idea. No resolutions. No certainty that there was a problem, really. Just that sort of gut feeling that either you are falling out of love or you're in some weird phase of self-discovery. Or you're crazy.

Sarah Anne told me that I was crazy. Not for feeling like I did but for expecting anything different. "I used to think of being older as that time when everything would finally make sense," she said. "But nothing ever makes sense. We've been trained to think things will, eventually. Like maybe when we're older. Or when we get a certain job. Or get married. The carrots always change. But the fact is, nothing will ever make sense completely, unless you're kidding yourself, or are very religious."

"Thanks for cheering me up," I teased.

"I'm just saying that, given the course of life, your discontent is not surprising."

I groaned in exasperation, kicking my feet up onto her coffee table. "This sucks."

"Well, if you want to know if you're boring, I'll tell you. No, you're not boring."

"He's irritating me."

"I usually know when a guy is gonna get it when I write a song about him," she said. "Do you feel like writing a song about him?"

"How should I know?"

Sarah and I talked until Luther returned from his run and I heard him open our door. By then I was feeling guilty for talking about him behind his back. And, of course, was still worried about being boring.

When I came back in, he was already showered. "Hey, lady," he said, giving me a hug. "It felt so great to go out and get some fresh air. I wish you'd have come."

"Yeah," I agreed.

He was drying his hair with a towel, which he snapped at me playfully. "So, what do you feel like doing tonight?"

We went to see a movie. Afterwards we went out for dessert and ended up talking about what we were going to do for New Year's Eve. And then he had an idea: a dinner party. He said that he knew a lot of his friends at the hospital had to work that same early shift on New Year's Day, so it'd be nice to have a little something that didn't go too late. And it would be a great way for me to meet a few of them. I asked him if Sarah Anne could come too.

"Of course she can. It would be great to get to know her better."

I was actually relieved that he wanted to do this. Not so much because I wanted to give a dinner party but because it would be a way to fill an entire day.

It seems an easy enough concept, the dinner party. Have a few people over for dinner. Cook a little bit of extra food. But inevitably it becomes a huge affair. I remember when it used to be Jeff's turn to host, we would spend an entire night planning what we were going to cook, usually with some sort of cheesy geographic theme.

Luther and I decided on the basics. Some turkey. Mashed potatoes. Green beans. Rolls. We were only going to have four guests, including Sarah Anne, but it still took all day to cook, mostly because of the turkey. Sarah Anne had agreed to help out, which was fortunate since our kitchen was so small that we needed two kitchens to make one meal. And, of course, because she is a much better cook than either Luther or I.

I was in charge of getting the wine and champagne. And of setting and decorating the table. I made a funky centerpiece thing out of wood scraps that was frankly pretty ugly. And then I set the table with the set of Luther's china that he insisted upon using.

Once the bird was in the oven, Luther suggested a toast. "To the cooks," he said, predictably, and we sat down and waited for our guests to arrive.

Meet the guests:

There is Simon. He is a surgery resident. I have heard of him before from Luther, mostly because no one in the program really likes him. Apparently he is one of those "ego-surgeons," the kind who have vanity plates that say something like DRHANDS. But nonetheless everyone acts like they like him anyway.

Then there is Joey. We like Joey. He is also in emergency pediatrics with Luther. He came from nothing in Queens and managed his way into college at Colgate and then into med school. He speaks in a concentrated accent, or lack of accent. Like he is afraid he might sound like somebody from the streets. I find this effort charming.

There is only one problem with Joey: his wife, Karen. She's an investment banker. She is also a classic assessor, someone who sizes up everyone in the room immediately, asking just enough questions to be able to sort people into groups with various headings (e.g., "college attended" and "profession"). And—perhaps her worst trait—she fancies herself hipper than anyone she works with, regarding herself as the pulse of . . . something. And I cannot forget her one last trait. She is schooled in politeness, and therefore has that annoying way of making sure that she remembers everyone's name by using it as much as possible.

There is Sarah Anne Hoecker, who rocks. Tonight she is wearing a silver, low-V-neck leisure suit in the *Staying Alive* style. She also has a mustache in her pocket, which she has agreed not to put on until she leaves our dinner to go to a costume party. She explains to our guests, when she arrives a few minutes late, that she is Lord of the Disco. When she says this, Karen senses hipness and makes a joke. "Well, Sarah Anne, shall I just call you Lord?" she says. Sarah Anne thinks for a second, taking her seriously. "Yes. I think I'd like that."

And there is Luther, who is in his typical good mood, turned up a notch. He's turned up to that notch that makes him dance to the radio and hug his girlfriend extra tight. He brags to me that he is known for his hosting. Sure enough, when Sarah Anne tells Karen that, yes, Karen should call her Lord, Luther bridges the awkward silence by belting out a laugh so loud that everyone easily blends into one another again, the antagonism gone.

And there's me. And right now I am thinking of my last run-ins with the dinner party. The Jeff ritual. I liked those, for the most part. Would I like this one? I, by the way, am wearing my new leather skirt.

• • •

There were many topics of conversation. First we were all assessed by
Karen. We talked about colleges, then saw that through to the do-you-
know-so-and-so game. This first phase was short, since neither I nor
Sarah Anne ever graduated. Simon then used our lack of college as a
segue into talk of an African safari that he went on when he took a year
off from college. This went on for too long, and only led to more talk
of travels. These people had dipped into more cities than I knew existed. We also talked about the market. I gave two points to Joey for trying to talk about sports, not that I was interested. But it would have at
least allowed everyone to bump down the vocabulary a notch. Sarah
Anne, up to this point, was simply nodding a lot. I imagined that she
was taking notes in her head, trying to remember these people as characters. The cadence of pretentiousness. Their phrases that alluded to
wealth, as in, "my housekeeper," blah blah. Or "my house in Stowe"
blah blah.

And then the conversation switched to politics.

Joey was making a simple observation that Mayor Giuliani had
done a lot to clean up New York. Joey said that he used to make a
game of walking through Washington Square Park and counting how
many men said "Smoke smoke smoke" to him, trying to sell him pot
"It used to be, I'm not kidding, fourteen or fifteen times. Now it's
maybe once. And if it does happen, the guy has to be more clever
about it, you know. No more 'Smoke smoke smoke.' Now they say
things like 'Nice shoes tonight, sir. Very nice shoes.'"

"It's just a shame he's such a nut job." This came from Sarah Anne.
And it wasn't mean-spirited. And it was not an unfamiliar debate. At
that time Guiliani was known for vehemently speaking out against a
painting of a dunged Virgin Mary and for generally thinking of the arts
as sort of take it or leave it. And Sarah Anne's whole world model was
based on what he, as mayor, tended to dismiss, or at least draw bound-
aries around.

Karen felt the need to chime in. "But he's done a lot for this city,
you have to admit that."

It was Sarah Anne's turn: "A lot of what? If you want to talk safety, fine. But if you want to talk schools or art, then we've got a whole new discussion on our hands."

Now this, to me, was just getting good. In the Jeff days, these were the moments when the group would pull their chairs in closer, lean forward in their seats, talk over each other's words. This was the point of discussion. When you dissect what people believe in and maybe even challenge other people's ways of thinking.

And this was the very moment when Luther, sensing an awkward moment, changed the subject. "You know what I say," he said, flashing his dimples. "I say that it's New Year's Eve and there are better things to talk about than politics."

Which led to more talk about work.

Which led to talk about *my* work.

"So, what do you do, Taylor?" Simon asked politely.

"I work in an antique store," I said. "It's called The Corner."

Karen said that she knew that place. It wasn't far from their apartment. She must stop by and say hello sometime.

"And she also builds furniture," Luther chimed in.

"Really?" Joey said.

And Luther opened up the closet and showed them the door I'd given him.

"Taylor, you're just like a modern-day cowgirl," Karen said.

"It's very interesting work," said Simon.

"Cool," said Joey.

"I helped her carry it home," offered Sarah Anne.

And Luther beamed.

I was not prepared for this reaction. It was like they had some strange curiosity about what it was like on the "other side." The questions just kept coming.

Did I go to a specialty school to learn how to do this? *No. I dropped out of college and learned from an old carpenter named Joe. Who I miss.*

Is it satisfying work? *Sometimes.*

What is it like to spend your day working with your hands? *Well, here I haven't done it much. But it used to be pleasant. Nice.*

"I think you have it right, Taylor," Karen said. "I just feel like so few people in this city get what is really important. Balance. We need balance."

"So, you don't like your work?" Sarah Anne dared to ask, and I loved her for it.

"Not the way that you like yours, Lord. You're an actress, right?"

Sarah Anne nodded, feeling the insult. Assuming someone is an actress is like telling them that you think they're hyperactive and a little loud. "Yes," she said, with practiced confidence. "I am."

"See," Karen said, "I just think that you two are following your passions, and it's so important that people do that."

Immediately I knew that Karen was the type of person who would walk up to a novelist and say, "I would have been a novelist, but I decided to be a banker instead." Sure enough, she delivered in her next words. "I just would love to spend my days like you do, Taylor. Get back in touch with those sorts of things that my schedule doesn't allow." She rolled her eyes when she said "schedule," as if to say that lately she had been experiencing uncontrollable demand.

"Well," I told her. "Maybe you can. I mean, some things are hard to fix and some things aren't. Like if I was sitting here saying I wanted to be an investment banker, then I'd have a problem. Because I could never do what you do. I would never be hired to do what you do, just by being a college dropout alone. But you. If you wanted to be like me, all you'd have to do is leave all that money at the side of the road and quit, and then you could be a carpenter or a painter or anything that sounded vaguely romantic to you at the time."

And everyone had a good laugh. Because Karen would never quit her job. She wasn't the type. And I would never have a conventional job. And that was just how it was. "What a delightful way of putting it, Taylor," she said.

"Well, you'll never catch me doing what you do," Simon assured us. "I love my work."

Again, I looked over at Luther to see what his reaction was. I knew he wasn't that close to these people. He couldn't be. But what kind of time was he having right now? It's true, I was testing him. It's a terrible thing to do, to make time add up to one question, one emblematic moment that says whether you're good or bad together. Whether you read each other or not. Apparently, we didn't. At least not tonight. All that irritation that was crawling up my spine was not visible in the least on his face. In fact, he was charming Karen right at the very moment I looked over. He has always been a good question asker. Someone who people like to talk to because he makes them feel comfortable, interesting. But I didn't assume he did this with just anybody. I was thinking of an expression I'd heard: that someone "suffers no fools." Looking at Luther that moment, it just appeared to me that he was suffering *all* fools willingly.

By this time, thank god, we were done with our meals. I got up to clear the table. Sarah Anne followed. We passed each other in the little kitchen just long enough for her to bug out her eyes. Once we were done clearing the table, we stayed in there to prepare the dessert. Or at least that was what we wanted to appear to be doing.

"Oh my god!" she said, and pulled out a joint. "That," she said, "is what I was trying to avoid by not going home for Christmas."

"Sorry?"

"Dude, I'm more sorry for you. At least I can ditch and go to another party."

"Fuck her," I said, knowing that Karen had gotten under Sarah Anne's skin.

"Yeah, fuck her."

She passed the joint back to me just as Luther walked in. He seemed out of "host mode," and I was hoping, praying he was on our side. That the three of us could sit and giggle in the kitchen, take a quick breather before having to head back into the land of the dominant witch. I held up the joint, waving it in front of him as if to offer him a hit.

"Taylor," he said, definitely not on our side, "what are you doing?"

I let out a laugh, which only made him madder.

Sarah Anne sensed the awkwardness and sat up a little, as if trying to appear more adult, which looked funny in her leisure suit. "So, I was just telling Taylor here thanks. I guess that goes for you, too," she said, leaning in to kiss him on the cheek. "Thanks again for dinner. But I have to get going before this neighborhood gets too crazy for me to get

to my party." And she was out of there. I heard her saying good-bye to
the other guests as Luther stared at me, disappointed.
   "Look, I didn't think it was a big deal," I said.
   "I just think you're being rude, that's all. We have guests out there."
   "I don't like them."
   "Well, you'd better learn," he said and walked back into the other
room, making up some ridiculous story to our guests about how we'd
been fixing a lamp in the kitchen or something like that. I remember
that it didn't make much sense.
   I stood like that for a minute, leaning against the counter, trying to
figure out what was going through my mind. The whole night was
just . . . Too much chatting. It was all chatting. And Luther was an ex-
pert at chatting. Fast on the comeback questions. Filled with positives.
Loving to listen. Making everyone feel comfortable. Accepted. And I
was surprised? I admonished myself in my head. How could I act like
this was news to me? I mean, that was why I'd liked him in the first
place. Back when there was nothing that I needed more than for him
to pretend that I was fine.
   I was about to have that little cry I'd been putting off for so long
when the wall started shaking. It was this slight rumbling sound. And
just the tiniest vibration in our floor. *Oh my god, I was thinking, it's a
fucking earthquake.*
   I walked out into the living room to see what the hell was happening. Everyone else was fixated on the TV. Dick Clark was leading mil-
lions of people in the Times Square countdown as the ball dropped
behind him. The apartment shook with every number, because our
building was so close to the commotion in the streets.
   "Ten!"
   "Nine!"
   "Eight!"
   "Seven!"
   Times Square was a full avenue away. But still you could feel the vi-
bration. And hear all the people screaming.
   "Six!"
   "Five!"

"Four!"

Louder and louder as the ball got closer and closer.

"Three!"

"Two!"

"One!"

"Happy New Year!"

And just then, I looked over at Luther. And we locked eyes. And we saw. Nothing. He came over and gave me a halfhearted kiss. And I was thinking to myself that for once he wasn't faking.

New Year's Day, Luther got up at 6:00 A.M. to go to the hospital. I immediately went across the hall and knocked on the door until Sarah Anne finally opened up.

"Oh my god. Taylor, you're killing me," she said, and walked back with me into the living room. On the way, she tripped on the corner of the table. "I think I'm still drunk."

And I sat down.

And I just started crying.

"I wasn't supposed to go after a Lula," I said, which made me feel worse because it reminded me of Joe. "And Joe's going to die while I'm living here."

"You're losing me here," she said. "Back up."

I told her what a Lula was. How Luther was my Lula. And now I didn't love him anymore. But I'd moved all the way out here.

"One thing at a time. First of all. You moved out here. Big whoop. People move all the time. Second. If you need to move out, you just have to haul some stuff across the hall. Mi sofa, tu sofa."

"Thanks," I said, not feeling better. "Why can't I just be happy for once? Why can't I just roll with it, like everybody else seems to do?"

"Because you're you" was her well-meaning reply.

I told her that I wanted to go home but I was afraid to. Because I'd made such a big deal about leaving Texas. I'd feel so dumb. All my life I wanted to go somewhere and now I was just chickening out.

"You're not chickening out. That's the dumbest thing I've heard. If you want to move back home," she said, "then you move."

She handed me one of her stuffed animals that she kept throughout her apartment. It was a big fluffy dog, which made me at least smile, thinking that she just did something that Maria would have done. She then continued her pep talk. "And if you're crying because of this whole Lula thing, well, it sounds like a myth if I've ever heard one."

"But he's so nice. I mean, there's nothing really wrong with him."

"A lot of people are nice, hon. It's not all about being nice."

I'd stopped blubbering by then, was feeling a little more myself. "Thanks," I said. "I feel a little better." And I'd no sooner said this than I realized that if I meant what I said, I was going to have to break up with him. How was I going to do that? I didn't want to do that. I didn't know if I could. I started to cry again.

"You're going to make it through this," she said.

"I know, but . . ."

Things were different between Luther and me, just like that. I couldn't tell whether it was because I'd changed and he sensed it, or what. But there was this hint of antagonism in both of our voices. We had sex, but we didn't linger. And if I thought we talked about nothing before, we were now both filling entire days with logistic-speak. "Have a good day at work." "When are you coming back?" "Do you need me to pick up anything on my way home?" That sort of thing.

Occasionally I would slip into my closet and make something I didn't need. Or want. I even started buying old pieces of junk from men with blankets on the street—like magazine racks, or little boxes— just so I'd have something to fiddle with.

It's so weird, living through these moments. When you can't quite articulate exactly what's wrong. What part of the whole thing is missing. You just feel it in your gut. And maybe you'll argue about a few things like doors or dinner parties. And maybe at some point you'll go to great lengths to describe your emotions, when both of you know that you're just waiting it out. You've crossed that line, and now it's just a matter of time before one of you has the courage to point out that fact.

• • •

A few weeks later, Luther and I spent our last night together. Nanette had mailed me pictures of J.J. and Luther when they were in college. She'd found them and thought I just had to see them because wasn't it so exciting that the two of us were dating and then maybe one day all four of us would be the happiest married people in the world.

Luther and I looked at the pictures the night after I got them. We'd just finished a very quiet dinner. He'd said he was tired. I'd said the same. And then we went to bed, slipped under the covers, and I pulled the pictures out of my bedside drawer. I was naked, and the pile was resting on the top of my chest, near my neck. He flipped through them one by one and told me the stories that went along with each.

Like the story about how great it was when he and J.J. went to this really huge pig roast. And Luther met a girl from Venezuela who only spoke Spanish. But they went home together anyway.

And the story about how great it was when he and J.J. worked on the bonfire at Texas A&M. Who'd have ever thought people could build something so miraculous?

And about how great it was at football games. Doing all those yells. About how there's nothing quite as great as a football game in Texas.

About how great everything was.

And then, I said the first thing I could think to unload that sinking feeling in my chest.

"How do you think you'd summarize our time together? What's great about it?"

"Why would I want to summarize our time together?"

"Never mind," I said.

"What are you getting at?"

"I don't know."

We lay like that for a while, staring at each other. Finally, I said, "Sometimes, I look at you, and everything that makes you happy is so different from me. And I can't help but wonder what the hell you see in me."

"You just have to know that I do see something, OK. I mean, I can't be your self-esteem."

"I'm not talking about my self-esteem. I know what *I* like about myself. I'm just not sure what *you* like."

"You're a beautiful girl," he said.

"How?"

"I'm not going to do this," he said, finally showing his irritation.

"OK. You don't have to answer that. Never mind."

"Tell me what's going on in there."

I was thinking right then that I'd never seen Luther cry. I'd never even seen him come close to it. "I feel like the things that I find the most beautiful in the world aren't the same things you do."

"Like what?"

"I don't know. I love weirdos and weakness. Messes. And you . . ." I didn't know what to say. I looked right at him, right through him. "Come on, Luther. It's OK to admit it."

"Admit what?"

"We're just different. Can't you see that?"

"Everybody's different."

"But everybody isn't sleeping together."

"Is that what this is to you?" he said. "We moved out here together. Remember that part?"

"I just think maybe . . ." Was I really going to say this? "Maybe we're making a mistake. I mean, it's not like we're failing or anything. We just . . . I moved out here. I didn't know a soul. And you didn't know a soul. And now I feel like we're together because we need that. To have someone. Or something. But . . . all the things I like most about myself are the things you either don't notice or think I need to 'get over.'"

"It doesn't matter," he said.

"If it doesn't matter, then why are we growing so far apart from each other?" was my reply.

He rolled onto his side, his back to me in what seemed like shame, maybe anger. "I wouldn't have asked you to move out here if I knew it was going to turn out like this," he said. And I knew what he was thinking. He was thinking that he'd ruined a girl. That he'd jumped the gun. That he'd misjudged. And that, to him, was a terrible offense.

I lay next to him, my body cradling his.

"I'm sorry," he said.

"This isn't your fault. Or mine. It just is."

"But I was the one who asked you to move out here. I mean, where are you going to go now?"

I began to put my clothes back on as he watched me, like he'd done so many times before. And I was thinking how strange this was. To suddenly feel the weight of expectations lifted off of me. The lightness of being on my own. Really on my own. How strange it was that the feelings used to be the other way around.

speaking in tongues

It was just a few days after Luther and I had broken up. I'd moved in with Sarah Anne. And I was having trouble sleeping. I kept trying to imagine what Luther was doing just across the hall. I'd wake up in the middle of the night, hear the sliding of the lock, and think that he was finally coming home from work. That he was about to curl into bed with me. And then I'd remember.

I was also a nervous wreck because I couldn't make up my mind. Did I want to stay in New York? Or did I want to go back home?

I asked Sarah Anne what she thought. She said that she would always want me in her city. But that she wasn't about to help me sort through everything, given her bias. This was my decision.

I decided to walk the city again.

It was a Saturday. Brisk but not cold. I decided to do the reverse of the loop I'd done before, still downtown. But this time east to west.

I made fewer stops this time.

One bar. One bookstore. One pet store.

Then I splurged on some fresh ceviche at a Latin place.

A photography shop. A trendy thrift store.

And then I stopped for a beer at the Soho Grand Hotel. I watched all the rich people come and go. These were people who were going somewhere, I was thinking to myself. With the exception of a few tourists, everybody looked important. It wasn't so evident from their cell phones. It was more in the eyes. That look that says, "Yes, I may be in therapy. But I'm smart and I know my shit."

When I went to the bathroom, I tried to make that look. It didn't
work.

I went back to Old St. Patrick's, and once I was inside I had to fight
the urge to scream. Or I guess yell is a better word. It was so damn
quiet in there. I wondered what would happen if I just shouted something, anything, at the top of my lungs. Like people do when they're in
the mountains and want to see if there's an echo. I'd almost made it
out the door when I thought to myself, *What the fuck?* I was paralyzed
for that moment that it took me to figure out what to say. "Hallelujah"?
Or "Jesus"? Or maybe "Cheez Doodles"? I closed my eyes as hard as I
could, trying to empty it of all thoughts so I could shout the first thing
that came to mind. "Kimineyo!" I shouted, and it did echo a little. I
did it one more time. "Kimineyo!" My mother occasionally went to
charismatic Catholic masses. She told me that if I was ever in a situation where I felt pressure to speak in tongues, a good thing to say was
"Kimineyo-ko-shek!" again and again. And to throw in one jubilant
"Kimineyo!" at the end. "Really," she said, "you just can't go wrong
with that." The other people in the church today didn't seem as appre-
ciative of my speaking in tongues. I saw two nuns making their way up
the aisle to me. Still, I left confident that no one had been injured by
my outburst. I admit, I found the whole thing exhilarating.

But it didn't enlighten me as to whether I should move back, that's
for sure.

In the end, it was the park that made up my mind. I was sitting on a
bench at the base of Central Park. On this little path where you're just
inside the park but can see outside of it to where all the horses and car-
riages are kept. Or watch the traffic go by on Central Park South. And
you can look up and see where the skyline meets the park. It's an
amazing view, really.

Behind me, only grass.

In front of me, only buildings.

Central Park is the embodiment of forward thinking. Someone
knowing that if they didn't block off a chunk of land from develop-
ment, it was going to be built over faster than they could spit. But I was
sitting there, listening to the strange mix of sounds that come in this

city. Nature sounds, like dogs barking and the low crooning of pigeons. And in the distance, the bustle of the city. The honking cabs. The cell phones ringing. The people speaking, energetic and crisp.

It was as if someone had drawn a line in the sand. And nobody was calling me from one side to the other. It was just me, looking at the line, deciding whether my center lay to the left or to the right.

I took one more look at the Plaza Hotel. Up to its top, towering above the trees and the people. And at the angels with their horns in front of it. And I knew.

That night I called my mom to tell her what I'd done. I got her machine, instead. "Mom," I said. "I want you to come visit in a few weeks. Give me a call so we can figure out what works. And I mean it this time," I added.

I knew she would never have forgiven me if I'd left New York without having her visit.

And I wouldn't have forgiven myself, either, for letting this chance pass.

you are here

It was raining outside, and Sarah Anne was late meeting me at the café Le Gamin, probably because of her audition. I'd gotten a table by the window and was watching the drops form patterns on the glass. Within five minutes of showing up, she was well into her Drake story, one I'd heard a few times before but indulged anyway. He was the first time she really fell in love. He was tall, handsome, and had eyes that sparkled when he talked. He was the first person who ever told Sarah Anne that he loved her. When he dumped her for a girl named Belle, she was devastated. But in the end she was better off, because she found out that, just three years into their marriage, he cheated on Belle, and wasn't she just so lucky? Because she'd rather be alone all her life than accept a cheating man. And this was just proof that everything turns out for the best. And I was just sitting there wishing I could be someplace where people didn't pass on stories as if they were your life. But I nodded as she told her story just the same. It was nice of her to try.

It wasn't Luther that was bothering me. Not exactly, anyway.

We were silent for a few more minutes, her staring at me again. Until, finally, "You look like shit, honey. I don't know how to tell you."

"I think you just did," I said, faking a smile.

There was a long pause, then Sarah Anne spoke again, gently, concentrated. "I feel like you're having one of those days where nothing I say is going to make the slightest difference."

I nodded, shredding my napkin, trying not to bite my nails.

"But if you want me to, I'm happy to just sit here and read, or drink my coffee. Just in case you feel like talking."

I shook my head no. "It's OK," I told her. "Stay however long you want."

So she stayed and calmly, quietly, finished her coffee, then offered to share a cab uptown with me.

"I'd rather walk," I said.

"But it's raining."

"I'll be OK," I said. And she let me go.

And I was walking.

I walked past a long, elegant woman with the slightly tanned cheeks and very tanned children that suggested a tropical winter vacation on an island somewhere. Her daughters were under ladybug umbrellas, pressing their noses against a toy store window, pointing until she gave in.

I walked past a middle-aged woman with glasses who was reciting lines as she kept her eyes on the sidewalk. Ignoring the rain. Probably on her way to an audition.

I walked past a woman wearing black, wheeling her cello in front of her, trying to avoid the puddles.

I walked past a woman talking on a cell phone as her tiny toy Doberman tried to keep up with her pace.

I walked past a manicured woman and her husband, who was holding an umbrella over her head, protecting her hairdo.

I wondered where each of them went at night. What their lives were like. Did they make more money than me? Probably. Were they more loved than me? Maybe. Were they happier than me? I had no idea. I was sure they'd faced things like I was facing.

I passed a couple fighting on the street. She'd just started to cry, and he finally started listening, chanting the I-love-you-babys that tend to follow tears. But I didn't believe him and neither did she. Would they look back and remember this minute on the street corner for the rest of their lives? All the people like me watching as they tore each other apart in the rain.

I tried to picture the spaces that Luther and I had shared. The bench where we used to wait to get into our favorite Italian restaurant. The corner where we used to meet each other before we went to movies. The bar where we got into a silly disagreement about birthday cards. About whether I was a bad person because I refused to send birthday cards to anyone, preferring instead to send letters whenever I was struck with something meaningful to say. As I walked by the bar, I thought about how Luther apologized to me by sending me a Hall-mark card with a poem inside that he'd signed, "Love, Luther." If I'd read into that gesture at the time, would I be here now?

I walked past the café where I used to sit, get caffeinated, eavesdrop, and think. Where I sat and decided that Luther and I were wrong for each other. That parts of me were being squashed one by one just by being with him, forming myself to his ways.

It was like the whole city was filled with people who might have been me. People who were me, once. And now, people who I would never be.

It was raining so hard I retreated into the subway. I waited in front of an enlarged map that covered one small wall. It was a detailed map of the surrounding area intended to help people get their bearings once they'd gotten off the train. All those streets. All those paths. All those corners with all those stories. And then that one red dot, slightly left of center, YOU ARE HERE.

I was here. Nothing was going to change that.

I'd imagined my life a million ways, down a million paths, but I was here.

I'd moved to another city.

I'd broken up with my boyfriend.

I thought I'd created my own world, defined by me.

But I was here.

In New York.

Alone.

And pregnant.

words to live by

These are the things that people have tried to teach me over the years.

Stay in school.
Find a career that makes you happy.
Work is not enough.
You can have it all.
Women are natural nurturers.
You have to stay focused on yourself because, in the end, nobody else will.
Birth control has allowed women, like men, to finally separate babies from sex.
Having an abortion fucks with your head.
You can have it all.
A woman without a career is bound to be empty.
A woman who has never given birth does not know what it means to be a woman.
Never shape your life around a man's.
You can't have it all.
Most women who try to have it all end up feeling inadequate all their lives.
You may not even want it all.

The walls in the clinic had been painted bright yellow ten years before and had faded to the color of nausea.

The other girl in the waiting room couldn't have been any older than fifteen. She was talking away her nervousness to me. She told me that she'd run off for the weekend, gotten high out of her mind, and ended up sleeping with a guy she didn't even know. "I mean, what else am I supposed to do?" she said, lighting a cigarette.

And I closed my eyes.

And thought.

About New Orleans.

About that night with Carlos.

How I could have ended up just like this girl.

Then.

But I wasn't like her.

Now.

i was going to teach my daughter

"I don't know what it is you're trying to pull," Luther said. We were sitting on the sofa in the living room. He was drinking a beer. I was drinking water, hungrily, eagerly, as if it were shots of tequila or something.

"Wow," I said.

"Wow is right."

"You knew me even less than I thought you did," I said. "Yeah, you're right. I just so wanted to ruin your life that I went ahead and fucked up everything I'd ever imagined for myself."

"I'm sorry. I just. Why did you wait so long to tell me?"

"I've only known for about a week."

"How late are you?" he wanted to know.

"I'm seven weeks pregnant," I said.

"Of course, you know I'll pay for it," he said, trying to sound sympathetic.

"Pay for what?" I just wanted to hear him say it.

"I think that's painfully obvious."

"Oh," I said.

"You can't be serious. Look, I'm thinking about you. But, you shouldn't have to feel guilty."

"I just don't feel separate from this . . ." I was thinking about how strange it was to have something alive inside of me. How terrifying. How miraculous.

Then, for the first time I'd ever seen, Luther started to cry. It was such a strain for him that I couldn't tell what he was doing at first. His face just bunched until it was all hard edges. But his eyes were watering. He quickly wiped them, the burst of sad, angry energy leaving as quickly as it came. "Are you sure it's mine?"

"I haven't been with anyone else."

"Why is this happening to us?" he said.

And now I was crying. Hard, uncomfortable sobs. "I wasn't going to tell you. I was just going to make everything go away. But I couldn't." And I was thinking, then, at the clinic, that nothing is ever neat. Yes, this whole thing is messier than most. It's probably the messiest thing around. But everything is messy. Messy now or later. And the only thing I could do wrong was to not follow my instincts, to listen to what I'd been taught instead of what I knew.

"It's amazing," he said, "that you never really think of this. As a possibility."

"*You* never think of it," I said. "I've been having pregnancy nightmares all my life. Every woman does." My mother once told me that she had a nightmare she was pregnant even when she was fifty and had already had a hysterectomy. She woke up in a cold sweat thinking, *I'm too old to have a baby. This can't be happening.*

His head was bowed, resting in his hands as he stared at the floor. "Can we talk about this again tomorrow?"

"I'm not going to change my mind," I said. In truth, I was starting to, but even that reconsideration made me angry. At myself. Because I was letting him control me, manipulate my instincts.

He threw a paperweight across the room. It hit the plastic base of a potted, dying plant, and bounced to the floor. Nothing broke.

"What happens now?" he asked.

"I don't know."

"What do you want me to do?"

"I don't know," I said. I had no idea.

"Maybe we could change."

"Change?"

"I don't know. Make everything different. I mean, why did you break up with me?"

"You know why."

"Yeah. I do. It was for twenty-something personal-angst bullshit reasons. Because we were different people."

"We broke up."

"For no good reason."

I couldn't believe what I was hearing. It just didn't make sense. Or maybe it made perfect sense. Because everything had to be neat in his life. He didn't want to be the kind of person who got a girl pregnant. He wanted to be a husband and a father who practiced medicine in Texas and lived around the corner from his parents. "What are you getting at?"

"Why don't we get married?"

I was going to teach my daughter that there is nothing glamorous about marriage. That it is hard work. That the merging of your life and identity with someone else's should not be taken lightly.

Why don't we get married? I let that question run circles in my mind for a week. And then I got a call.

"Taylor, it's your mother."

"Hey."

"So, what's the weather like? I'm packing and just can't make up my mind about which coat to bring."

"When do you get in?" I had completely forgotten she was coming.

"This Friday."

"Right. It's not too bad. In the high forties. The fifties maybe," I told her.

"I'd better bring the heavy stuff, then."

"It's really not that cold."

"It's cold for me. Now, tell me. What do I do to make sure that the taxicab driver isn't ripping me off?"

I was going to teach my daughter that there is nothing more annoying, and more irreplaceable, than your mother.

• • •

I wasn't going to tell her. I decided that in advance. I was not going to tell my mother that I was pregnant.

And I wasn't going to give Luther an answer about getting married for another week or so. "I don't understand what is taking you so long," he said. "What is there to think about?"

I listed them off in my mind: whether I love you, whether we would end up hating each other, whether you would end up hating the baby, whether I could support myself without your help. "Look, two weeks ago we were over. And now we're thinking about getting married. That doesn't make sense. Yet. I have to let it all sink in."

"It's the right thing to do," he said.

That word again. *Right*. A week ago the right thing was to make this whole baby situation go away. As fast as possible.

"Do you want me to go out with you and your mother?" he asked.

"Do you want to come?"

"I don't even think I have time this weekend."

"That's cool," I said. "I hadn't really expected you to come anyway." This conversation was so bizarre. What, were we playing house or something?

I was going to teach my daughter to trust her instincts. That women's intuition does exist.

The first thing my mother said when she walked into Sarah Anne's apartment was "You could lease a whole house in Houston for what you pay for this little dump. Why, it's no bigger than a cricket's ass."

We went out to dinner and I heard all about Hilton. And their house. And their two little Pekingese. She had always wanted Pekingese. She ordered a Coke with lime in it emphatically, to show me that she wasn't drinking. And once, during dinner, she even said, "I look younger, don't I? Having some money around will do that to you. It's so nice to have money to spare for once."

"I bet," I said.

"How's the world of carpentry?" she said, a big grin on her face. She was so happy for me these days, so proud of what I was doing. But still I was annoyed at the way she asked the question. I resisted the temptation to act irritable. And I told her about the door. That it was my first significant piece of restoration work.

"And Luther?" she wanted to know. "How is Luther?"

"We broke up, Mom."

"You did?" she asked, and I could tell she wanted to know who dumped who.

I told her how he was the type of person who woke up every morning, looked out the window, and said, "What a great day I have ahead of me! Just think how lucky I am to be alive and able to share this beautiful day with all the beautiful people on this earth."

"Well, then it sounds like maybe he'd be a good complement to your personality," she said.

"I'm not that kind of person."

"No shit," she said.

"It's not that I'm negative. We just didn't get each other. He wanted things to be neat and easy. And . . . My life is like having sand stuck between your toes," I said.

"I don't get it" was her response.

"Never mind," I said.

The waiter came with our food. Relieved, we began eating our pasta. Then she stifled a giggle.

"What?" I wanted to know what was so funny.

"I used to want to live in New York. I used to tell my friends that I was going to be a dancer. Did I ever tell you that?"

I nodded yes. Countless times.

She continued. "Really? It's just too embarrassing. Especially with these explosive thighs of mine."

"Explosive?"

"That's what Hilton calls them."

"Too much information, Ma."

"Sorry."

"So, when did you stop dancing?"

"Oh, when I was about twelve, I guess. I never really was any good. And then when I gave up that dream, the only dream I had left was getting married. That's how it was back then. Not like you. Today. Moving all the way to New York."

"I think I'm coming back to Texas," I said, consciously mumbling because it was such a strange thing to admit in this particular conversation.

But my mother hadn't heard me. "Oh my god," she said. "There's that redheaded girl."

I craned my neck just in time to see Molly Ringwald sit down to eat dinner a few tables down. I tried not to be impressed.

"She was always in those teenage nerd movies," my mom said.

I thought about that kiss she gives Andrew McCarthy in *Pretty in Pink*. "I used to be addicted to those movies."

"What do you think it's like, to be famous like that? Have people staring at you while you make a mess with your pasta."

"I don't know."

"In another life, Taylor. Maybe in another life. That's what Hilton always says. In another life I'll be a famous something. It's fun to think about, anyway."

I was going to teach my daughter to listen to her mother, because every generation of women goes through the same things. They just express them differently.

The next morning I got a call at about 6:00 A.M. "Meet me at Alice," he said. It was Luther, just getting off work.

"It's six in the morning."

"Just do it, OK?"

"OK. Give me a half hour."

"Done," he said.

Alice was this big statue of Alice in Wonderland in Central Park. It's right next to a playground where Luther and I used to sit and watch the kids play, imagining (but never admitting to it) that one day we might be watching our own kids.

When I got there he had two bagels, two coffees. He had changed into his favorite khaki shorts and a button-down. How did it take me so long to notice how eager he was?

"Thanks," I said, taking the coffee that he'd already sugared. So nice. "What's going on?" I asked.

And he pulled out a box.

From which he pulled out a ring.

"Marry me," he said.

"You asked me this a few days ago," I told him. I felt horrible being irked. I did. A few months ago this would have been everything I'd wanted. Or thought I'd wanted. And now it was just annoying.

"I just wanted to make sure I'd given you a proper proposal. I mean, how horrible would it be to look back on this time and think that I proposed right after a fight? I don't want to remember it that way."

"But that's the way it was," I said.

"Not anymore." He took the ring out of the box and held it in front of me. "Taylor Jessup," he said, dropping to his knees, "will you be my wife?"

I wanted to say yes. I did. It was romantic. Romantic-ish. A little embarrassing, really. But I couldn't help but feel pressured. How was everything supposed to be different just because there was a ring involved? Why should this one little thing make the difference? It was a ring. Just a ring and a tradition. That didn't make the two people any less flawed.

"Look, just put it on," he said, already sliding it onto my finger. "It doesn't mean you have to say yes. It's just a little reminder." He was sitting beside me again, brushing the dirt off his knees.

"OK," I said.

And then we sat like that, side by side, as the first set of parents and child showed up and started to play on the slide.

"Well, I think I'd better get going," he said.

"Yeah," I said. "Me too."

• • •

I was going to teach my daughter that tradition is one thing, and life is another.

That afternoon my mother and I spent two hours at TKTS, and finally ended up getting tickets to the miraculously-still-on-Broadway show *Five Guys Named Moe*.

"Maybe next time we should splurge and get full price," my mother said. But by then we'd laughed so hard making fun of the show that we'd decided bad theater was sometimes more entertaining than good theater.

Something is happening, I was thinking as we walked through the city. Then, "I forget how fun you can be," she said to me.

"Me, too," I said. But I was thinking about Hilton. How amazing it was that he had taught her how to be fun. Again. But I didn't want to tell her that. I was afraid that she would stop.

I was going to teach my daughter that it is OK to change. To grow up. At any time.

We were still walking, our feet dragging, when I asked my mom to come with me into a parking garage.

"What are we doing?"

I wouldn't tell her. "Just trust me," I said.

And as the parking garage attendant looked on, I asked her to do a dance step.

"You mean like Shuffling-off-to-Buffalo?"

I told her that would be fine. And so she did a clumsy Shuffle-off-to-Buffalo or two, swinging her arms. She turned to the attendant. "I think my daughter has lost her mind."

He gave a smile that said he had gotten used to exuberant tourists.

As we walked out, I pointed to the sign on the building. "Now you can say that you've danced at the Met."

• • •

I was going to teach my daughter that dreams are OK. Even if they are foolish. Because, what isn't foolish, really?

The next morning I brought croissants and coffee to my mom's hotel. She was wearing the fluffy white robe and watching one of those Sunday morning newsy debate shows, without the sound. "I just like to watch them get excited about things," she said.

So we watched the suited men argue and yell in silence as we ate our breakfast. Then she turned to me, closed her eyes for a moment as if to gather strength, and said something she had clearly rehearsed.

"I wanted to tell you that." She paused, nervous. And then she came out with it. "I'm sorry I was not a better mother to you. I tried, I did. But sometimes you just do your best. And it's a mess. But it's your best."

"I'm fine," I said.

"I am very proud of you," she said, without a hint of sarcasm. "You really are on your own. And it sounds like you have a few good friends here. You always were strong. You didn't know it. And I loved to forget it. But you were."

"I'm pregnant," I said, just like that.

"What?"

I couldn't say it again. I just bowed my head, shamed.

"Oh, Lord."

"Oh, Lord," I repeated.

"What are you going to do?" A long silence. "I'm sure your brother and Nanette would raise him. Or her. If."

"I'm twenty-five."

"That's young."

"Not that young. Younger than I'd ever expected. But."

"Whose is it?"

"Luther's."

"And let me guess. He won't have a thing to do with you."

My lips were trembling, I was trying so hard not to cry. "He wants to get married."

She stared at me. For a long time. Her hand on my shoulder. Examining.

"And you don't want to marry him."

"I feel like I should." *Should. Should. Should.*

"What's wrong with him?"

"He's just not . . . me. But that's so selfish. It's not about me anymore," I said.

"You think that baby is going to be happy with a mother who cries at the thought of her husband? Grow up."

I couldn't think of a response. And she couldn't bear the silence.

"Let me just tell you one thing. I never imagined this for you. I never hoped this for you. But I still respect you. I mean, why is it that it's the woman who has to be marked? A guy gets a girl pregnant and he still walks around, free as all get-out. A girl starts giving up things, from that very first moment. But I'm here for you, I am." She looked right at me, into me, wouldn't speak until our eyes were locked. And then she said it: "I won't let you drown." Then added, "And from what I know about you, you won't let yourself drown, either."

I was going to teach my daughter that there are certain things that only mothers understand.

We were sitting on the sofa in Luther's apartment. He was fidgeting with batteries from the remote control, nervous in a way I'd never seen before.

"So?" he said, tossing the batteries back and forth and back and forth between his hands.

And that's when I told Luther that my answer was no. That I'd decided we shouldn't get married.

He took a second, then sighed, then told me he'd been awake all night thinking the same thing. "I didn't sleep all night," he said. "I even threw up once."

"But what if I'd decided that I wanted to get married?" I asked. "What if I'd said yes?"

"Then I would have gone along with it."

That thought still terrifies me to this day.

How close.

How far.

We all are.

Or were.

From something else.

the way to somewhere

"I love the smell of gasoline," I told the attendant as he filled up the tank.

"Should I spill some on you?" he joked, waving the nozzle near my window.

I laughed and shook my head no.

"Where you headed?" The attendant couldn't have been older than sixteen. And he seemed genuinely curious about my moving. Or about moving in general. About taking a long trip. Away.

"Somewhere," I told him.

"Oh," he responded, annoyed by my answer.

"Texas," I said.

"Texas?"

"Yeah."

"Cool," he said.

I was driving a truck I'd rented. Originally I'd planned to rent a U-Haul, but the thought of driving cross-country in that thing was stifling. So I went with the truck. It wasn't like I was ever going to get the chance to do this again. At least not anytime soon.

I'd filled the truck with the few things I had. Sarah Anne had helped me pack. She even went into her bedroom and packed an extra box of things for me. "It's just a mishmash," she said. "Just some books and stuff."

She also helped me carry the church door back down, with the assistance of two of her friends. It was funny how much more careful we were carrying it down the stairs than we had been going up.

As we were strapping it in with bungee cords, a curious man with a mustache came to help us, as if he were concerned that we couldn't do it right. That the door would just go flying out the back without his expertise. Still, his effort was nice, so we took his help graciously.

Until this exchange:

"What are you going to do with this thing?" he wanted to know.

I told him I had no idea.

"That's a lot to carry for no good reason," he said. Sarah Anne responded with a dirty look.

Sarah Anne was sad to see me go but was trying her best not to be emotional. "Make sure you drive safe," she said. And she hugged me. Hard. And I was sure then that she knew. She knew she was going to be one of those perfect bubbles in my life, someone who had affected me, had supported me. On my way.

To somewhere.

The way to somewhere was long. It took me five days to get there. I stayed in Super 8's, La Quintas, anything along the highway that wasn't falling apart. I ate alone in diners, read a lot, called my mother a few times. Thought about my dad whenever truckers passed me by.

It rained in Louisiana. There was a heat wave in Kentucky. And the best sunset was in Oklahoma. It was so good I pulled over, sat on the hood of the truck, opened a Little Debbie, and took in everything. I started thinking about the time I stole the ice-cream truck. What it felt like then. To know you were changing.

How that feeling still comes, almost every day.

And now, looking back on my drive to Texas, I think about all the things I didn't know.

Then.

There were hardships I couldn't have even imagined. Like that first year with Taylor Jr., raising her on my own. It would redefine my personality—giving me more joy than I thought possible, and sometimes

more despair than I'd ever known before, nights when I thought I'd
never be able to support her on my own. When there was never
enough money. And never enough of me to give her what she needed.
And as she grew up, I couldn't have imagined how difficult it would be
to explain the world to her, what it had become.

But, mostly, what I didn't know were the little victories that lay
ahead.

I didn't know that the door I was dragging all the way from New
York to Texas would become the door to my first house. That it would
mark the beginning of my reputation as a restorer in Houston who
doesn't say no. No piece is too shabby. No effort too much.

I didn't know that two years later I would meet another man altogether. A man who, just like me, was rebuilding himself every day. I
didn't know that this beautiful man would become Taylor's adopted father. My husband. And that we, as a family, would spend Christmases
with Joe, and occasionally even Sarah Anne.

I didn't know that my mother and I would become even closer.
That Hilton would become a priceless friend.

I didn't know that Luther would be such a good father. That he
would end up moving to Dallas and marrying Priscilla Banks, who had
spent her life changing as well, into a likable person.

I didn't know that, unlike my mom, unlike Luther, I wouldn't try to
forget the bumps and bruises of my life. That I would even want to pass
on a few of these stories to my daughter someday—if she turns out to be
one of those rare children who realize that they should be interested.

I didn't know that the way to somewhere could be the same as the
way home.

That the unexpected things are the things that you would least want
to change.

If you could.

But, of course, you can't.

At least not until you drag them out of the garbage.

And begin to build.

Again.

about the author

ANGIE DAY is a television producer and editor. She lives in New York City.